The Cost Of Kindness

A Dash Hammond Novel

By
E. M. Munsch

The Dash Hammond Series:

The Price of Being Neighborly

The Cost of Kindness

Copyright 2017 by Elaine Munsch. All rights reserved. No part of this publication may be reproduced, stored in a retrieval system, or transmitted in any form or by any means, digital, electronic, mechanical, photocopying, recording or otherwise, or conveyed via the internet or a website without prior written permission of the publisher, except in the case of brief quotations embodied in critical articles and reviews.

This is a work of fiction. Characters, organizations, products, locals and events portrayed in this novel either are products of the author's imagination or are used fictitiously.

I.S.B.N. 978-1974022267

For my dad, Paul J. Daniels,

and

my brother, Douglas.

Prologue

Dash Hammond gazed out the window. At 6'4" he didn't have to stand on his tiptoes or hang from the bars to enjoy the view of Lake Erie. Sighing, he moved away to sit on the cot. Elbows on his knees, he rested his chin on his clasped hands.

He sighed again. Deeper this time. He closed his baby blues to wonder, for the umpteenth time, just how he landed in the Lakota County Jail.

That damn picnic. Celebration of Freedom! Well, not so much for this favorite son of Clover Pointe, Ohio, the little town that billed itself as the hidden gem on the coast of Lake Erie.

The retired Army colonel got up, stretched his back and began pacing his cell. No clock, so he didn't know if he had to wait ten minutes or another hour before being called for his arraignment. Arraignment for murder. Another mystery to him.

He walked back to the window, more like a slit in the wall. Did he want to see the sunshine or would it upset him? Unable to feel the sun on his face, depressing!

That damn picnic. It all started at the picnic.

"It was the best of times. It was the worst of times." Charles Dickens must have visited Clover Pointe at some point.

Last Saturday, when Dash uttered that phrase to Annie Dewitt, his neighbor and now his nemesis, he had no idea it would be so relevant.

One

Lake Park ran across the top of Lakota County. The town of Clover Pointe sat in the center, dividing the park into east and west. The eastern part, deeper of the two, had the gazebo and pavilion. Sunday afternoons there was an ice cream social and band concerts. Once a month dancing under the stars took place on Saturday nights. Being close to the beach, families gathered in this area of the park.

Dash and Annie made their way from the parking lot, looking for the tables reserved for the 1983 Class Reunion. He rolled a cooler full of fried chicken, potato salad and brownies behind him. On top of the cooler was a box filled with stuff, the Lord only knew exactly what stuff, but Billy Mac, his cousin and the former class president, had asked him to bring it.

They stopped so Dash could survey the grounds, looking for the banner announcing the class reunion. Annie removed the 'stuff' box so she could sit on the cooler.

"See him?" she asked.

Shaking his head, Dash answered "No." Looking down at his petite companion, he asked, "Do you think we can use not finding Billy as an excuse to head back home? You look a little peaked to me. Told you not to drink so much last night."

Annie scrunched up her face, brushing her blonde hair aside. "I didn't drink too much; you drank too little."

Dash watched as a tallish woman with curly auburn hair made her way towards them. A pale, slender man followed her. Both were dressed in crisp white tees and shorts more suitable for the tennis courts than this lawn.

"Doctor Summers, what a surprise," Dash said as he glanced at his watch, "You out of bed before noon on a day off. What brings you to town so early in the morning?"

"Our schedule changed so we had extra time. We drove in late last night," the man answered.

"Amazing, Mae. I never saw your lips move. Quite the life-like dummy you have there," Dash said.

"Dashiell, talk about getting out of bed on the wrong side. I'd like you to meet Doctor Chandler Allen, a colleague of mine." Turning to her companion, she continued, "This cranky man is Colonel Dashiell Hammond, U.S. Army retired. I believe I may have mentioned him once or twice. The ex-husband."

Extending his hand, Dash said, "Pardon me. Welcome to our little town, Doctor Allen. Interesting. You have either two first names or two last names."

Shaking Dash's hand, Chandler said, "And you, sir, must be named after the famous mystery writer, Dashiell Hammett. Interesting as well."

"Yes, my mother was a big fan of his."

"Ah, but did she know his first name was really Samuel?" Chandler asked.

Smacking his hand to his forehead, Dash said, "So that's why my older brother is called Samuel. Thanks for clearing that up."

Mae stepped in. "Where's this dog you adopted? What's his name?"

"Charlie Dog. Left him at home. Not sure how he'd behave with crowds; probably have to muzzle him. Figured he would be happier at home. I know I would be." Dash answered.

"Someone should have thought to muzzle you," Mae mumbled.

Annie stepped forward. "In case anyone is interested, I'm Annie Dewitt, Dash's next door neighbor."

Mae said, "Yes, so very convenient. How are you, Annie?"

"Fine. It's good to see you again, Doctor Summers." Annie said insincerely.

Looking straight at Dash, Mae continued. "Chandler lives in my complex. Also convenient, don't you think, Dash?" With that said, Mae took Chandler by the hand and walked away.

Dash turned to Annie. "He's a loser. She has such rotten taste in men."

"Didn't she marry you?" Annie asked.

"My point exactly. I'm Exhibit A." Dash frowned as he watched Mae and Chandler from a distance.

Conversation stopped when Dash and Annie heard their names being called by Billy. He stood by several tables across the lawn waving his arms, motioning for everyone to join him. They did as ordered.

Once the minions were assembled, the ginger-headed general, Billy Mac, issued orders so the area was set up for the upcoming reunion. He opened the Pandora's Box, pulling out balloons and rope and other accoutrements for game-time. Balloons were filled with water; beach balls blown up. When everything was to his liking, Billy gave his final approval and dismissed his troops.

Dash stepped back, pulling out a day glow orange vest from his voluminous pockets in his camo shorts. He added sunglasses and his Go Army ball cap.

"Heigh, ho, heigh, ho, it's off to work I go. Should be back around noon so please save some food for me."

Billy looked his cousin up and down. "Do you not own anything that doesn't shout 'look at me I was in the Army'? Surely you have tee shirts in another color than olive drab. What the hell do you have in all those pockets?"

"Water, tissues, hand-wipes for all those snot-nosed kiddies who will be crying because they lost their mommies. And..." Dash was interrupted when Mae walked over, laughing out loud.

"How did Sam talk you into doing this? You managed to avoid it the last two years. Thought you said you'd never get corralled into it." She asked.

Shrugging, Dash said, "You know Sam, blah, blah, blah. A thousand words a minute. Something about someone about to have a baby, or maybe just had the baby, or more likely someone wants to stay home to make a baby. I tuned him out, then discovered I had agreed before I realized what he was asking. Really need to pay more attention."

He rolled his eyes, "Maybe I'll get parking lot duty rather than patrolling the grounds. Either way, I need to check in with the powers that be over at command central, what most normal people call the gazebo. Later, gators." Leaning down, he glanced at Mae but kissed Annie. "Sweetheart."

Billy called out, "Goodbye, Deputy Fife."

Dash looked back. "Even Barney got one bullet and at this close range I won't miss, so mind your mouth, my friend."

Over the next few hours his friends watched as Dash walked the grounds, talking to the various picnickers. A regular Pied Piper, he gathered a following of teens and children, all vying for his attention. Finally, he passed by holding the hand of a sniffling child heading to the lost parent station. Looking over at Billy, he waved the tissue packet, giving a thumbs up.

He finally trotted over to the table, pulling off the day-glow vest. He sat down, picked up a drumstick, announcing, "next year it's a fishing trip for me. So far so good but I have a feeling disaster is just around the corner."

He saluted his friends then bit into his piece of fried chicken. Turning around he saw Trigger, a lanky man with a pony tail, approaching. He was the owner of the local strip joint, Lulu's Lounge, located on the other side of the county, closer to the turnpike exit.

Standing up and stepping over the bench, Dash nodded a hello. "What's happening, Trigger? This is the last place I thought I'd see you."

Trigger laughed. "And the last place I thought I would be. Hey, wanted you and the other vets who may not want to watch the fireworks to know that the girls have worked up a few sparkling effects of their own. Show starts at nine and will run until midnight. Since they've worked so hard, I thought I should spread the news. If you see any of the vets, tell them please. Would break the girls' hearts if no one showed."

"Love to, Trig, but" and he motioned his head toward Annie, "doubt if she would want to attend. But, here's a thought, maybe I can get her interested in joining in the festivities. She does a mean pole dance."

Annie joined the men. "I'm not sure I want to know what's going on but I saw that look, Dash. What's up?"

Before Dash could answer, his attention was turned to the sound of a man yelling and a woman screaming. He handed his drumstick to Trigger saying, "Hold this. Be right back."

"What the hell?" as he stared at the half-eaten drumstick. He looked at Annie who said, "Don't give it to me. He entrusted you with it."

The rest of the party watched Dash run across the park to where the man slapped the woman.

"Carter, you ass. Stop it right now. You want to hit someone, try me. Give me a reason to beat the crap out of you, why don't you." Dash yelled as he approached.

The heavy set man pushed the woman away, turning his attention to Dash. Carter had a weight advantage but the ex-soldier had height and skill.

"You and what army? This is none of your business, Hammond. Now back off."

Dash walked up to Carter, tapping him in the chest. "You just made it my business when you hit your wife." Turning, he said, "Chrissy, get the kids and head to the gazebo. I'll meet you there."

A crowd began to assemble. Phones were pulled out to film whatever was about to happen.

Carter hauled off and punched Dash first in the mouth and then in the gut, knocking him to the ground. "See what I said. You and what army?" While Dash was down, his opponent kicked him in the ribs, then backed off, signaling for Dash to get up.

Dash staggered to his feet, holding his side. "Carter, you're beginning to tick me off. That's it. I'm going to make a citizen's arrest. Come on, I'm taking you in."

Murmurs of 'citizen's arrest' ran through the crowd. Billy stepped forward yelling, "Enough. The *real* police are on the way. Dash, step back."

"Billy, you step back and let me handle this. I'm a trained warrior after all." Dash winked at his cousin.

"Trained fool more like it," Mae stated as she approached the fray.

Trigger yelled, "Dash, you want me to shoot him?"

Billy turned to yell at Trigger, "No guns!"

Carter seized that moment to rush Dash. The surprise was on Carter as Dash side-stepped him, sticking out his foot. Carter went down cursing but jumped back up, ready to run at Dash again.

Dancing around, shifting from one foot to the other, Dash quoted Ali, "Float like a butterfly, sting like a bee." He stepped forward and then back, moving left and right, jabbing at the air.

Carter moved in sync with Dash, then he crouched and ran straight ahead. Dash braced himself for a hit then quickly stepped out of the way so the charger hit a tree. Carter's head thumped, bark being embedded in his forehead. He slid slowly to the ground.

The crowd burst into applause which Dash acknowledged with a bow. He waved but stopped when a sheriff's car pulled up, lights flashing. An EMT ambulance followed.

Out stepped his brother, Sheriff Sam Hammond. Besides his sheriff's uniform, Sam wore a not-so-happy face. He yelled to his younger brother, "Why didn't you radio for help? Where's the walkie-talkie we gave you?"

"Carter would have beaten her bloody if I had waited for you to arrive." He pointed to Chrissy who stood on the sidelines crying. Mae moved to comfort the teary-eyed woman.

"You okay?" Sam asked his brother.

"Nothing a beer won't cure." Dash said, rubbing his side and grimacing. He wiped the blood trickling from his lip.

"Get yourself looked at." Sam walked over to the semi-conscious Carter. He pulled him into a sitting position, telling Deputy Collins to stand guard until the EMT's could check him out. "Then arrest the bastard."

Turning to the assembled picnickers, the sheriff announced, "Can you all hang for a minute until my assistant, Ruthie Malloy, gets here? She'll collect names and numbers. We'll get in touch later for statements. Have fun, be safe."

Dash stood waiting for instructions. Annie joined him while the rest of the party milled around. Hearing the whir of a golf cart, he watched as a silver-haired man and a woman wearing a Sheriff's department uniform pulled up. The elderly man whose spine was straight as a pike walked toward him. In spite of the heat, the man looked as crisp and clean as a new dollar bill. Ruthie Malloy, the engine that kept the sheriff's department running smoothly, followed.

"Son." Owen Hammond, retired sheriff, acknowledged his youngest.

"Father, good of you to stop by. Miss Ruthie, how are you this fine day? Sam's got you working as well."

"Always, Dash, always. What happened? I thought you were on lost kids patrol, or did I have that recorded wrong?" she asked. Hearing her name being called, she excused herself to get instructions from the sheriff.

Dash's father reiterated Ruthie's question. "What happened, Dash?"

"Ah, Carter was slapping Chrissy and, um, I intervened," Dash mumbled. "Never can get the protocol right. I mean, how long do you let a cretin like Carter beat on his wife before you jump in? If nothing else, I thought I'd distract him until the cavalry arrived." Dash rubbed his side.

"Hop in, son, I'll drive you to your truck and go with you to the ER. Get those ribs looked at." Seeing his son's face, he added, "Humor me. I'm an old man. Don't want you dropping dead in the middle of the picnic."

Annie chimed in. "I'll come along for company."

Dash shook his head. "Nah, no reason for you to waste your time. Got your bikini, right? Head to the beach, no sense both of us sitting indoors on this nice day. Be back as soon as I can." He bent down to kiss her cheek and retrieved his half-eaten drumstick which had somehow found its way into her hand.

She studied his face. His eyes pleaded with her not to argue, so she nodded. "See you in a bit."

Annie watched Dash climb into the golf cart. His dad started talking non-stop, probably chastising Dash for jumping in without backup. Owen worried terribly about his son.

St. Mary's Catholic Church sat on the Lake Erie shore. Good Catholic immigrants, both German and Irish, bought the parcel of land over a hundred years ago and cherished it through the years. The Irish stonemasons handcrafted the exterior of the church while the Germans carved a beautiful wooden altar. When the Italians arrived in Clover Pointe, they added fine stained glass to complete the building.

A churchyard cemetery served as the final resting place for the parishioners who sacrificed so much to build and maintain the church and its eventual school.

Dash knelt before a small headstone. He brushed away some debris, making sure the engraved words were clean. He read: Beloved daughter, Grace Marie Hammond, 3 months, 4 days. Always with us.

He heard the car on the gravel drive as it pulled up. He stood to watch Mae exit and walk toward him.

"What are you doing here? Shouldn't you be at the ER getting your ribs and head checked?" She asked.

"Owen wanted me to drop him here. Father Tom officiated at a wedding this morning so Dad is catching a ride with him." Holding his hand up, he added, "I promised him, and now you, I'll stop on my way through town." Glancing down at the headstone he smiled, "Just thought…"

"I know." She said. "Wanted to get away from the picnic for a few minutes. I should have stopped on my way into town last night but it got later and later."

Mae took his hand and they stood, heads bowed, in silent prayer. After making the sign of the cross, she turned to Dash, tears streaming down her cheeks.

He slowly wiped away them away with his thumbs. "You know she'd be starting her senior year this fall." He said as he wrapped his arms around her.

She pulled back. "We'd be up to our knees in college catalogs. Time sure flies."

"Seems like yesterday to me." Dash shook his head sighing, "Sweetheart, we need to get back to the picnic *and* with smiles on our faces. Think we can do that?"

"You're right. If we stay here talking about 'what might have been', Sam will find us collapsed on the grave. Might need more therapy. Both of us."

Laughing Dash said, "There aren't enough hours in the day for all that I need." He guided his ex-wife toward her car. "Hey, where's Chancer or Chandelier or whatever? Didn't he want to come with you?"

9

Stopping she turned to Dash, "I didn't ask him. He and Billy are jawing up a storm. No, this is about me, and, well, you. Now be a good soldier and get those x-rays. Promise me you'll come back."

"See you soon, or so I hope. Remember how long the wait can be ...." He smiled as he opened the door for her. Pecking her cheek one more time, he said, "Drive safely. See you for fun and games with the ringmaster, good old Billy Mac."

He walked to his truck but waited for Mae to pull out before he drove off in the opposite direction.

Two hours later Dash arrived at the picnic grounds. He danced over to the table, moving to a tune only heard by him.

"Well ladies, here I am! Clean, smiling and positively adorable, if I may say so myself." Leaning down, he kissed Billy's wife Elena on the cheek, then one for Annie and stepped around the table to Mae. He stood in front of her, hands on his hips. Seeing the look on her face, he asked, "What? You wanted me here and here I am. My mind is right..."

"And your snoot is full. Please tell me you didn't drive here in that condition. How much have you had to drink?"

"Am I still standing and walking? Then not enough." He pulled Mae to him and kissed her quickly before she could react. He stepped back, dancing over to the other side. He sat down next to Annie, laying the truck keys in front of her. "Owen drove me here after making me promise to give you the keys. Is there any food left? Not much at the house."

"So you've been drinking on an empty stomach?" Annie asked.

"Of course not. I put some liquid in first." Sighing he said, "The ever so helpful doc at the ER told me to 'suck it up' when I mentioned some pain. So I decided to suck up some Jameson." Waving his arms about, he said, "The world is a better place after you've had a few."

"Are you drunk?" Elena asked coyly.

He held up one hand, thumb and forefinger about an inch apart. "This close. But I'll be fine. I'm almost sober."

Annie filled a plate and set it in front of him. "Eat. Slowly. I'm going to see if anyone has coffee."

Dash ate everything and then some. When Annie returned with a thermos of coffee, she demanded he drink a cup or two. He obeyed, complaining the whole time.

Sitting back, he winced, rubbing his ribs.

Mae cocked her head. "What did the x-rays show? Broken or bruised."

"Bruised. Everything inside seems okay, not like after the accident." Shaking his head, he added, "Tomorrow, though, I'm going to be one sorry puppy, probably unable to move."

"Mae, Dash! Come on. We're starting the games," Billy yelled across to them.

Dash's shoulders slumped. He leaned toward Elena. "What the hell is he talking about?"

Trying hard not to laugh, she said. "He's arranged for a three-legged race, something with water balloons, etc. All the games little kids play when having a backyard bash. I'm pretty sure he forgot this is a *high school* reunion, not grade school."

He stepped over the bench, backing away. "No! No! No! No! I'm not drunk enough for that." He looked at Annie. "I'll give you fifty bucks if you come home with me right now."

"So I've gone from girlfriend to low-end hooker in one afternoon. Like you said, the best of times, the worst of times."

"Hey, I don't know how much a hooker costs. Name your price." Pointing at Mae, he added, "I just always had Mae."

Mae put her hand to her head saying, "I'm hoping there's a compliment in there somewhere." She looked over to Annie. "Eejit, feckin' eejit." Grabbing Dash's hand, she pulled him along as he began another round of "No! No! No!" Then he added, "Remember the ribs!"

Annie shouted, "No Dash, it's 'Remember the Maine!'" She burst out laughing as he scowled at her.

Passing Billy, he muttered to him. "I'd say I'm going to kill you but Elena might miss you." Unfazed Billy continued to orchestrate the games to the amusement of all.

Dash and Mae won the first heat of the three-legged competition.

"Won! We're done!" Dash led Mae back to the table. He found Annie doubled over in laughter. Changing his mind, he pulled her to the starting line. Even as Annie protested that she was a foot shorter than he was and this would never work, he bound their legs together. At the sound of the starter's pistol, Dash lifted her up, wincing. He held her like a football and walked the race. Her left foot never touched the ground. Winners again.

This time Dash announced to all. "Finished, forever! Games over. Proceed to have rational fun."

Billy sputtered, "No, not finished. Don't listen to him. Aw, come on!"

Annie untied the rope and glared at Dash.

"Next time take the fifty bucks," he said as they walked back to the table. They barely sat down when his classmates began calling his name, motioning for him to join them as they sat in the shade of the trees.

"Want to come along? After all, this was your idea." he asked Annie.

Wrinkling her nose, she politely declined. "Doubt if I'll ever see them again. Too hot to strain my brain. I need to get something from the truck anyway." Sarcastically, she added, "I'll be back in time to sing the school song. Always brought tears to my eyes." She handed him a copy of the song that had been passed out by the ever-efficient Billy.

"Gawd, I forgot about that; don't think I ever knew the words." Pointing, he said, "Hey, there's Trigger. Ask him how much a high-end hooker costs. Bet he'll know. Match him dollar for dollar unless it's really expensive."

"And what a conversation starter that will be!" Kissing him on the cheek, she said, "Later." Waving at Trigger, she yelled, "Wait up. I've got a question for you."

Dash looked around then reached into his cargo pants pocket and pulled out a flask. Taking a swig, he said to himself, "Loins girded. Off to meet the Lakota County High Lions and Lionesses." He wandered around greeting the late comers. A lot of back slapping and hugging took place. He moaned and groaned about his ribs. The chatter grew louder with all the "Oh my God, you made it" and the ubiquitous lie "You haven't changed a bit" in spite of the balding pates and growing stomachs. The last thirty-odd years were reduced to two or three sentences.

Annie rejoined Elena at the picnic table. She sat watching Dash kiss and hug all his female classmates. Turning to Elena, she asked, "How long have you known Dash?"

"We met as freshmen at Ohio State so I guess a little over thirty years. He introduced me to Billy but I dated him first. Why?"

Nodding toward Dash who now stood with his arms around two female classmates. Annie asked, "Isn't that unusual behavior for him? The only social events we've attended have been with his family and there I expected him to greet his sister and sister-in-law with kisses. That seems out of place for him, cozying up to his classmates."

Elena cocked her head. "That's right, you've only known him for a couple of months." Taking a deep breath, she continued. "What is unusual is that Dash agreed to come. The kissing and hugging is icing on the cake." Laughing she added, "That's why he needed the Dutch courage, or more precisely, the Irish whiskey. He's nervous. Hasn't been comfortable with crowds, especially mixed company, for years. See how he's fidgeting with his hands."

Mae sat down on the other side of Annie. Elena leaned across to say to Mae. "I was telling Annie about Dash's tells, running his left thumb across his fingers. Nervous."

"Don't look at me like that, Elena. I'm not going to rescue him. He needs to be uncomfortable every once in a while." To Annie she said, "He'll do that for a bit and then calm down. I bet he's taken a swig or two from his flask."

"How do you know he brought one?" Annie asked.

"Fifty years of sharing time, space and thoughts with him. You'll get to know him in about ten years. It takes that long for him to open up and talk."

Annie studied the women on either side. Both tallish, one auburn and one brunette, both curly-headed. One dated Dash; the other grew up with him, only to marry, then divorce him. Both women clearly cared for him.

Feeling like the square peg in a round hole, Annie of the limited height and blonde hair asked Mae her million-dollar question: "Does he still talk to you about everything?"

Mae cocked her head. "You want the truth?"

Suddenly deciding she already knew the answer, Annie shook her head no.

"You know Annie, I'll give you one word of advice, if you haven't figured this out already. Watch out for the damsel in distress, his Achilles's heel. Think back to this morning. If Carter had been pummeling his brother or some guy, Dash would have called the sheriff and finished eating his drumstick."

Accentuating the next point by raising a finger in the air, Mae said, "But, and this is the big *but*, a woman was in danger so he felt he had to act."

Pulling back, she asked, "Hey, didn't he pull you from some man-eating plant or other? Classic damsel in distress."

The three women watched as the men separated themselves from the women. A latecomer joined the group yelling loudly as he pointed at Dash. "You're alive! Dammit, Dash! Come here, you bastard and let me shake your hand." The handshake turned into a bear hug. Dash's back was slapped so hard his whole body shook. Everyone could hear him groan as he rubbed his ribs.

One of the men turned, then nudged the guy next to him. The nudging went on until the circle was complete. They watched as Emmysue Miller strutted toward them. Dash heard Duke Ellington's *Jeep Blues* in his head. Each step accentuated by the drum beat in his brain.

She wore an itsy bitsy teeny weeny stars and stripes bikini. She looked closer to fifteen than fifty. A large sun hat shaded her face hiding any wrinkles she might have. She waved to all the guys.

The man next to Dash murmured, "Be still my heart." Dash added, "And my other parts." He leaned into his classmates whispering, "What she paid for that body and those boobs she could have treated all of us to a trip to Hawaii."

She smiled coyly, very aware of her effect on the men. "Howdy, y'all. I missed the memo about the games and that y'all would be up here. I thought everyone would be on the beach. Glad Frank and Will found me so I can join you."

Dash performed a courtly bow. "Not as happy as we are. Emmysue the Prom Queen! You are a sight for sore eyes. Hard to believe, but you look better now than you did in high school. What's the secret of your youth?"

"Money, honey. And tons of it." Running her hands down her sides, she said. "Texas oil. Enough to pay for the best plastic surgeon and, if we're talking about looking good, Dash, you seem to have held up rather well considering."

"Considering what, if I may ask?"

"Considering Portia told me you were dead, killed in some gawd awful place. I cried for a week." Reaching out to touch his biceps, she continued, "Toting all those guns around seems to have agreed with you." This time she touched his cheek, saying, "Oh, Dashman, I'm so happy you're not dead."

"Now I know why I fought so hard to keep this country free." He returned the gesture touching her cheek, "I'm so glad I didn't die in that gawd awful place, though seeing you just might cause this old heart to stop ticking." Dash nodded in the direction of Mae and the other female classmates who were all watching.

"I'm sure Mae and the girls would love to say hi. Shall I escort you over?"

"Only if you mean to protect me when they started tearing me to shreds. Should I cover up? You and Mae still together?"

"Sadly no, married then divorced."

"Then I finally have a shot."

"Aren't you married or did you strike oil on your own?"

Emmysue looked around. Winking at Dash, she said, "Don't see Travis Tycoon anywhere? Believe I left him alone in the Lone Star state. Besides ours was always an open marriage. I opened my legs and he opened his checkbook."

Dash threw his head back laughing. He took her in his arms, bending her backwards. He whispered, "Let's see if that skimpy halter holds. If not, we'll see how many guys pass out." He gave her a big kiss.

The halter held. They joined the distaff side of the class. Mae welcomed Emmysue with a very cordial air-kiss on the cheeks. The others followed Mae's lead. Annie and Elena distanced themselves from the group.

Dash walked over to Annie, grinning like the Cheshire Cat. "Miss Annie, I'm so glad you convinced me to come."

Practically bouncing on his toes, he asked Elena where Billy was. She replied suspiciously that she hadn't seen him in a bit. "Why? Why do you want to see him?"

"Because I'm sure the Prom King would want to visit with his Prom Queen. My, but they made a good looking couple, all regal like."

Annie jumped in. "Don't stir up trouble. Come on, let's go home. I'll make it worth your while."

"Too late. Oh I can't wait to see Billy's face." Turning he added, "And it won't be long."

He spotted his cousin and waved to him, encouraging him to join the class. The males had crossed the field to mingle with the females. A circle had closed around Emmysue.

When Billy walked up, Dash grabbed his arm. "You'll never believe who's here." Then gesturing with his arm, the classmates parted to reveal the bikinied Emmysue.

"King William, meet your Queen."

Billy's smile faded, then reappeared. Regaining his composure, he approached the Prom queen, arms outstretched to hug her.

Elena stepped next to Dash. "Okay, spill the beans. So they were Prom King and Queen. Why the Cheshire grin?"

"Do you know what we called her? The 'virgin' queen. She took all the male virgins and made them feel like kings. And the worst was William Patrick McCafferty, the boy who was saving himself for God. He rarely dated, rarely kissed anyone, and sermonized on and on about the sins of the flesh. Then came prom night. The thought of the priesthood flew right out of his head after a night with Emmysue. They had a very passionate affair until graduation when she dumped him like a rotten tomato. He mooned about all summer, very pathetic."

"So I guess I should thank her." Elena said.

Dash looked incredulous.

"I'm assuming she taught him all he knows." Smiling, she winked at Dash, "And all he knows is pretty good by me."

Annie laughed and looked at Dash. Nodding toward Emmysue, she asked, "Yours?"

Shaking his head, Dash said. "Hell no. Mae. Always Mae for me."

Annie ground her teeth, swallowing a comment.

Speaking of 'his first', Mae walked over to join them, slipping her arm around Dash's waist and quietly laughing. "Revenge on Father McCafferty, is it? He's going to kill you, you know that."

"But sweetheart, it would be *worth* it. Just watching him squirming over there. When Emmysue gets under your skin, or more appropriately in your pants, thirty or thirty-five years is but a second." Looking very guilty, Dash added. "Or so I am told." Sighing. "Ah, the sweet taste of revenge."

Dash walked over to Billy who was still conversing with Emmysue. He whispered in his cousin's ear. "Bless me, Father, for I have sinned."

Billy excused himself, grabbing Dash by the arm and led him away. "You bastard. Did you plan this?"

"Honestly, Billy, no. No idea she was coming. But this *is* the best day ever. The look on your face."

Glancing over Dash's shoulder, Billy's eyes met Elena's. She shook her finger at him. "You told her, didn't you? All these years I never mentioned my romance with the Prom queen and in two seconds you ruin my marriage."

In response Dash planted a kiss on Billy's lips, roaring, "It's a grand day to be alive, me Irish cousin. Five Our Fathers and five Hail Marys if you will. And a bunch of roses for Elena."

Dash swaggered back to Emmysue. She took his hand, suggesting they find a place to talk, get caught up. They found a vacant table at the edge of the park. She stopped to open her bag, slipping on a pair of shorts and a tee shirt. Tucking her long hair into her hat, she donned a pair of oversized sunglasses and said, "I know I came alone, but I can't believe you're flying solo. You said you and Mae are divorced, but surely you're not all by your lonesome."

Dash pointed out Annie who wiggled her fingers at them. She pointed at Trigger and waved goodbye. Dash gave her a thumbs up.

Emmysue shook her head, "Dash, I don't want to come between you two."

Dash countered, "Nothing serious. We met a few months ago and are dating. She's a good egg. She'll understand my wanting to renew old acquaintances. Hell, it was her idea to come. And having you here makes the whole thing worthwhile."

Sitting down, he patted his pocket. "Want a swig of some good Irish whiskey?"

"No. I was hoping that was a gun you had in there."

Seeing the look of surprise on his face, she took a deep breath, saying, "Dash, I need some help. I'm being followed, stalked. No one believes me, least of all my husband. But I *know* it's so. When I traveled up here I was hoping Billy would agree to help me. He's the smartest guy I've ever known but he seems distracted. And, voila, you appeared, rising from the dead." She reached out to take his hand. "Dash, someone is watching me."

Dash rocked back. Under his breath, he said, "Of course everyone is watching you. You're gorgeous." Lowering his voice he asked, "Gotta description?"

Smiling widely as if he said something funny, she said, "No, just a sense. This has been going on for about a month. My husband thinks I'm crazy. I don't know whether he is having me watched, thinking I'm cheating on him." She reached for his hand. "I swear I'm not. But something is wrong. Everything is wrong. I just don't know what. All I know is I'm scared, boogey man and all. Scared no matter what."

Dash stood, helping Emmysue up. "Let's walk a bit and then you join the class. Stay close to them. I'll do a bit of surveying. Don't worry, this colonel has your back, your front and everything in between."

Two

Annie returned to the picnic table where she sat watching Dash and Emmysue mingle with the class of '83. Mae walked to the table, grabbing a bottle of water.

"What's the deal with Dash and the Prom Queen? He seems particularly pleased to see her." Annie asked.

Mae took a swig of water. Looking toward Dash and Emmysue, she said, "Oh, she was one of his projects."

Annie raised her eyebrows. "Projects?"

Sitting down, Mae said. "She moved here from some little town in the mountains of Tennessee. Her mom was a working girl, or so it was rumored. She arrived with a chip on her shoulder. All brassy blonde hair, brassy mouth, begging for someone to ridicule her so she could pull out her brass knuckles."

"A problem fitting in?" Annie said.

Mae smiled. "Good old Dash, who hated for anyone to be left out, made her one of his projects." Looking directly at Annie, she said, "He's forever picking up stray animals *and* people. No matter how much she pushed him away he literally killed her with kindness. He dug deep and found a very funny girl who then spent hours regaling us with silly stories of growing up in the mountains. I'm sure most of them were made up, but with that southern drawl and knack for exaggeration, she had us rolling on the floor."

"Weren't you and Dash a couple then? You were okay with him spending time with her? Don't think I'd be so agreeable. In fact, I know I wouldn't. Didn't take it from my husband; wouldn't take it now," Annie said as she glanced over to Dash and the Prom Queen.

Mae said, "Emmysue posed no threat. Dash is as faithful as he is tall. Sure, he'd ask my advice about how to get her to open up. Actually it was fun, watching him trying to figure out the female mind. He's really intrigued by the opposite sex. Couldn't understand us then and *definitely* doesn't understand us now." She sighed. "What you're seeing here, today, is the old Dash. Naïve, silly, social and wonderfully innocent. He used to love everyone, trust everyone. Only saw the good in people."

She stood, turning away. "Those were the days, my friend. Lord, I'm depressing myself." Sniffling, she said to Annie. "Do what you want. Sit here or join him. The music should start soon. Good excuse to pull him back to your side. Since he's a bit lit, he'll be dancing like crazy. Speaking of partners, I need to find Chandler. Later."

She waved goodbye with one hand and wiped her nose with the other.

In truth Mae wanted to get away from the reunion. Why she had told Billy this would be a good idea escaped her at this moment. Shaking her head, she meandered through the crowd.

Smiling faces greeted her, inquired how she was doing in her new job. Several told Mae they missed seeing her around the town. All wished her well and reminded her 'not to be stranger'.

She smiled, thanked them for their good wishes and agreed to drive back more often. Jeez, Mae thought, you think I'd been gone for years rather than weeks. Uncomfortable with praise, all her childish insecurities flooded back. She never trusted that the person wasn't being especially kind to her because her mom died when she was only eleven and then her father, not that she wanted to acknowledge that brute as being a blood relative, ended up in prison for beating up Dash when he came to her aid. The irony of her brawler dad getting his due in prison. Picking a fight with a lifer was a far cry from beating on her mother or Dash. A shiv in the chest put paid to her dad's career as a tough guy.

Leaning against a tree, one foot propped against it, she sighed. No, she was at her best when working, caring for the sick, diagnosing problems. She leaned her head back against the rough bark, closing her eyes.

A few minutes later she walked toward the old pavilion dodging folks. Suddenly she felt a hand on her breast. She turned to see a stocky man next to her. He was her height, possibly her age. Not at all attractive.

"Nice rack you got there." He said, pointing at her chest leaning into her.

Mae put out her hand, pushing him away. "That line ever work for you?"

"Doll, you all alone? 'Cuz I can fix that. Whatta you say? I can show you a good time, babe." He put his arm out as if to touch her again.

She knocked his hand away, pulling out her phone to snap his photo.

"My brother-in-law is the sheriff in this county and his number is on speed dial. You have two seconds to get out of my sight. *If* I see you again, you will regret coming here."

The slovenly dressed man cocked his head. "Is that right, Busty? Lots of threats." Looking around, he continued, "Don't see no army coming to your aid. Whaddaya say? Let's start over and we can have a beautiful ending."

"Look you piece of shit! Don't press your luck. If I call on my army, you really will be sorry you set foot in this park. Now I suggest you scram."

Mae looked up and saw Chandler. She called to him and he started to walk her way. The man watched him, saying under his breath, "See you later, Dollface. Next time..." And he drifted into the crowd of picnickers heading for the fireworks show at the beach.

Annie wandered over to the pavilion where the class of 1983 had assembled, but couldn't find Dash. When she didn't see Emmysue either, she decided she had had enough. She walked over to Elena announcing she was leaving, taking Dash's truck and he could walk home.

A few minutes later, Dash approached Elena. "Have you seen Annie? I've been looking for her."

"Well, honey, she looked for you. When she couldn't find you, she decided to go home. Said you could walk there. Where were you? Where's the infamous Prom queen?"

Dash pointed to the long lines at the port-a-potty. "I don't know where Emmysue is but I took a trip into the woods."

Elena made a face. "You're fifty, not five."

"Hey, in the last thirty years I've peed outside more than inside. Blame the Army and all those deployments for my bad manners. But I did find some soap and water so my hands are clean." Holding them out and flipping them back and forth, he said, "See?"

"Dashiell Hammond, I love you." Elena kissed his cheek and hugged him.

Billy walked over. "What the hell? First you ruin my picnic and now you're kissing my wife."

Elena punched her husband's shoulder. "Stupid. *I* kissed him."

"Why?"

"Because I could. Now come along or I'll dance with him and not you." Elena led Billy to the stage.

Dash looked around for Emmysue. He spotted her talking to a group of the girls -- that's how he still thought of them. He waved and danced his way over. True to his high school reputation he made a point of dancing with every female classmate when he wasn't goofing off with the guys. During his dance with Emmysue, they made plans to meet in her room at Little Biff's motel after the fireworks; topic of discussion would be her stalker problem.

As the sky darkened, the dance floor emptied; people moved toward the beach to await the fireworks. The last dance was announced.

Dash spotted Mae and Chandler about to take the floor. Dash intercepted them. Taking Mae's hand he said, "Sorry, Doctor Allen, but the last dance is always mine."

Chandler pulled back, none too happy to relinquish his partner. "Trust me, Dash, this *will* be your last dance with her."

Ignoring the last shot, Dash pulled Mae into his arms.

As they swayed to the music, Mae asked, "Where's Annie? Shouldn't you be dancing with the girl you brought?"

"Sadly I do believe she is angry with me. She sent me a text telling me to do to myself what I did to her last night. Will spare you the language. I just hope she doesn't put my truck in the lake. Any idea why she's mad at me because, and I hate to admit it, I'm a little fuzzy on what I did or did not do."

Mae laughed. "Start with kissing all your female classmates and end with spending time with Emmysue. Your sweet little Annie has greener eyes than I do. Forget about her and hold me tightly."

When the dance ended, she leaned into Dash whispering, "I need to talk to you."

Dash's shoulders slumped. "Dammit, Mae, never in my life has good news followed that sentence. Let's get it over." He let her lead him to the edge of the woods.

"Dashiell, Chandler and I are thinking of getting married."

"And," rubbing his face, he said, "I don't think you're about to ask me to be your best man. Spit it out, Mae."

She ran her fingers through her hair. "He, I mean we, I mean me, think, um, that you and I should not talk or text each other. I mean you have Annie now so I think I should find someone else. Need to make a clean break here."

Dash leaned back against a tree. "Fess up. His idea or yours? And I'm not going to get upset. I just don't understand. When we were married, I couldn't get you to do the laundry but he can convince you to give up your best friend of fifty years. Which one of you is not confident of the other?" When he saw the tears glistening in her eyes, he took her hands in his.

"Okay, okay. Not at all happy with this arrangement but if anyone deserves a good marriage it is you. Lord knows I'm not marriage material. I think cutting all ties is a bit much but....."

"Thank you for understanding." She kissed his cheek. "I'm so sorry, Dash. You'll always be my best friend."

As she started to walk away, he pulled her back. Hugging her he said, "Mae, you saved my life and I can't thank you enough for that. Listen, if you ever, and I mean *ever*, need me just snap your fingers." Releasing her he added, "And if he lays a hand you, don't worry about filing for divorce."

"He's not Richard, Dash."

He kissed her forehead, whispering as she walked away. "Good bye my dear heart."

Chandler waited for her, staring back at Dash who had walked to the pavilion. Hands in his pockets Dash muttered to himself, "Don't say a word. Let them leave. Be the man she thinks you are."

When they were out of sight and earshot, he picked up a folding chair and began to smash it into the ground. He wanted to scream obscenities but caught himself. He finally just flung the mangled chair. He turned to watch it fly directly at Elena who was walking with Billy over to him.

"Elena, look out!"

The chair grazed her leg causing her to stumble a bit. Billy grabbed her before she could fall. Dash rushed over to them only to be confronted by Billy.

He swung at Dash re-opening the gash on his lip. He stepped back to yell. "You bastard. What the hell is the matter with you? Crazy? Drunk? Or both?"

"I'm sorry, I'm sorry. I didn't look." Turning to Elena, he asked if she was okay. He licked his lip, tasting blood.

"Just startled." She pulled at Billy. "We wanted to know if you were going to the fireworks or needed a lift home."

Billy waved her off. "What the hell did you say to Mae? When she passed us she was crying."

"Why assume I said something to her? Why is it always me?"

"Because it usually is you, stupid! You, acting like Wyatt Earp today. Always looking for a fight." Billy shouted.

Elena tried to pull him back but he wouldn't budge. Instead he continued, "You just had to show off and then you got hurt, hero again. Always you, always center-stage."

"Billy, for God's sake, shut up." Elena pleaded with her husband as she watched Dash's face. Turning to Dash, she begged, "Ignore him. He's been out in the sun too long."

"He has no idea what 'being out in the sun too long' really feels like. He'd melt like ice cream if he had to spend a day with us in the sandbox." Dash replied.

But Billy wouldn't shut up. He continued to verbally jab at Dash, dredging up old slights, real and imagined. Then he started ragging on Dash's beloved Army and how the only thing it did for Dash was to make him insane.

Dash stood stone-faced, never blinking. When he sensed Billy was finished ranting, he stepped closer. Through gritted teeth, he said slowly and quietly, "I know you think *I'm* crazy and I don't care. But don't start on the Army. We're the reason you're able to sit behind your fancy desk on your fat ass." Taking another step forward he said, "Now get out of my sight before I pull out your fucking tongue."

Billy backed up, blinking, suddenly aware the effect his words had on Dash. He shook his head, "Sorry, I didn't mean…I…"

Dash executed a military about-face and walked toward the woods.

Elena pulled Billy away, yelling "Sorry" to Dash.

Three

Dash collapsed onto the ground. Looking up at the sky, he said, "It was the best of times, it was the worst of times." Yelling to the heavens, he asked, "Okay, got the worst of times part. Today I lost my two best friends and my girl. Okay I'll take responsibility for the last one. But where the hell is my 'best of'? And please don't say it was winning those stupid races. Some rotten sense of humor here."

He lay with his eyes closed, trying to breathe calmly, decompress. Sensing someone standing over him and praying 'please don't be my brother', he opened his eyes to see Miss Ruthie standing there, still dressed in the department uniform, the setting sun giving her graying hair silver highlights. He looked up at her, raising his eyebrows. Moving his lips around, he finally asked, "What?"

"Well, I came looking to see if you were in one piece. A few minutes ago I passed Mae who was crying and her stud was prancing like he just won the rodeo. Then I see Billy. When I asked where you were, he told me to look for you in hell. Elena kept punching his arm and called him a moron over and over. Hours ago Annie almost ran me over in her haste to get to the parking lot. Not so much as a goodbye. Had a good day, did you?" She sat down next to him, taking his chin in her hand, clucking over his bloody lip.

"Miss Ruthie, do you know I could have been fishing all day? Had the cabin all set; it still is. Probably have six or seven steelheads by now ready to clean and cook. Charlie Dog and I would be ready to curl up with a good book and a cold beer. But noooo I had to listen to *that* woman." He began to mimic Annie's southern accent. "Oh Dash, go to the picnic. See your friends. It will be sooo much fun." He looked at Ruthie. "Damn Southern belle. Shouldn't let 'em cross the Mason-Dixon line. Just because she's smart and cute and funny she thinks she can rule the world. Well, not this fella. No, that's it. Off women forever."

When Ruthie started to chuckle, he sat up. "You laugh but I mean it this time. No more women; I'm officially celibate."

Ruthie broke into a laugh. He scowled at her. "Stop it! I thought you were my friend. Oh wait, that's right, *I have no friends!*"

She sighed. "Your father is right. You can be tiresome. Come on, Pitiful. Got some fine Irish whiskey that would make your ma proud.

Think of me as a substitute mother. Helene-Marie always said a good belt cured a lot of ails."

Dash stared at her. "My mother never said that."

"Well she should have. Get your ass up and let's get going. If you don't want a drink, fine, but you'd be a sorry excuse for an Irishman. Or would you rather me drive you home?"

"Lord no. Billy and Elena might be there, picking up their stuff. Hopefully they'll let Charlie Dog out. No, give me a lift to your house. I'm supposed to meet a classmate at Little Biff's later. I can walk from your house. Who knows? Maybe Emmysue will put me up for the night."

After he stood, he reached over to help Ruthie stand. As she was brushing off the seat of her pants, she said, "So, let's see. 'Off women forever' lasted about three minutes. Or is Emmysue one of those strangely named guys?"

Dash made a face. "It's not like that, Miss Ruthie. Emmysue is just an old friend I haven't seen in a long time. She's got a problem that she needs to discuss with me. Get your mind out of the gutter, woman."

Ruthie cocked her head. "Poor you. That accident did a number on your brain. Well, think what you want but sounds like trouble to me."

The bungalow where Ruthie lived was three streets behind and six blocks over from Little Biff's. This was the edge of the town limits. By the time they pulled into her drive the fireworks had begun. Ruthie stopped to admire the colorful display. Dash just walked onto the porch.

"Don't you want to watch?" she asked.

"Nah, saw the real stuff years ago and I have no fondness for a lit night sky. If you're going to stand there gawking, give me the key. I do need that whiskey."

They went inside. Dash wandered a bit, checking out the bookcases he made for her last year. Ruthie announced she would make her famous omelet since they shouldn't drink on an empty stomach.

She said, "This won't take long. Take a shower if you want."

After cleaning up, Dash climbed onto one of the bar stools next to the prep area. Propping his elbows on the counter, he rested his chin on his hands, watching Ruthie stir the ingredients, pouring them into the pan.

"Owen still come for dinner?" he asked with a mischievous smile on his face.

Ruthie reached over with her wooden spoon to tap his hands. "Wipe that smirk off your face. Your father and I are just good friends. We worked very well together so don't go thinking there were or are any shenanigans going on. Your parents were too good to me when Wally died for me to even think about... okay I thought but did nothing. I know you don't see it but your father can be a charming man."

Setting out two plates, she dished up the omelet. "Hey, tall guy, get some of the good glasses down from over there. You know where the whiskey is."

They raised their glasses in a salute to Helene-Marie. Dash gobbled down his omelet and drained his glass. "Mind if I have another?" he asked.

"No, but go slowly this time. Don't need you passing out on the floor. I'd hate to call Sam and ask for his assistance moving you. Oh, before we do anything else, let me get your statement about the Carter incident."

"Damn, Miss Ruthie, feels like two weeks ago. But fine. I don't need Sam chewing my ass out."

They moved to her computer where Dash dictated his side of the story. By the time they finished he was yawning. She pointed to the guest room.

"Why don't you stretch out in there? I'm going outside to watch the rest of the fireworks. I promise to wake you."

His eyes flickered open. His brain registered the bright sunlight. The rest of his body registered pain. Dash slowly pulled himself up, unwrapping his arms from the pillow he clung to like a life jacket. Slinging his legs over the side of the bed, he sat. Out of the corner of his eye he saw Ruthie leaning against the door jamb.

Covering his yawn, he said, "Miss Ruthie, did you beat me with a bat last night? Can't believe how much I hurt."

Smiling Ruthie said, "A little fuzzy headed, are we? No, I didn't take a bat to you. Carter took his fists to you."

"Shit. Tell me I put the bastard in the hospital so I know he hurts as much as I do." Dash implored.

"Well, not the hospital but the jail. So to answer your question, I imagine he'll be in pain for a while longer than you will. Now would you like some coffee? No whiskey added."

Dash nodded slowly. "Hey, last thing I remember you saying was 'I promise to wake you up.' Guess I should have specified what time, what day." Flexing his shoulders, he added, "Fess up old lady. What did you put in the omelet? 'Coz I never sleep more than four hours at a time unless I am sick or have been drugged."

Ruthie laughed. "I'm invoking the fifth. You'll never prove I added anything. Not with the day you had and the booze you drank. No, mum's the word." As she stepped away, she added, "And I did try to wake you but you snored on."

"What did you do? Stand in the front yard and whisper my name?"

"Hell, Dash, I could have clanged cymbals over your head last night and you wouldn't have budged. Off to get you some caffeine."

Dash looked at the alarm clock sitting on the bed stand. "Nine o'clock? Poor Charlie Dog. Gotta get moving."

Ruthie returned holding up her hand. "Wait. I've been out there so Charlie's had his morning constitutional and breakfast. So rest easy on that account."

"How the hell did you get in? No, don't tell me. You too have a key and a code. Thank you Owen. His sense of security defeats me every day. Any evidence Billy and Elena stayed there last night?"

She handed him a note from Billy: 'Took care of your dog for you. Here are your keys.' Dash crumbled the note tossing it across the room. Standing, he grabbed at the pajama bottoms that started to slip.

"My clothes?"

Ruthie pointed to the chair. "I washed them thinking you wouldn't want to meet your Emmysue in them, kinda rank."

"Well, there's that. Thanks. I'm going to take a shower to wake up." He took a step. "Hey, you want to go to JoJo's for breakfast? My treat, if I can find my wallet."

"You're on. Check the bed stand for your wallet. Take your time. I'm going to read the paper on the back porch. Oh Annie left your truck keys on the kitchen table."

Dash muttered, "At least she didn't burn down the house and ditch the truck into the lake. Hey, did you check to see if she slashed all my clothes or trashed my office? Woman scorned and all that. Well, maybe not scorned as much as ignored. Probably not a good thing either."

He gingerly hoisted himself off the bed, moaning and groaning the whole time. In his head he could hear his father telling him he got what he deserved for over-indulging in the whiskey. Hated it when the old man was right.

Breakfast turned into an hour long affair with plenty of laughing. Dash figured he was still punch drunk, or maybe just drunk, but Ruthie was so droll. He was enjoying himself; something he had given up on last night.

"Want to go fishing? I still have a few days at the cabin I've borrowed from an old Army pal. We could drive up, see what's biting. What do you say? I'm sure Sam owes you about a million days off."

"You're on, kiddo. Just a few days, right? I need to let Sam know I'll be gone. Let's get moving."

Ruthie dropped him off at the old homestead. He promised to be back at her place in just a bit. After packing a few things, grabbing his fishing gear and settling Charlie Dog into the truck, he glanced out the back window to see if Annie was outside. A bit of groveling needed there. If he only had a good explanation for his churlish behavior yesterday, but the head injury thing only went so far. Being chicken-hearted where women were concerned he decided a nice bunch of flowers might soften her up a bit. He'd take her out to dinner and maybe even spring for a piece of jewelry.

Back in town, he walked down the street to the Petal Pusher florist. There was a sign on the door saying the shop was closed. Just as he was about to turn around, the door opened and Peggy McCafferty ushered him in.

"I've been waiting for you. Saw big brother Billy at Mass where he told everyone who would listen what a prick you were at the picnic yesterday."

"Billy better watch it or I'll sue him for slander." Dash said.

Laughing Peg said, "Think you have to prove he's wrong first." Snapping her fingers, she said, "Anyway, a lightbulb went off in my tiny brain. Cousin Dash will be contrite and that means flowers for everyone. I couldn't pass up a chance to make my financial goal for the year today. So order away!"

"First, I need a nice cheerful bouquet that says sorry for being a jerk even though I'm pretty sure I wasn't one. That goes to Annie Dewitt. She's next door at Franklin's. The next one is for Elena. Is she still in town or have they gone back to Columbus?"

Glancing at the clock, Peg said, "They're probably pulling out now. Spent the night at Tommy's; you'll hear from him about that. So you want a bouquet sent to her house or office?"

"Doesn't matter unless you think Billy will throw it out if it arrives at their home."

"He wouldn't dare. Elena will throw him out first."

"Now, the biggest best bouquet of red roses for Mae. No card. You have her new address, don't you?"

Peg leaned on the counter, pencil to her lips. "And what would the boyfriend think of you sending her flowers? Two things will happen: one, he claims the roses are from him; two, he pitches them. Either way you lose. What's her office address? Best bet, agree?"

"How the hell did you find out about the boyfriend? Did Mae tell everyone before she told me?"

Shaking her head, his cousin said, "You've forgotten about the Peg Pipeline. I know who's going to die three weeks before they even get sick. And I start planning the wedding flowers before people meet."

Dash laughed. "Why aren't you working for Homeland Security? You *will* let me know if the Taliban or al-Qaida comes to town, won't you?"

"You're number one on *that* call list. Now back to the flowers. It might be more effective if you send Mae a small bouquet every week, no card. Should keep you in her thoughts." Peg snorted, "Like she's able to forget you. We might be skirting the no-call, no-text agreement but we'll plead ignorance after the fact."

"What don't you know about this triangle? You've not started planning the wedding flowers yet have you?"

Peg rolled her eyes. "It won't last. He's a loser. I can spot them miles away."

Looking to the ceiling, he added, "Oh what the hell. Send flowers to your mom with my love, to my sister and my sister-in-law, and to any female McCafferty and Hammond. One for my neighbor, Mrs. Guzy, she of the perfect apple pie. What the hell! Even make one for yourself while you're spending all my money."

She wriggled with pleasure. Reaching over the counter, she gave him a peck on the cheek. "Have fun fishing."

Throwing his hand into the air, he asked, "Okay, how did you know I'm going fishing?"

"Silly. You always go fishing when you're upset. *And* your fishing rods are sticking out over the edge of the truck bed. Love you! Be safe."

With a deep sigh he left the Petal Pusher laughing.

Next stop was Little Biff's motel to see if Emmysue was still there. Maybe she would want to go fishing as well, but he was informed she checked out early that morning. No message was left for him. Batting zero!

Dash, Ruthie and Charlie Dog pulled into the Landings' Cabin resort area. The drive up north was pleasant. No traffic since the fourth of July had been on a Saturday so most weekenders had traveled on Friday.

Exiting the truck, Dash stopped to stretch out his back. Charlie Dog jumped down and began sniffing around. Ruthie came round the truck.

"Why are we stopping here?" she asked.

"A couple named Chatworthy keep the cabin keys. They also run a little grocery/bait shop. Thought we'd pick up a few provisions. A word of caution---they live up to the name, very chatty so don't engage or we'll never get out of here."

Dash wasn't exaggerating. After a litany of questions to which Dash either nodded or shrugged, he loaded the groceries and his companions into the truck. It was a short drive around the inlet to the cabin. Part of Dash's rental agreement was he would do a few repairs to cover his rent.

Chuckling, Ruthie told him she told Mrs. Chatworthy they were having a romantic getaway. She thought it was a 'hoot', an expression she used often.

Not enamored of her ruse, Dash looked sternly at her. "Please. Low key. Pretend we're on the run from the law. No need to be memorable."

Once at the cabin site, Dash surveyed his upcoming projects while Ruthie and Charlie Dog explored the environs.

Sitting on the steps, Dash made notes on the work ahead. Ruthie and Charlie Dog walked up, "Hey, we gonna eat anytime soon? I know CD's food is ready made, but if you think I'm doing all the cooking, you are sadly mistaken my friend." She joined him on the steps, waiting for an answer.

He handed her a precise timeline of work/eat/fishing/exercise. She studied it, handed it back to him with an under-the-breath comment which soundly suspiciously like mutiny to Dash.

Standing, he said, "Okay, revised agenda. You do whatever you want and I'll do whatever I need." That pronouncement earned him a salute.

The next two days went according to the new non-plan. The only wrinkle, Dash discovered he lacked several tools to finish his project. Hating to, but seeing no alternative, he drove back to the Chatworthy store and rented the implements. No need to buy since somewhere in Clover Pointe one of his co-workers was probably prying something up or out with the missing crowbar.

Four

Sheriff Sam had taken the fifth of July off so when he sauntered into his office on Monday, the sixth, he was surprised to find his desk littered with messages. Ruthie usually handled all this, leaving only the most important for him to read.

He opened the door and yelled for her, only to be informed she had decided to take several days off. He retreated to his office and began to plow through all the papers. A knock on the door caused him to stop and cry 'enter'. Deputy Collins came in bearing a sheet of paper.

"Thought I'd bring this to you rather than dump it on your desk."

After glancing at it, Sam pulled out his phone and texted his brother, 'Where are you? Have questions.' He then texted Ruthie, asking her the same question. Figuring he would give Billy Mac and Mae a shout out as well. Finally he texted Annie. Asking everyone if they knew where Dash was.

The answers came flying back from Billy, Mae and Annie. The gist was they didn't know, didn't care and if they never saw him again, so be it.

He opened his door again, this time calling for Collins.

"Any idea what that brother of mine did on the Fourth, beside the Carter incident. Judging from the responses from his closest friends, he made an ass of himself, offending them in the bargain."

Answering that she had no idea what went on as she had been assigned to the other end of the park, she suggested Sam call his sister Dolly.

He rang the bookstore to learn Dolly was out of the store having lunch. Since Annie was filling in, Sam decided to broach the 'where is Dash' question.

"Why don't you ask Emmysue the Prom Queen?"

"Enough said, Annie. So sorry. I guess he'll turn up when he does. Big boy and all. Take care."

Sam wondered if he could convince the Army to take Dash back. His phone pinged twice. Reply from Dash: Gone fishing. Ruthie's only said:

Me too! Shaking his head, he texted back to both of them: Thanks. Bring some home for me. Don't be gone too long.

Returning to the paper Collins handed him, he discovered it was the statement from Dash about the Carter incident. He noted that it had been emailed to the office at midnight on the Fourth from Ruthie's home computer. A picture was beginning to develop and he didn't like it.

The interior of Lulu's strip joint looked like any other strip joint in any other town. The dusty light fixtures added to the atmosphere of dingy and dim. Two bright lights were focused on the runway stage where, on this Monday afternoon, two emaciated-looking young women gyrated to the sounds of a scratch-ridden record.

The stocky man slid onto a stool at the bar, signaling the bartender he was ready to order. Scotch on the rocks was placed in front of the customer.

"Is it always this empty in here?" he asked.

"Nah, you just caught us at a bad time. Today is a bit of a holiday since the Fourth was on Saturday. Lots of people went out of town; they just ain't back yet. You new in town or just passing through?"

"Just passing through. Supposed to meet a friend here. Business associate. Figured this would be a good place to grease his gullet and maybe I can swing a bigger deal than planned." He took a sip of his drink, turning to watch the girls on stage.

He ordered another drink. A man sat next to him even though the rest of the stools were unoccupied. Glancing at the newcomer, he snarled, "You lonely? Any particular reason you've decided to crowd me?"

The newcomer flexed his back, stretching out his arms displaying well-developed biceps. He looked over at the stocky man.

"I saw you at the picnic and wanted to ask you a question." He reached into his back pocket to pull out his wallet, removing a photo. He slid it over to the older man. "By any chance did you see this woman on Saturday?"

Looking at the picture, the stocky man replied, "Crap, in this light I can't see anything. Hey, barkeep, you got a flashlight under that counter? I can't see my hand in this place."

The bartender slid a flashlight down to the customer who turned it on, shining the light on the photo. The picture was of a beautiful woman with very long blonde hair. She wore diamonds on her ears and around her neck. She wasn't smiling broadly, just a hint. Turning the photo over to see if a name was attached to the face, he shook his head.

"Sorry pal. I'm pretty sure if I saw this broad I'd remember her. Hell, I probably would have tried to screw her." Handing the photo back, he asked, "She in some trouble? Runaway wife? Hate to say it but she looks a bit old for you."

The younger man swiveled on the stool so he could put his arms on the bar. "My boss's old lady. I mean to him she's a young one, probably by fifteen or twenty years. Trophy wife. He's offering a reward to anyone who helps find her. That's why I'm here, trying to ferret out where she might be. Seems she was coming to town for some corny class reunion which was held at the Fourth of July picnic."

"You said you saw me there. A reason I was so memorable?" The older man sipped his scotch.

"Not particularly. You just didn't seem to fit in. Kept moving around, watching the ladies."

"Didn't know that was a crime. You a cop?"

"No, I told you I work for the lady's old man and I do mean old. And no, I'm not a P.I. just one of his security crew." Tapping the photo, he said, "I'm just tired of being in this shithole. Need to find this broad so I can get back to my lady, at least the one in Texas. Listen, are you going to be around for a few days? Let me give you his card. I've written my number on the back. If you see her, give me a call. There's a nice reward in it for you. How's twenty-five g's sound?"

The recipient of this information looked askance. "Hey, don't kid a kidder. What's going on? Nobody offers that kind of cash just for a piece of ass. What'd the broad do or what is she going to do that has the old man's balls twisted in a knot?"

The young man shrugged. "Not sure. I'm only privy to a small part of what goes on in the old man's world. I'm muscle, not brains." He tucked the photo and his business card into the other man's shirt pocket. Tapping it, he said, "Call anytime and I'll come running. You blend in better than I do. Don't be a stranger."

He slid off the bar stool, dropping a fifty dollar bill onto the bar. "Keep 'em coming for my friend."

The door to Lulu's opened, flooding the bar area with bright sunshine. In walked another stocky man who stepped aside as the young muscled man exited, bumping into him.

"Well, excuse me, Arnold. Sorry to be in your way."

The young man tossed over his shoulder, "My name ain't Arnold, jerk."

"Yeah, it's Einstein." The newcomer walked over to the man still seated at the bar. He sat down next to him. "Is that what passes for intelligentsia here?" He waved to the barkeep, pointing to the glass in front of his comrade. Noticing the fifty dollar bill on the bar, he said, "That yours? Big spender!"

Ralph Scott turned to Jock Hadley. "Let's take our drinks to a table." Glancing at the barkeep, he added, "A little more private. Got something to share."

As they carried their drinks to a table in the corner, Jock asked, "I'm hoping you found Annie. Pretty sure I know where she is but I'd like to make sure I don't surprise the wrong woman."

After they were seated, Ralph leaned into Jock. "A couple of things. I did see Annie at the picnic. She was bouncing between two guys. One pretty tall and clean cut, the other a bit shorter, scruffier. Both look like they could be ex-military so either could be the stud your son told you about. What's your next move?"

"I'll wait a day or two. Verify Annie's whereabouts and check out this stud; see how dangerous he could be. Then I'll approach her for the money."

"Still don't know why you're so sure she'll pony up big bucks to get you out of her life. I mean, she already thinks you're gone."

Jock smiled. "Like the proverbial bad penny, here I am again. She hates me. Don't worry. Her money is almost in my pocket."

Ralph motioned for Jock to get closer. "Know that bodybuilder you bumped into on the way out. Well, he's looking for a broad who came up here over the Fourth. He's offering a 25 grand reward for information leading to her whereabouts. I think we should do some looking. Another 25 would go a long way into helping us get out of this town, this country. Whaddya think?"

Jock reached out and tapped Ralph on the head. "Let's just stick to the plan. We probably don't have a whole lot of time for snooping. And, genius, what's to say this jerk is really going to pay you the money?"

Seeing the chagrined look on Ralph's face, he added, "Well, okay. You can look around as soon as we verify where my darling ex-wife is staying. Hopefully which ever stud she's bonking won't be staying with her. And, if you find this broad, you can have all the money. Deal?"

"Yeah, thanks. Listen I've booked a room at the Blue Belle B&B off Route 2, other side of town. Where are you staying, if I may ask?" Ralph said.

"About as far away from here as I can. Next turnpike exit, Motel 6. I'll just dart back and forth for now." Smirking he added, "Unless the sweet little Annie decides she wants a real man around. Wonder if I can convince her to hit the road with me, I mean, us."

Pushing back his chair he rose. "Keep in touch. And for God's sake stay under the radar if you can."

He walked over to the door and pushed it open, again flooding the joint with bright sunlight. Everyone inside groaned as they squinted.

Five

The Blue Belle Bed and Breakfast, located off Route 2 in the eastern end of Lakota County, had been in operation for almost three years. Wanda and Mason Handke bought the old Carson mansion with the idea to create their own little oasis of happiness, one they could share with those people lucky enough to stay with them.

There wasn't a blue bell flower anywhere on the property. Instead the name was in honor of Wanda's first kitten, a pleasant but distant memory. Wanda, never one to skimp on detail, ordered special paper to hang on the walls of the main floor. The reception area had to have blue flowered paper whereas the breakfast parlor needed sunny yellow flowers to set the happy tone for the day ahead. The very formal dining room looked like something out of a British magazine featuring country homes. The bedrooms, on the other hand, were simply painted. The wall color was complimented by the drapes and furniture. The key handed to the guest upon registration, after forking over his/her credit card, was color coded to his/her temporary home away from home.

What Wanda and Mason did not factor into their 'little oasis of happiness' were the number of repair/renovation projects necessary to keep a leak-free roof above their heads and a solid floor beneath their feet. The cost wasn't what bothered them, but rather it was the noise and clutter as these repairs were being done that was upsetting.

Once they learned the local military hero, one Dash Hammond, had formed a small renovation company with other veterans, the Handkes felt it was their civic duty to hire Dash and his band of merry men. It was the beginning of a nice relationship: '4B ranch' as Dash called the property needed a bit of this and that consistently; no job so big Dash and his guys couldn't handle it. The current project was replacing the small porch and stairs exiting the back of the building. Since this egress wasn't in constant use, the work wouldn't interrupt the tranquility.

The assignment fell to Sam's twin boys. Fairly straightforward: dismantle the steps and replace the treads and railings. The tools and lumber necessary were provided by Dash. The instructions were for Johnny and Joey to be as inconspicuous as possible, and neat, a priority at any work site.

Johnny was the oldest by 20 minutes but the less responsible of the two. Everyone in town remarked how, even though the boys were twins, they were different in looks and temperament. Johnny resembled his sheriff father, stocky, brown hair, a few inches shorter than Joey who inherited whatever gene created his uncle Dash. With the curly black hair and piercing blue eyes, plus the added inches and slender build, he was often mistaken for Dash's son, if only Dash had had one.

The boys, about to enter their senior year at Ohio State, spent the summer working for their uncle. Most of the time they were faithful to the schedule devised by Dash. 'Most of the time' did not include the week following Fourth of July.

Johnny was in love, again, as his brother would add. So when the twins received the text from their uncle that he was leaving town for a short fishing trip, Johnny declared an extended holiday for himself. He would be knocking off after his shift on Tuesday heading to Cleveland to visit the latest inamorata aptly named Aphrodite.

Three o'clock Tuesday afternoon found the twins cleaning up the work site. They were gathering the old treads and flooring when one of the guests approached them.

"Hey guys, nice job. I've been watching you from the garden area. Good team work. Do you have your own company or are you working for someone else?" The stocky man asked.

Joey stopped piling the lumber, stepping over to the man. "Thanks for the compliment. We work for our uncle's company. Are you in need of any renovation work? I'll give you his card if you like." Extending his hand, he introduced himself.

The man replied, "My friends call me Ralph. I'm looking around at some of the real estate available in the area. Hoping to find a summer cottage close to the lake. Figure anything I find will probably need some work. Yeah, if you have a card, I'd take it."

Reaching into his back pocket for his wallet, Joey pulled out a business card. When he handed it to the stocky man, he looked closely at the man.

"Were you at the picnic the other day? I think I saw you talking to my aunt. Beautiful lady, auburn or red hair. Though now that I think of it she seemed rather angry with you."

Ralph shook his head. "Yeah, I accidentally stepped on her toes. Quite the temper. Hey, won't keep you any longer. If I find a property I'm really interested in, I'll give you or" glancing at the card, "Dash Hammond a call." He walked back to the garden area.

"Hurry up stupid. I don't want to spend all day doing this." Johnny yelled at his brother.

"Okay, okay, I'll move the lumber to the truck; you pick up the tools." Joey said as he gathered an armful of old treads to be discarded.

The twins worked furiously. Johnny finally yelled "I'm off. See you Thursday or Friday or even later if I get lucky." And he sprinted for his car.

Joey stood there muttering under his breath. Wiping his brow, he headed for his truck and the recycling center to drop off the lumber. Wondering how Danny, Dash's partner, would feel about Johnny abandoning the project, he left the 4B.

The stocky man walked back to the work site. He bent down to retrieve the crowbar he had surreptitiously pushed under the skeletal porch. Handling it carefully, he smiled thinking how his partner might use this to coerce the ex-wife into relinquishing her hefty divorce settlement.

Dash was up and out early Tuesday morning. Again, he and Charlie Dog did their stretching exercises and then ran for an hour. When he returned Ruthie was still in her room. Not wanting to disturb her he went down to the boat and pushed off. He and Charlie Dog did a bit of fishing and swimming. As they were motoring back to the shore, Dash spotted Ruthie running towards him, waving something in her hand.

Hopping out of the boat, he ran toward her. "Is there a problem? What's going on?"

Ruthie handed him his phone. There were four messages from Annie, all right in a row, all this morning.

He opened the last: 'Pls pls come! Jock here! Trouble!' The other three messages were about the same. Annie's ex-husband had shown up and was causing some kind of hassle.

Dash texted back: 'eta 3-4 hrs, call Sam or Trigger.'

He called Sam who picked up immediately.

"Finally back in town are you little brother? Got several bones to pick with you...."

Before Sam could finish, Dash stopped him. "Shut up and listen, please. Annie's ex-husband is in town. She sent me four texts, very upset. Could you get out there? I'm three to four hours away. I'll pack up and hit the road immediately, but would appreciate it if you would check on her. Please."

"On it. Let me know when you get into town. Drive safely. And bring Ruthie back, you bastard."

Dash turned to Ruthie. "Get the lead out. We're needed back in town. I'll start packing up the truck. I'll pay the Chatworthys extra to do the cleaning so we can leave right away."

The trip down from Michigan was less pleasant. Only one bathroom break and only because Ruthie swore she was about to burst. She then had to listen to Dash going on and on about drinking so much coffee. She glared at him, effectively shutting him up.

They rolled into Clover Pointe. Dash practically pushed Ruthie out of the truck as he flew by her place. Calling Sam, he asked what his brother had found out at Annie's.

"Nothing. The two of them were sitting at the kitchen table. Annie looks fine; she was smiling. The husband looks dodgy but that's just a professional opinion. I asked to speak with her in private but she declined. Said she overreacted this morning when Jock showed up. Things were good; hoped she didn't put me out any. Told me to text you to stay where you were and enjoy the fishing."

"What do you think I should do?"

"Go home. Unpack. Walk over to say hi and see what you think. Don't get confrontational; call for backup. Deep breath, brother, deep breath."

So Dash did most of that. Once home he dug around in his files to find a contract his cousin had drawn up six years ago when he had to leave town for nine months. Franklin gave Dash permission to handle the property as he saw fit, rent it or not. Neither cousin ever gave much thought to the paper, but Dash figured he could use it now.

Dash knocked on the back door of Annie's, well actually his Cousin Franklin's house. She answered the door, very politely thanking him for coming.

Inside the kitchen a stocky man with a salt and pepper goatee stood next to the table. Suitcases were at the bottom of the stairs.

"Dash, this is Jock Hadley. I'm sorry I bothered you. A misunderstanding, that's all."

Jock walked over to Dash who stood with his arms crossed. Everything in his stance shouted his displeasure.

"Well, so this is the 'super stud' I've been hearing about. Ex-military. Annie forgot to add that I'm her husband, not her *ex*, just in case you didn't know."

Dash looked over at Annie. She shrugged.

"Oh, my wife didn't tell you. We're not divorced. I've come to take her back where she belongs, by my side. So what do you think of the lying bitch now? She really screwed you didn't she? Or maybe I should say you really screwed her."

Ignoring the man standing very close to him, Dash asked Annie if she invited Jock to stay, nodding towards the suitcases.

"No, I didn't invite him to stay. That's why I called you in the first place, but I don't want any trouble. Jock, *please!* Just leave?"

Instead he jabbed at Dash's chest. "So what you gonna do, big guy? Throw me out?"

"I'm not going to throw you out, but if you touch me again, I will take your finger and shove it where the sun don't shine. Now if I break a few bones in the process, so be it. Now, *step back*."

Hearing the menace in Dash's voice, Jock took two giant steps back.

Dash pulled out the contracts. "My good cousin Franklin is quite anal. He has a contract for everything; I think he even has one to make sure the sun comes up every morning. A few years back he drew up this baby giving me control over his property in his absence. There is a clause pertaining to unwanted guests and my right to evict them. Annie, I don't suppose you read the fine print in your contract as house sitter. Again, there is a clause about guests. I have final say. If, as in this case, I feel the guest to be unsavory I can have him removed."

Dash moved to open the back door. He ushered in two deputies from the Sheriff's department.

"Deputies, please remove this man and his suitcases from the premises. If you can escort him out of the county that would be wonderful. If not, please remind him if he comes onto this property he will be trespassing and I will have his ass thrown in jail."

Jock turned to Annie saying, "This isn't over." Stopping in front of Dash, he said, "Watch out, big guy. I've cut bigger men than you off at the knees. We'll see who has the most broken bones then."

After they left, Dash sat down gesturing for Annie to join him. While gathering his thoughts, he admired the flowers he had sent her, turning the vase round and round.

"Well, Lucy, you've got some 'splaining' to do. Husband, ex-husband. Small prefix but crucial."

She sat down, rubbing her forehead and smiling faintly at him.

"I am soooo stupid. When I left South Carolina, I thought he had signed all the papers. The marriage was over. Didn't think I needed any papers; figured I would get them eventually. My Aunt Delia told me the attorney died a few months ago. Didn't think it was a big deal. I honestly don't know what to do."

"Well, it's an excuse. Not a good one but knowing you, I can see you forgetting the little details like signatures and copies. Not happy with you, Miss Annie. You dump me at the picnic and then beg me to come back to save your ass, nice as it is. But that's another discussion for another day. Do you know exactly what he wants?"

Seeing her reaction, he added, "Not that any man wouldn't love to have you for a wife, companion. You're pretty, intelligent, sexy. Can I stop now or do I need to find a few more of your assets to list? I'm never digging myself out of this, am I?"

Annie leaned back in her chair and shook her head. "When I opened the door, bang, there he was; I went into a kind of shock. When I left Charleston only my aunt knew where I was going. Didn't even tell the kids, though I eventually told Timothy. The last few conversations with

Jock were very nasty although the division of assets was fairly quick and equal. We both wanted out so badly."

Shivering at the memory, she continued. "After I recovered from seeing him again, I went into the john, threw up and texted you. I honestly don't know what he said. I think something about what a neat hideout I found for myself. Then he started on about how we weren't really divorced. I watched his mouth move but not much of what he said registered. Then he asked me for some money, saying everything would be fine if I just gave him what he wanted. All I can think of is he has run through his part of our estate. I told you he made a lot of money but also frittered a lot away as well."

Dash gestured to her. "I recall you saying something like that. So I take it he wanted some money from you. Figured he didn't come all this way for $100. None of my business but dare I ask how much?"

"Add three more zeroes." Annie answered.

Sitting back in the chair, he tilted his head to ask, "Did I hear you correctly? One hundred grand? Now this *really* is none of my business, but do you have that close at hand?"

Shrugging, Annie nodded.

"Dammit woman. Next time we go out to eat you're picking up the tab. And we'll rethink that trip to Paris; you just might be paying for that as well." Muttering to himself, he continued, "I may have to reconsider our relationship."

"Dolly said you still had your First Communion money. Not sure exactly what that means but I'm thinking she means you're a tightwad. She said you got a boatload of an insurance settlement from the accident. So does it kill you to spend a few bucks?" Annie spouted off to him.

"My sister is quite the ingrate. And, for your information, the settlement was more the row boat size than freighter and most of it is in a fund set up to pay for care when my brain turns to mush, which is happening sooner than anticipated if this conversation is any example of how I'm thinking. But we digress. Annie, it's your money but if you were to ask for my advice, I'd say don't do it. Seriously what can he do to you? I suppose if he can prove you're still married he might be able to tap into your resources. Don't know. We could ask cousin Tommy Mac if he knows. He handles a lot of people's money."

"It's not that I want to give it to him or that I'm really afraid of him but he could make things uncomfortable. I just want this to end, for him to go away forever." She looked hopefully at Dash. "You could...."

Dash stood and started backing up. "No, Annie. Don't even go there. I don't know what you think I could or would do, but forget about it. No way. Tell him no. No money."

"I'm not sure what you think I was asking but it wasn't that." Pursing her lips, she asked, "What if it was Mae asking, not me?"

He took a few steps around the kitchen. "Discussion over. Quite the couple you and Jock. All that aside, he *is* quite the catch. Question, do you feel comfortable staying here on your own or would you rather be my guest, in the guest bedroom, mind you? Tonight you should call your aunt, maybe she knows who took over your attorney's practice. You need to find this person 'toot sweet' as my old French teacher would say."

Releasing a held breath, Annie smiled. "I'll take you up on the offer for a room. If he comes back tonight at least he won't be able to harass me further. Should I pack for a couple of days or just overnight? And, just so you know that I haven't forgotten, when this is over, we'll talk about who ditched whom at the picnic. I'm not happy with you either." Screwing up her nose at him, she added, "So there."

Ignoring her, he said, "Couple of days. If we can't figure out something by then, you may have to go back to Charleston to straighten this out. I'm going to check the doors and windows to make sure they're all locked. Don't dawdle, okay?"

They removed to Dash's house where he told her to pick out a bedroom. She dutifully carried her bags up the stairs not asking for assistance. The usually gentlemanly Dash wandered around his kitchen, making sure all items were lined up properly as if a military inspection were due.

When Annie came down, she asked him how long he was going to be mad at her.

"Well, let me put it this way. That song, *Let It Go*, is not my anthem. Call Mae. Ask her how long I can hold a grudge. Learned all I know from her."

He set a pad and pencil in front of her. "Write down everything you know about him. Social, birthdate, birthplace, education, blood type, any places of employment. Hell, if you know how often he pisses, add that. You remember my old Army buddy, Grady Lennington and his 'eye in the sky' security firm. Think I'm going to call Grady and ask him to start a search. Let's see what his firm can dig up."

Charlie Dog followed Dash into the office. Dash announced, "It's going to be an early night for me. You can do whatever you want. Just don't leave the house. I have no idea if there is any food, but have at it."

"Do you want something to eat?" Annie asked.

"See what's there. You know what I like. A sandwich would be good." And he closed the door.

Several minutes later, Annie tapped on the door. She opened it to present Dash with a ham sandwich on rye, a pickle and a beer.

"Trying to worm your way back into my good graces, are you? Thanks."

He picked up the plate and followed her back to the kitchen table. Dash wolfed down the sandwich while Annie picked at hers.

"Did you remember to bring your laptop? Why not see if you can get your divorce records online? Might not have to bother your aunt." He suggested.

When Annie didn't move, didn't make eye contact, Dash added the ubiquitous 'whatever?'

After letting Charlie Dog out for one last run, he locked the door and said goodnight.

He was drifting off to sleep when he heard a timid knock. He looked up to see Annie's silhouette in the doorway.

"Dash, I really could use a hug. I'm so sorry," she sniffled.

Dash sat up, pulling back the covers. "In for a penny, in for a pound. Come on. Get in here. A hug and that's all."

"Thanks."

She slid under the covers wiggling over to him. He pulled her close, squeezing her. After cuddling with her for a few minutes he began to make love to her.

When it was over, Annie whispered, "You sure know how to give a hug."

He grunted. "Last time until we get this straightened out. Now go to sleep."

She smiled, saying, "Well, in the morning, if it's alright, maybe I'll give you a hug."

Six

Dash slid out of bed around five. He dressed for his run. Charlie Dog waited eagerly. The duo did their warm ups and trotted down the slope heading for the beach. When they returned, Dash threw some food in the dog's bowl and grabbed a handful of cereal for himself. He slipped into his sweats and headed into town to pick up his mail and grab a decent breakfast at JoJo's.

As he sat in the booth sorting his mail, his brother Sam joined him. They discussed the removal of the interloper from the house yesterday. Sam reported Jock got a room at Little Biff's Motel.

After Dash related the exchange of words with Hadley, Sam asked, "If I may ask, what set Hadley off? I mean when I was there he was polite, smiling and so was Annie. So what happened in that hour or two? Why the hostility toward you? On a scale from one to ten, how threatened did you feel?"

"He didn't have a weapon so, one or under. Now if he shows up with a gun, or even indicates he might have one, game changer." Dash stated.

"Were you carrying?" Sam asked.

Chuckling, Dash smiled. "What do you think? Of course I was, am. Not quite comfortable without my sidearm."

"Changing the subject, did you and Annie ever discuss her marital status before this? Or didn't it matter to you?"

"Early on she said something about a shotgun wedding. Jock kept her barefoot and pregnant the first several years of the marriage. He made a ton of money and she lived comfortably. Then she got ticked off at something he did, nasty divorce followed and she moved north. Got the feeling he was a serial adulterer. And, yes, it would have mattered to me. I'm not as immoral as you would like me to be."

Leaning back into the booth, Dash looked at his brother. "Sam, need some brotherly advice. There is a good chance Annie isn't divorced. Apparently she never asked for nor received the final papers. He says they're not; she thought they were. I want to help out but not sure what to do. Suggestions?"

The brotherly advice was very succinct: Remarry Mae and forget about other women.

Dash replied, "Leaving women alone is going to be the easy part. You must be the last person on the face of the earth to learn this but Mae and that Doctor Chandler are talking marriage. And, get this, I'm not to call or text her. Clean cut. Between you and me, I'm not comfortable with that guy."

All Sam could do was shake his head. "You wouldn't be comfortable with any guy, just like she's not comfortable with Annie or any woman with you."

After staring into space for a few minutes, Dash turned to his brother. "Billy and I had words Saturday night. Well, he had words for me, but he's been ragging on me all our lives. Usually I give as good as I get, but this... I don't know. Tired of it all." He pointed to a box sitting on the table. "All my files from Billy. His very professional letter explained he felt he could no longer represent me in any matters. It would be in my best interests to find a lawyer here in town."

Throwing his head back, Dash looked toward the ceiling. "Man, when things go south. Two best friends in one night. New world record. You want my tickets to the Ohio State games? I'll find others; can't sit next to him. Spilling his blood might give a new meaning to 'scarlet'."

"Take a deep breath, little brother. Put your head down and get back to finishing all those remodeling jobs you have on your plate. Then we'll go fishing or just bum around the lake on the boat. Not much in the wisdom department, but I'm told time heals some wounds. Okay?" Sam cocked his head.

Throwing down some bills for a tip, Dash stood, saying he had better get back to the house. Hopefully Jock would see some sense and leave town to turn this into a legal battle back in South Carolina. Gathering up his mail, he waved goodbye.

Sam pulled out his phone, calling Ruthie. "Miss Ruthie, run a check on Jock Hadley lately of Charleston, South Carolina. Let's see what floats to the surface. I need to head off any trouble before little brother finds himself in deep shit. He really has no idea how to operate in the real world. Then again, this just might start a war in our little county."

Annie was sitting at the kitchen table, Charlie Dog's head on her thigh when Dash came through the back door.

"I thought maybe you abandoned me again."

"Again? Hardly abandoned. I couldn't very well 'reunite' with the old gang glued to the picnic bench you refused to abandon. I asked you to join me, not my problem you suddenly decided to turn into the proverbial lump on a log. Would seem like a poor reunion if I never even spoke to them." Screwing up his face, he added, "I'd offer to fill you in on what happened but doubt if you're interested. And, just for the record, I wouldn't leave the dog behind. How are you feeling today? Any great insights into what you might do. Sam said Jock is at Little Biff's Motel in town."

After he put the mail on the table, he threw his hands open. "Anything?"

"I have to work at the bookstore today, ten until two. Would you drive me and then bring me back here? If my car's not there, Jock might not look for me in town. Oh, I did get online and ordered a copy of my divorce records. Unfortunately it will take several days for them to get here. I just don't want to ask Aunt Delia to head downtown and fuss with all this. Would you call Billy Mac for some advice or do you think I should do that?"

Pointing to the box, Dash explained how Billy cut their ties, not elaborating on the incident. "If you want his advice, you make the call. Why don't you try Elena? She works on divorce cases, family law, etc. where Billy is very good with the criminal element. She is one sharp lady and I bet she would be willing to help if she can."

"Did you eat breakfast without me?"

"Yes, Lucy, Ricky ate breakfast without you. I'm still pretty upset. You've put me in a very poor position. I don't have many rules in my life but one is that I don't knowingly get involved with married women. Wouldn't want it to happen to me so don't want to do it anyone else. Though I will admit Jock almost makes me happy he got some payback."

Annie tried to smile but couldn't. "Shall I take the first shower? I'll try not use all the hot water." Glancing at the clock, she added, "I'll be quick."

Dash sorted his mail, trashing most of it. The rest he moved to his office. He secured his legal files in the small safe below the gun safe. He checked email to see if Grady had found anything on Hadley. Nothing yet.

He sent another request: "One more favor. Toss Doctor Chandler Allen, U of M, into your little computer. Let me see what pops. Thanks, G-man. If I ever have a son, I'll name him after you."

Grady replied that a bit of cold cash and a bottle of good Irish whiskey would pay the bill.

As Annie came down, Dash jogged up the stairs for his shower. He returned dressed in khakis and a white shirt raising Annie's eyebrows.

"What no scarlet and gray or Army green? Special occasion?"

"Don't know what the day holds. Let's see what awaits."

After dropping Annie at the bookstore, he parked the Vette behind the City/County administration building. Inside were offices and courtrooms. In the basement was the jail which served both the city and county. Dash headed for the sheriff's department. Ruthie waved at him. Pointing toward his brother's office, he knocked and was told to enter.

Dash took a chair opposite his brother. He rested his chin on his hand as he leaned on the desk, listening while Sam recounted his conversation with his counterpart for Clover Pointe, Chief Robbie Rakestraw. All professional encounters with Robbie were delicate as he was also dating their sister Dolly. She seemed to really like Robbie, but the brothers' jury was still out.

Hadley appeared to be settling in at Little Biff's and the chief of police saw no reason to keep watch on him as he had done nothing within the town limits to warrant more than a hello.

Sam discouraged Dash from setting up surveillance. "Let things take their course. I'm sure Annie will figure out what to do. She's a bright lady. Just sit in the background and keep your cool."

Dash left to wander the town a bit before returning to The Bookshop, the store he co-owned with his sister. Originally purchased to give Dolly a distraction while mourning her husband, Dash also found solace in the stacks of books. After his premature retirement from the Army, he discovered a hideaway.

The old wooden door clanged as Dash pushed it open. The bell hanging from it added a Dickensian flavor to the shop. He took a deep breath, inhaling the scent of old books and new wood polish. He spent hours refinishing the oaken shelves so they glistened, worthy of the books they held. The stock was a mix of old and new books, leather-bound and paperbacks.

He walked over to Tracy, his part-time bookseller. Tall and slender, with almond colored skin, she leaned ever so slightly into him. She motioned her head toward the office at the back of the store, saying, "Annie's in the back with some creepy guy. She wasn't happy to see him but when he started to talk loudly she led him back to the office. It's been pretty quiet. I was hoping you'd stop by. Getting a bad vibe."

Thanking her, he set the lunch down on the counter and made his way to the office. Knocking, he didn't wait to be invited in. Annie stood with her back against the wall; Jock was in her face but talking quietly. He looked over at Dash, saying, "Get out. This doesn't concern you."

Shaking his head, Dash replied, "Sadly it does. Once again you're trespassing. Sorry pal but I own this bookstore. Annie works for me. I get the impression she is feeling threatened. One of my jobs as owner is to protect my booksellers."

He walked over to Jock, looking down at him. "Don't make me say it twice. Get out of my store."

"Nice gig. You pay her to work here. Do you pay her for sex as well?"

Dash glanced at Annie, then back to Jock. "There you go getting stupid, making a bad situation worse. If you weren't such an idiot I'd take you outside and beat the crap out of you. But, being the intelligent one here, I'll pretend I didn't hear that slur about Annie. One, two..."

Jock backed away, saying over his shoulder as he made to leave. "This isn't over."

"Oh for God's sake, Hadley, yes it is! And get yourself a new exit line. Hell, get out of my store, out of my town, out of my county and out of my state. Go back to whatever you crawled out from under. Call Annie on the phone if you want to talk to her. Get your attorney to talk to her attorney. Get out of my sight. NOW!"

Dash took a step toward Jock who had the good sense to retreat, slamming the door.

Annie whispered, "Thank you."

Hugging her, he asked if she was okay. When she nodded in the affirmative, he added, "Lunch is out on the counter, if you're hungry. I've got a few calls to make."

The first call was to the chief of police. He explained what transpired in the bookstore, telling Robbie he did not want Jock anywhere near the store, his house or Franklin's. Robbie simply told him to get a restraining order. His words were along the lines of 'you know where the courthouse is; you're here often enough'.

Next, he called Sam to bring him up to date. Sam's response, he was happy to hear Dash followed his advice, leaving things alone. He hung up.

He stood with his hands on his hips looking around the office. Stacks of papers and books were everywhere. His sister's idea of order was hell and gone from his. But first things first. He needed a new attorney. He walked onto the sales floor, his brow furrowed. Tracy looked over at him.

Finally, he asked, "Tracy, do you know a good attorney?"

A young man who was browsing turned around. He walked over to Dash opening his wallet as he approached. He presented Dash with a card and a newspaper article.

Dash read the article and then asked, "Are you Matthew Livingstone? If you are, you look nothing like the picture in the paper."

"That's my cousin. I'm helping him set up his practice. We rent an office over Sweetie's Pie. You hafta enter from the alley. We know it's not the best but he's just starting out. Want to stroll over there and see what he can do for you. I assure you the rates are very reasonable." Under his breath he mumbled, almost non-existent.

"What the hell! How bad can he be? He graduated law school and passed the bar. Local kid makes good. And, best of all, he's a Buckeye. Lead on Macduff."

Annie peeked out of the small stockroom. "Tracy, has he left?"

"That man, yeah, he left right away."

"No, I meant Dash."

"He's gone as well. What's going on, Annie? You look positively ashen."

"Listen, I've got run an errand. Can I borrow your car? And, if Dash comes back looking for me, just say I had to go out; don't mention the car. Please!" Annie implored.

Tracy frowned but shook her head yes. "The keys are in my purse in the office. You look like I should add, be careful."

The young man introduced himself as Adam Livingstone, first cousin to the burgeoning Perry Mason, except that Matt had no experience with criminal law.

The office of Matthew Livingstone, Esquire, was one big room, partitioned for a reception area. The small desk had a name plate with Adam Livingstone on it.

Calling out to his cousin as they entered, Matt answered, telling him to come on back. 'Back' was just a few feet. The future Perry Mason's portion of the office was sparse but functional. The desk was a bit larger than his cousin's. The wall contained a framed diplomas from Ohio State, undergraduate and the law school. Matthew Livingstone reminded him of Ichabod Crane from the old Disney movie. Tall and thin, Matt's suit needed pressing and the sleeves shortened. He extended his hand to Dash, motioning to him to sit down. There were two padded chairs in front of the desk. Dash guessed they came right from his parents' living room.

Once seated Dash explained what he needed: a restraining order to keep one Jock Hadley out of the bookstore, his house and his cousin's house. He also filled Matt in on the problem Annie had but made it clear that was not what he wanted Matt to handle. Dash could see the eagerness in Matt's eyes. He wondered if he was the first non-related client. The kid seemed to ask all the right questions, made neat notes on the ubiquitous legal pad. At the end of the conversation, Dash asked the price. After hearing a ridiculously low price, Dash pulled out his checkbook. Matt looked relieved.

"If this works out, I'll retain you for my legal services. Any additional billings should be referred to Thomas McCafferty. He handles my financial affairs. You know him? His offices are at the other end of Erie Street."

"Yes sir, I do. I had his sister, Miss Colleen McCafferty, for my ninth grade history class. You probably don't remember but you spoke to our class about the conflict in the Middle East. Very impressive, sir."

"Well, *now* I don't feel at all old. And about the McCaffertys, you can barely stretch your arms without hitting one of them. I'm certain we'll be calling ourselves McCaffertyville in another generation or so. Thanks, kid."

"Sir, I want to reassure you that you'll be in good hands."

They stood to shake hands. As Dash left the office, he turned to his attorney, saying "O-H" to which Matt properly answered "I-O". Giving him a thumbs up, Dash left, thanking Adam on the way out.

Feeling good with the day's work he went back to the bookstore where he spent a ridiculous amount on books for goat farming and cheese making. Tracy kidded him about his new avocation. Collecting Annie they drove home. Dash explained what he had asked his new attorney to do.

"Maybe your Aunt Delia has a line on the attorney who holds your files by now. First order of business should be to call her."

"Dash, I am tempted to just give Jock whatever he wants to finish this. I'll figure out some way to get more money if that is the reason for all this."

"Don't be so brash; you're not always going to be so cute and perky. Trigger might be able to use you as a pole dancer but the tips are only going to carry you so far."

Annie took this ribbing as a good sign Dash was thawing a bit. Taking her phone she borrowed his office. He grabbed a beer to settle in on the porch, telling Charlie Dog all about the goats they were going to buy. He hoped the shepherd part of Charlie's breeding would come in handy. Charlie just listened, unimpressed with the new plan for the backyard.

While Annie talked to her aunt, Dash received a call from his sister-in-law, Marie. She invited them to join Sam and her for some pizza. He gave a tentative yes but said he'd see how Annie was feeling after her call to Charleston. They agreed to meet at Papa's Pizza Parlor at seven, if all went well.

Leaving his office, phone in hand, Annie said, "Aunt Delia's pretty upset about all this." Shoulders slumping, she continued, "I really don't want to mess with this anymore. Think he'd settle for a smaller amount if I promise to send him more money later on."

Dash threw his hands up. "Since I wasn't there for any of the discussions, I don't know what he is thinking. If you have his phone number, call him. I'm guessing he figures being in your face is more intimidating than yelling at you over the phone. As for getting your records, the faster the better would be my vote. Settle the thing once and forever, if possible. Up to you, babe."

Shrugging, Annie walked over to him. Putting her arms around him, she snuggled up to him.

"Annie, Annie, you're a hard woman to resist. Go do whatever you think you need to do so you're ready for pizza tonight. I'm going to make a grocery list; we'll stop on the way home. Now skedaddle."

Seven o'clock found the four fussing about how many toppings they wanted on how many pizzas. The conversation stayed general. Dash rolled out his plan for a goat farm and cheese making business. The women rolled their eyes while Sam shook his head, muttering about head injuries and the need for a keeper for the keeper of the goats. The couples parted in good spirits. Dash reminded Annie of the grocery run.

They were wheeling the overflowing cart out to the truck when Jock stepped out from between cars. Dash couldn't believe his eyes.

"What is *wrong* with you? Just leave us alone."

Jock answered by throwing a punch, connecting with Dash's chin. The ex-soldier countered and a fight was on. Several patrons gathered; most had their phones out to take photos or videos. Annie called 911. By the time the police arrived, Dash had pummeled Jock pretty good. The two officers jumped out almost before the car stopped.

Dash explained what happened, saying he was only defending himself from Jock's onslaught. A report was filed while Jock screamed that Dash was the aggressor. Annie and two patrons backed Dash's version.

Finally everyone was released with warnings to stay away from each other. Dash couldn't have agreed more. Stepping away, he loaded the groceries into the truck. Once Annie got in, he peeled out of the parking lot, yelling to Jock "Get the hell out of my town."

When they arrived home, Annie pleaded a headache, retreating to her chosen bedroom. Dash muttered the whole time he put the provisions away. Final chores: Charlie Dog's evening outing and lock up the homestead. He made an icepack for his right hand and decided to watch ESPN for the rest of the evening.

Seven

Dash woke up in the recliner. The sun had come up, but just barely. Sitting up, he listened for the noise that woke him. Cars. He looked out the front window to see two Clover Pointe police cars in Franklin's driveway. When the police got no answer, they returned to their cars but only to drive to his house.

"Crap." Walking up the stairs he knocked on Annie's door. "Wake up. We've got company. Good old Robbie Rakestraw and some of Clover Pointe's finest. Get dressed before you come down."

The chief of police stood at the back door. He had two officers with him. He was about to knock when Dash opened the door.

"Robbie. Bit early for a social call. What's up?"

Chief Rakestraw answered rather formally, "Mr. Hammond, may we come in? I'm looking for Annie Dewitt Hadley. Since she's not next door, any chance she is here? Need to speak to her."

Robbie looked at the swollen knuckles on Dash's hand but said nothing.

"Not a social visit then. She'll be down in a minute. Coffee anyone? I haven't had my morning cup yet."

He had no takers. As Annie came down the stairs, Dash's phone rang: Grady. Dash stepped aside to talk.

Grady asked, "What's going on Dash? Just saw the cops pull into your driveway. Anything I should know or do?"

"Funny you should ask. Not sure what this is about. They want to talk to Annie probably about her husband. Last night he and I got into a fistfight, can you believe that? Hadn't done that since high school and this week I've been in two! Anyway, not sure what's going to follow."

He glanced over at Rakestraw who motioned for him to join the group. Dash told Grady he would get back as soon as possible. Walking over to where Annie stood nervously eyeing the police, Dash put his arm around her waist.

"Robbie." Dash said.

"The body of a man, possibly Jock Hadley, has been found behind Little Biff's Motel. I'd like Annie to make a formal identification, if possible." Robbie made a point of looking at Dash's fist.

Dash felt Annie tense, then she squeezed his hand. He winced. She turned to the chief of police asking him if Dash could accompany her.

"Of course. I was about to invite Mr. Hammond to come along anyway. The fight last night and all." Rakestraw said.

Dash jumped right in. "Am I giving a statement or is this a formal interview? Should I be making my one phone call? I sense I should have an attorney present."

"Go ahead and call Billy Mac. We can wait for him to get here from Columbus before we start the interview."

"Billy's no longer my attorney. Give me a second."

With that he pulled out his phone, texting Grady: Shit, fan, go. He called Livingstone asking him to meet Dash at the police station. Turning back to Rakestraw, he explained to him he was going to let his dog out, eat a bowl of cereal and he would follow along shortly.

The chief in turn informed him one of the officers would wait and escort him downtown. After that announcement Annie started to panic, asking if she needed an attorney. Not waiting for an answer, she grabbed Dash's phone texting Billy Mac that she, not Dash, needed him.

Dash took her aside. "Annie, I know you don't usually listen to me, but a word of caution. Don't say anything until you hear from Billy. If it is Jock, identify him but make that the extent of your conversation with the cops."

She nodded while Robbie shot angry glances at Dash.

Escorting Annie out, Rakestraw tossed this over his shoulder to his officer. "Get him downtown as soon as possible. Don't let him out of your sight. Check for weapons."

"Tsk, tsk. Robbie, such a lack of trust on your part. I'm kinda glad it's over between you and my sister, never did warm to idea of another lawman in the family."

"Who said it's over?" Robbie asked, confused by the statement.

"Dolly. As soon as she hears you're bringing me in. Oh well, I'm sure she'll eventually find someone worthy of her and the kids."

Rakestraw slammed the door. Dash smiled at the officer, again offering coffee.

Dash cooled his heels in an interview room. Rakestraw was nowhere to be seen and Livingstone was taking his time getting here. The door popped open. The young attorney looked in.

"Oh here you are. Hate to say it but I got lost. I asked to use the bathroom and then got all the directions mixed up. Sorry."

Dash rubbed his forehead wondering if he should give Billy Mac a pass. Instead he smiled, motioning for his attorney to sit.

"Thanks for coming. I realize this is a bit of surprise; it was to me as well. Not sure what's going on. No one has come to visit me since I was given such a charming room." Clearing his throat, he leaned in. "You did take all the criminal law type courses, right? Please tell me you passed them or at least remember being in the classroom."

"I sense a little reluctance on your part, Mr. Hammond, and rightly so. Criminal law was never going to be my specialty but I think I can get you through this interview. But, if this goes further, like a trial, I'm going to suggest you might want to retain someone else."

"Hey, you'll do alright. First thing I want you to do is write down every question they ask me. That way we can form some idea of what, when, how it happened. Hadley's death must be at the very least suspicious."

Dash filled Livingstone in on the fistfight and the arrival of the police this morning. The attorney scribbled notes left and right, repeatedly saying 'got it'. Dash explained what role Grady Lennington would play in all this, passing on his number.

"Listen kid. I've got some reinforcements available if this thing gets too far. Trust me. Use this as a learning experience. We'll be okay."

Since Rakestraw didn't seem to be in a hurry to interview Dash, he and Livingstone took the time to make lists of possible information that they would need: security camera footage, if any was available, from Little Biff's Motel, witnesses to the fight in the parking lot, security footage from his home, etc. Dash explained Grady's security firm and how he already asked Grady to dig into Hadley's past. Relating his first impression of Annie's ex, he added, "There are, sorry, were probably people lining up to kill him."

It was mid-morning when the chief finally showed. "Mr. Hammond, this is Sergeant Poole. She will be assisting me with the interview which you probably can guess is being filmed as well as recorded." After setting down several files, Rakestraw read Dash his rights, asking him to state his name and occupation.

The interview commenced.

"Mr. Hammond, you are a person of interest in the death of Jock Hadley, mainly because you and Hadley had a fight last evening. I know you left the parking lot in the company of Annie Dewitt Hadley. We have security footage showing that and our officers' report. What I don't know is if you decided to pay a visit to Hadley later that night or the wee hours of the morning. Would you please tell us what you did last evening until the time we arrived on your doorstep?"

Dash began a step-by-step telling of the evening with Sam and Marie, ending with the ill-fated trip to the Magic Mart for groceries. "We were heading for my truck when out steps Hadley. He immediately began yelling. Not sure what his exact words were but he was going to make me pay for screwing his wife, to clean it up a bit. Then he swung at me, hitting me in the chin. I punched him back. A fight ensued, ending with me slamming him into my truck and pummeling him, hence the swollen knuckles. Annie, and probably half a dozen others, called your lot. The security guard arrived promptly."

Scratching his head, Dash said, "The whole thing lasted maybe five, ten minutes tops. He got in a couple of shots and I got in more. The cop who caught the call was York. He wrote up what happened and then told us to go home, stay away from each other."

"How much alcohol did you consume last night before the encounter with Hadley?" Poole asked.

"I had a beer when we got home from the bookstore and one while eating." Pulling out the receipt from last night, he pushed it over to her. "You can see what we had. One beer, two cokes, that was me; Annie had the two glasses of wine. I'm sure you can check with Sheriff Hammond or his wife to verify, though I would be surprised if they were paying attention to what Annie and I had."

"So you were sober."

"Yes."

"Would you be surprised if I told you one of the witnesses said you seemed drunk?"

"No, witnesses are notoriously inaccurate. How did he or she describe Hadley's demeanor?"

"I don't believe that's any of your business."

Dash leaned over to Livingstone. "This is where you jump in and tell her that it *is* our business."

"Oh." Livingstone did just that.

Poole and Rakestraw shuffled the folders. Dash and Livingstone leaned back. After minutes of silence, Dash asked, "Care to share how I killed him? Drawing a blank on that."

Rakestraw looked up. "Do you often draw a blank on what you've done? I am aware that you suffered a severe head injury years ago. Is this one of the residual effects?"

Chuckling, Dash said, "You don't recognize sarcasm when you hear it, do you? Residual effect of having a poker up your ass?"

Before he had a chance to answer there was scuffling at the door. It was thrust open by five foot two inches one hundred twenty pounds of fury. Dolly Hammond had arrived.

"So it *is* true!" She looked at her brother asking, "Are you alright?" Dash had to smile at his 'big' sister's protectiveness.

The officer at the door reached out to grab her arm. She shook him off. Both Dash and Rakestraw came to her aid. The chief told the officer to back off.

"Dolly, please. This doesn't concern you. Just go home and I'll call you later." Rakestraw said.

She turned to him, hands on hips, eyes narrowed. "Like hell you will, you mother...."

"Brigid Marie, watch that mouth. *Our* mother would not be pleased to hear you say what you were going to say." Dash said more loudly than he intended.

"How come you get to say all the nasty stuff?" she asked.

"It comes with being a soldier. You, sister dear, are supposed to be an example to me. Don't lead me into trouble. That was Mae's job."

She walked over to him, pulling his head down so she could kiss him lightly on the cheek.

Dash escorted her to the door. "Now run along. Robbie is just doing his job, no matter how poorly. The guy *is* trying. Go sell some books in case I need money for bail."

Scowling at Rakestraw, she mumbled something and left, slamming the door.

Dash tilted his head, trying hard not say 'told you'. He sat back down trying to look angelic.

"Now, where were we? That's right, I've drawn a blank," he said.

Rakestraw reached over and turned off the recorder. "We're taking a break. If you want to use the bathroom, an officer will accompany you."

Looking at Poole, Dash winked. "Oh please, can it be Officer Poole?"

She shot him a nasty look, "Be careful what you wish for, Hammond." She stared at him until he said, "Sorry. That was inappropriate. Begging your pardon, ma'am. I have utmost respect for women who serve and protect." She stood, about to exit when he winked again.

Livingstone put down his pen. He stood up unable to contain his laughter. He finally tapped Dash's shoulder.

"Quite the performance. Do you plan these things or do they just happen to you? On a more serious note, what evidence do you think they have? I can't believe they pulled you in because you bloodied Hadley's nose, if you indeed did that. Or are you just convenient?"

Standing, Dash started to stretch out his back, leaning this way and that.

"That, my man, is the sixty-four thousand dollar question *and* the reason we will continue to play this game. Robbie never did say how

Hadley died. Need to get that bit of information. I'm going down the hall; if you leave, take your notes with you. Be back in a bit."

He collected the officer guarding the door and they headed toward the restroom. Dash chatted him up with sports talk. When they returned to the room, the guard walked inside continuing the conversation about the Cleveland Browns upcoming season. Dash thought it looked as dire as his afternoon was shaping up to be.

Officer Poole returned to the interview room. She slid several sheets of typed paper over to Dash. "This is a typed statement covering your whereabouts last evening. Please review it and sign it unless we need to amend it."

As Dash read the statement, passing each sheet over to Matt to review, Poole continued. "We have more questions for you about your relationship with Jock Hadley and his death."

Dash signed the statement, asking if he would receive a copy. Poole nodded in the affirmative.

Sitting back, Poole flipped on the recorder and began to question Dash starting with when he first met Hadley to their last encounter in the parking lot. One sticking point for Poole was whether Annie could have left the house without waking Dash as he slept in the recliner.

Dash answered, "Honestly, I doubt it because I think my dog would have stirred. Pretty sure I would have heard that and been jolted awake. But, no way can I be sure. I was tired, not drunk but clearly ready to rest. Listen, why don't you just review my home security film? Ask the Sheriff's department; they are linked into it."

He stood to stretch his back. "If I may be so bold as to ask, how did Hadley die? I'm guessing his death is at least a bit suspicious, right? And you don't seriously think Annie...."

Before he could finish, Rakestraw entered the room, carrying a long paper bag. Dash knew it didn't contain a loaf of French bread. After setting it down on the table, the chief nodded to Poole.

She continued, "Mr. Hammond, it is well-known that you build furniture and do home repairs, renovations. Correct?"

"Well-known, doubtful but yes, ma'am, I do woodworking and repairs."

"You own a lot of tools, wouldn't you say?"

Dash pointed to Livingstone's pad and whispered to him, "Here we go." Turning to Poole, he answered, "I own a fair amount. You might consider them a lot and another might think the selection was paltry."

"Do you own a crowbar?"

Leaning forward, Dash said, "So Hadley was killed by a crowbar. Answers that question."

"I didn't say that. I just asked..."

"About a crowbar, really! If Hadley had been sawn in half you would have asked me how many saws I own. Not a gigantic leap here, Poole. And, yes, I own one, no make that two, crowbars."

"Can you tell me where these crowbars are? Right now?"

Blowing air out of his cheeks, Dash admitted, "No. Earlier in the week I was up in Michigan doing work for a friend. The crowbar that usually is kept in my tool box had gone missing. I rented one from a guy named Chatworthy. He can confirm this if necessary. Give me a bit to think and I might be able to backtrack my movements. I do know for certain that I did not use it last night on Hadley."

He added, "I have three jobs going right now: renovation of the building next to the bookstore where the bottom floor will provide additional sales space for children's books; the upstairs apartment is being turned into a meeting room for our vets' group and finally some repair work out at the Blue Belle Bed and Breakfast on Route 2."

He rubbed his forehead. "Danny Jerome, my partner, and I employ maybe six to ten men a day; they all have access to the tools. The rule is everything should be returned to the box at the end of the day." Shaking his head, he said, "One of my dumber moves is the fishing trip I took at the beginning of the week. I wasn't at any of the sites." Returning to the table, he borrowed Matt's legal pad. "Here are the names of the crew. Check with Danny to verify that everyone worked this past week. All I got for you, Chief."

Rakestraw reviewed the names, only stopping at Joey and Johnny Hammond, the sheriff's sons. "I didn't know your nephews worked for you. Aren't they still in college? "

"They are, but every summer since I've been home, they've helped me out, either at the homestead or on a job I might have going. Good kids. Sure they'll be happy to talk to you. Might want their dad next to them but, hey, what are parents for?"

Poole looked at Rakestraw. He sighed. He pulled an evidence bag containing a crowbar out of the brown bag.

"Does this look familiar? I mean this is one huge crowbar. What's it weigh? Ten, twelve pounds. Do some damage, eh?"

"Look familiar, yes. It's similar to one that I bought last year. You think it's mine?"

"Mr. Hammond, 'DJH' are etched into the handle. I understand your name is Dashiell Joseph Hammond. Initials on tools, one way to identify yours from anyone else's. Could this be your missing crowbar?"

Before Dash could answer, the door opened. An officer handed several sheets of paper to Rakestraw. After reading them, he turned to Dash. "This is Mrs. Hadley's statement identifying the body as that of her husband, Jock Hadley. I also have her statement saying she could not be sure you didn't leave the house during the night since she was upstairs and you were downstairs. She notes that, in the past, you have left her bed without waking her. Almost made a point of saying you move around very silently." The chief leaned back in his chair.

When he leaned forward, he pointed to the crowbar. "If I were a betting man, I would bet that this is yours. You know where it was found, next to the body. Anything to add?"

Dash reached into his wallet pulling out a business card. Handing it to Rakestraw, he said, "Guess I forgot to leave this. You're making a big mistake, Robbie. I didn't do this. Take a deep breath before you say another word. Think about this. Isn't this a bit too neat? You really should take some more time before you do anything rash."

"Give you time to escape. I don't think so. I..."

Dash interrupted, slamming the palm of his hand into his forehead. "Escape! Dammit, I knew there was something I was supposed to do.

But no, I went home to get my beauty sleep. Silly me. Robbie, I will say this once more, but with feeling. *I did not kill Hadley.* You *will be* sorry if you arrest me."

"Oh, so now you're threatening me. Not wise, Hammond."

"I'm not threatening you. Just advising you that, when this is over, the lawsuit I'm going to file will have you shitting bricks. Think a bit longer. Look around. Take your time."

"So the mighty Hammond family will be upset that their shining star has fallen. Dash, I wouldn't do this if I didn't think it was the right thing to do. Maybe insanity can be your plea. Dolly's told me of your problems."

Dash closed his eyes and counted slowly to ten. "Robbie, two things. One, keep looking because you've got the wrong man. Two, polish up that resume."

Rakestraw, reddened by that last comment, quickly changed the subject. "Is that dog of yours dangerous? I've sent some officers to search your place and Annie's. And before you ask, they have all the proper documentation. Just want to know if I need to send a guy from Animal Services."

"Call my father. He can handle the dog and witness the search."

Poole pulled out her phone to call Owen.

Standing, Rakestraw sighed. "You have the motive, one Annie Dewitt Hadley; the means, this incredibly heavy crowbar; and the opportunity, probably talked him into a rematch of your earlier fistfight. Dashiell Hammond, I'm arresting you for the murder of George aka Jock Hadley. Is there anything you wish to add to your statement?"

Dash shook his head no. He looked at Livingstone who said, "Grady, on it." He gathered his things and ran from the room.

Annie glanced at her watch. It had been almost three hours since she identified the remains of her ex-husband. Three boring hours. She answered all the questions, gave her statement and then waited until it was typed so she could sign it.

There must be something written somewhere that leaving someone sitting in an interview room for almost three hours was impolite, if not illegal.

The door opened. An officer said, "Sorry, ma'am. You're free to go. The Chief will call you if he needs to talk again."

Annie half-smiled and turned to walk toward the reception area. She flopped down on the bench and wondered what happened to Dash. She sat there for ten minutes and then approached the officer at the desk.

"Sir, do you know if Dash Hammond is still here?" she asked.

Annie watched as the officer glanced away from her gaze. He swallowed then turned back to her.

"I'm sorry, ma'am. But the colonel has been arrested….for the murder of your husband if you are Ms. Dewitt as I suspect you are."

Her eyes grew wide as she uttered "What the…." She looked around angrily. "Where is that son of a bitch Robbie Rakestraw? Get him out here right now or I swear I'll go looking for him."

Standing, the young man said, "Now ma'am…"

"If you or any of these bastards 'ma'am' me again, I'll pull your tongues out. Get Robbie Rakestraw now!" Annie yelled.

Phone in hand, the officer dialed. "Chief, Ms. Dewitt would like to talk to you. Sir, she's in reception and I just told her Colonel Hammond has been arrested. She is rather upset."

Annie reached over and grabbed the phone. "Robbie Rakestraw get your ass out here now! You don't want me to come looking for you."

To her surprise, the Chief of Police was not on the other end of the phone. A female voice said, "Ms. Dewitt, the chief is unable to meet with you right now. I'll relay your message to him and I'm sure he'll get in touch with you as soon as he can."

Annie slammed the phone down. She started to reach across the desk to grab the officer but, at the last second, she stopped.

Glaring at him, she stomped out of the Police Department to cross the hall to the Sheriff's Department. She pushed the door open so hard it almost came off its hinges. Slamming it shut for emphasis, she stomped down the hall, pushing the door open to Sheriff Sam Hammond's office.

"Did you know that idiot Robbie arrested your brother? Can't you do something about that?"

Sam sighed, closing the folder he was reading and pushing it aside.

"Know, yes. Do something, no. Not my jurisdiction." Pointing to a chair, he said, "Have a seat."

For the second time that day, Annie flopped down.

"He's going to kill me, isn't he?" She asked.

Trying hard not to smile, Sam replied. "Well, look at it this way, you have probably twenty years before they let him out. Plenty of time to get out of town."

"Not funny. How did Billy get here so fast? I mean, they can't arrest Dash without proper representation, can they?"

"Billy's not Dash's attorney right now. He's got some kid who's so fresh from law school he hasn't had time to frame the diploma yet, but he did sit and pass the bar. Understand he's a Buckeye, so, in Dash's mind, the kid is competent. To him, anyone who can sing the alma mater is competent. Strange people, those Buckeyes."

Annie and Sam stared at each other for a few minutes. Standing Annie announced that she probably should head home, hoping that would be enough of a hint for Sam to offer to drive her there.

He just tilted his head, saying, "Owen is at the homestead while the police search the house and grounds, looking for God only knows since they already have the weapon."

"They do? What weapon?"

"Big ass crowbar. Probably could crush a rhino's skull with the right torque. Dash's initials on it. Motive, you; means, crowbar; opportunity, any time he wanted."

Annie collapsed into the chair again.

"Owen is going to skin me alive, isn't he? Always felt he wasn't quite sure Dash and I should be involved." Her eyes suddenly opened wide.

"Holy and unholy crap! *Mae.* Does she know? God, when she finishes with me, it won't just be my head that's pulverized."

Taking a deep breath, she said, "The Hammonds vs. one little ole' Dewitt. Guess I should head for the hills."

Sam shook his head. "Wouldn't advise that tactic. Rakestraw will get the notion that maybe you're the one who should be in jail. Annie, just go home. Have a glass of wine and sit still. Dash will be in touch as soon as he's able."

He stood to escort Annie to the door. "Keep that pretty little head down, Miss Annie. The shit is about to start flying."

She walked out the door and right into Deputy Collins, a friendly face.

"How are you doing, Annie? Look a bit worse for the wear and it's only noon." Collins said.

"Do you have an hour? I can fill it with grievances large and small. Can I interest you in a cup of JoJo's finest coffee?"

"Sure, and I bet you could use a ride home. Let's go."

Annie spent the rest of the day glancing out a variety of windows to get whatever view she could of the activities next door. She watched Owen take Charlie Dog for a walk around the perimeter. Even from a distance she could feel the displeasure radiating from Dash's father. The look on his face when he glanced her way kept her inside.

She sat staring at her phone, waiting for her son Timothy to answer her text. A helluva way to learn your father was dead but he hadn't picked up her call.

It was almost six when Tim called her, announcing he was at the Cleveland airport and would drive out to Clover Pointe immediately. The two hour wait was excruciating.

She hugged her youngest child until he pushed her away.

"Mom, what the hell is going on? Sit down and tell me everything. A text saying 'hate to tell you but your dad is dead' doesn't quite answer any of the questions rattling around in my head."

Tears welled up in her eyes; not for Jock, but for the mess she and Dash were in. Slowly Annie gave Tim a blow-by-blow accounting of events starting when Jock knocked on her back door.

She reached across the table to take her son's hand.

"Tim, there's something I need you to do. Yesterday I took an envelope of money to the abandoned bus depot. It was supposed to be for your father, his get out of town money. I reckon he won't be needing it now and I sure will. When it gets dark would you retrieve it for me?"

"And you can't go because..."

"Because I'm pretty sure either the police or the Hammonds have staked out this house. I can't leave it but you can. If anyone asks, you're heading down to Lulu's Strip Joint. You can park there, go inside, exit from the rear and make your way through the woods to the bus station. Once you have the envelope you reverse your steps. Simple enough."

Tim took a stroll around the room, glancing out the windows wondering if his mom was right about being watched. He saw no one but then he figured you rarely did.

"Okay, mom. I'll do it. Once it's dark I'll head over to Lulu's. Directions, please and hiding place for the money since I'm assuming you didn't just leave it nailed to the door."

Mother and son sat down to begin the plotting and planning.

Once the sun had gone down and all was quietly dark, Tim drove off as planned.

Annie waited, thinking about all the time she spent today waiting followed by more waiting.

Finally she heard Tim's car pull into the drive. He rushed into the house.

"No money! I looked everywhere, even in places I would never want to look again."

Annie walked over to the kitchen counter, grabbed the bottle of bourbon and poured two good sized portions. She handed one to Tim and chugged the other.

Looking her son up and down, she announced, "We are so screwed."

Eight

A Clover Pointe police officer led Dash, dressed in the usual orange garb complete with handcuffs, into the courtroom. Matt Livingstone walked nervously by his client's side. The young lawyer, almost as tall as Dash but half his weight, sweated more than the prisoner who kept telling him to relax.

Settling into the defense table, Dash heard his name being called. He turned to find his father in the first row. Owen Hammond moved forward so he could talk to his son.

"I'm so thankful that your mother isn't alive to see you like this." Owen said, shaking his head.

"I know, Dad. She would be livid to see me head-to-toe in the orange. I asked if they had anything in Kelly green but sadly they were out of my size. No respect for the Irish." Dash said with a smile. He motioned for Matt to join him. Introductions were made.

Shaking his head, Owen asked, "I'm sorry, son, but this young man seems barely over twelve. Just where the hell is Billy Mac, if I may ask? No offense Mr. Livingstone but, even though my son doesn't realize the gravity of his situation, I hoped his counselor had a few trials under his belt before tackling this one."

"No offense taken, Sheriff Hammond. But the Colonel assures me he has reinforcements if needed." Matt said.

Dash winked at his Dad. "Don't worry. The cavalry should arrive shortly." He looked around then asked his father. "Is Annie here? I don't see her."

Owen shook his head, "I haven't seen her. All the McCafferty cousins are here as well as Father Tom and Dolly. The family has rallied."

The bailiff appeared to call the court to order. Owen reached out to Livingstone whispering, "When asked how he pleads, say 'not guilty by reason of insanity'."

The prosecutor, Harry Crownover, stood at his table ready to begin. He wore his sixty-plus years like an old sweater, frayed at the edges. He had a fringe of gray hair around his shining pate. He had a reputation as a law-and-order man, 'do the crime, serve the time' kind of man.

The packed courtroom stood as Judge Martin Pope entered the room. Being told to 'be seated' everyone complied, eager for the arraignment to begin.

The bailiff read the charges: Dashiell Joseph Hammond, charged with first degree murder of Percival Hadley also known as 'Jock' Hadley.

Judge Pope looked down from his bench to the defense table. "I'm sorry sir but I don't know your name."

Standing, Matthew Livingstone introduced himself to the Judge and nodded toward the prosecutor. "My client pleads not guilty, Your Honor."

"Again, my apologies. Mr. Livingstone, have you much experience in the courtroom specifically with murder charges? I only ask because this is not where you enter your client's plea."

Matt's face reddened. "Oh, Your Honor. I'm sorry but this will be my first."

Now asking the defendant, the Judge spoke. "Colonel Hammond, you realize the gravity of the situation. I'm not questioning Mr. Livingstone's ability but, Mr. McCafferty, your usual attorney, is well-known in the criminal defense field. His absence is notable."

Standing, Dash responded. "Your Honor, I am confident of Mr. Livingstone's skills. And, as you will see, additional forces will arrive to help in my defense, if needed."

As if on cue, the courtroom doors opened and in marched three men, all wearing sunglasses and well-fitting civilian suits, though their bearing betrayed their military training. They were tall and well-built. The last man in walked with a cane but stepped in time with his fellow officers. They walked to the front; two of the men stepped into the first row while the lead gentleman continued to the defense table.

Tall, tan, he wore a gray-silver suit which cost more than the clothes on the backs of all the Clover Pointe citizens. When he stopped next to Dash, he tugged at his shirt cuffs ala James Bond causing the defendant to smile and shake his head.

The courtroom broke out in applause. Some yelling 'go get 'em Dash'. The judge pounded his gavel, threatening to empty the room unless order was immediately restored. The prosecutor looked angrily at the defense team. Dash winked at him, shrugging.

"Order in the court. The movie isn't being filmed just yet. Quiet! Gentlemen, I strongly suggest you take off the sunglasses. There hasn't been a ray of sunshine within these walls for a long time."

All three took off their sunglasses.

Once order was restored, the silver-suited man apologized to the judge for the uproar.

"I'm sorry, Your Honor. I had no idea our entrance would be received so favorably by the constituents of your fair town." Leaning over to Livingstone, he introduced himself, handed him a folder, then nodded toward the bench.

Mr. Livingstone addressed the judge, reading from the file. "Your Honor, this is Beau Saylor, retired Judge Advocate General. He will be assisting me." He walked over to the prosecutor and handed him the folder. "Mr. Saylor's credentials are enclosed."

Returning to his table, Livingstone asked, "Your Honor, if it pleases the court, might I request a short recess while I bring Mr. Saylor up to speed on the case against Colonel Hammond?"

The judge pulled his reading glasses down and studied the defense team. "Request granted. Will a half hour be sufficient? And, Mr. Saylor, might I caution you about the speed bumps located in small towns."

Bringing his gavel down, the judge announced, "Court recessed. We'll reconvene in half an hour."

Dash and his legal team paraded out of the courtroom to a small conference room. Beau Saylor, Frederick Caverly III aka The Cav and Grady Lennington, Dash's right hand man through many combat missions, settled around the room. Last to enter was Matthew Livingstone, a look of awe on his face.

Shaking hands with Beau and Cav, Dash said, "Thank you for coming. Sorry about this mess I've found myself in but I'm hoping you guys will bring some sanity to all this."

He embraced Grady, rubbing his head. "Loving the chocolate baldness. And the cane is a nice touch. Kinda Fred Astaire. All you need is a top hat."

"Enough already. Seats, gentlemen." Beau instructed as he pulled out a chair and sat down. "Last night I was about to indulge in an evening of sinful decadence when my phone pinged. Text message from Grady: 'Dash Hammond arrested for murder. Can you help?' That was enough of a teaser for me to make the call, see what I could learn. Unfortunately the conversations I had with Grady and this young man were totally disjointed. Care to clarify?"

Dash smiled. "Well you know how it is. Woke up in the wee hours of Thursday morning and realized I had forgotten to kill someone this week. So I drove over to Little Biff's Motel and persuaded Jock Hadley to leave his room, follow me behind the motel. See earlier that evening we had gotten into a fist fight so of course he had no qualms about meeting me, dead of night, secluded area. Then, dammit, I discovered I had left my weapon at home."

The Cav interrupted, "I just hate when that happens."

"So rather than drive back home I grabbed a hefty crowbar, making sure it was the one with my initials etched on it, and beat the crap out of Hadley. Rather than take the tool home with me, I left it there so the police might have a head start in solving the case. Went home and fell asleep in my recliner."

Beau turned to The Cav. "See, I was right. This is going to make the world forget about the O.J. trial. I just have to come up with a catchy rhyme."

"There you have it. Questions?" Dash shrugged.

"Is this a love triangle? A hit for hire? Any classification?" The Cav asked.

"Definitely not a love triangle. The husband, ex-husband, now the deceased, showed up on the scene Tuesday, or at least that is what I understand. Annie, ex-wife, texted that Jock was here and would I come home. I was out of town at the time so I scurried back. To be honest I'm not sure what she wanted me to do. Provide moral support would be my first guess." Pausing, he then added, "We attended the Fourth of July picnic where apparently she was upset with the manner in which I renewed acquaintance with some high school friends, the female ones. She left me there and the next I heard from her was a 'please come' message. And stupidly I showed up."

"Tell me about Annie Dewitt. She doesn't use Hadley?" Beau asked.

Dash stood to move around the room, finally leaning against a wall. "Annie is house-sitting and doing some garden design next door for a distant cousin, Franklin Hammond. I'm trying to remember exactly what she said about how she got the job. Think she met him through a mutual friend in Charleston; that's where she's from. She moved in last February but I didn't meet her until April since I was out of town from January until then." Smiling at the memory, he said, "We met under a rose bush, funny story for another time. We really haven't been together, if that's what we are, for very long. Six weeks give or take a few days."

Beau said, "Six weeks and you're up for murder. Interesting doesn't seem to cover it. More about Annie, please."

"Well, she is smart, sexy and silly. Often all three things at once. And a very good cook if that counts for anything. When I returned from rehab," He held his hand up to avoid questions, continuing, "I asked, no, we mutually agreed upon a night of incredible sex. Since then we do things together, and it's not all sexual in nature. If you call saying 'hey want to go for pizza' a date then we date. We've gone to Toledo for dinner and a movie; spent the night. Usually, since we both have things to do during the day, we spend evenings sitting on my back porch. I'll have a beer, she has wine and we just talk about things, books, mainly. She works part-time at the bookstore my sister and I own. We enjoy each other's company, or we did until I messed things up at the picnic."

"Okay, I have more questions but let's get back to court so we can get you out of here. Then we can talk in more comfortable surroundings. And I want to interview Annie."

Beau looked at Matthew. "Listen, from first glance, the prosecutor appears to be under a lot of pressure. I think he'll ask for a million dollar cash bail."

Matthew's eyes opened wide. "What?"

"I've scribbled a few words for you to say when you ask for a lower bail. Use this as a starting point." Handing a scrap of paper to him, Beau ended with, "Make it your own."

"Shouldn't you do this? I mean, you have more experience and, frankly, panache. I don't think I can carry this off." Matthew said.

Both Dash and Beau shook their heads. Dash said, "No, kid, you'll be fine."

Beau asked the team if he might have a private word with Dash. The men obliged.

"First, I want to say how much better you're looking today than when I saw you, what four years ago. Of course that was right after your mom had died and it was obvious you were still very much in the recovery, rehab mode from the auto accident. You were very gaunt and being propped up by the woman who was your Iraqi 'terp' or don't we use that term back home, so your interpreter."

"Her name is Jamillah but I call her Millie." Dash mumbled.

"Since not many saw either of you after the conference workshops, rumor had it you were using what energy you had to teach her some maneuvers of the horizontal kind. Not relevant right now. Glad to see you've put on some weight, still need more if you want my opinion. But get a goddam haircut. Look like a hippie."

Making a face, Dash thanked him, waiting for the real reason for this *tete a tete*.

Beau let out a breath. "When you asked me to help, I moved a few cases around so I could get up here. It's been a while since we worked together and that was when we were both in the Army and you had rank. Let's get this cleared up right now. If you want me on your team, you do as I say. I want twenty-four, seven access to you. This trip I can only stay until Monday but will be back as needed. Cav will stay until he feels there is nothing more to be learned. With me on this?"

"Of course, Beau, you're right." Raising his right hand, he said, "I swear I'll listen to you; do whatever you want. I need this to be over. I know I didn't kill Hadley but can't be sure Robbie Law hasn't given up looking since he thinks the evidence is damning. After you, Counselor."

Back in the courtroom, the bailiff again instructed, "All rise." After Judge Pope took his seat, he asked Mr. Livingstone how his client pleaded.

"Not guilty, Your Honor." Looking over his shoulder at the former sheriff, he smiled weakly. At the last second, he was tempted to add 'by reason of insanity' but decided he was more afraid of the son than the father.

Papers were shuffled between the tables and the bench.

"Mr. Crownover, bond?"

The prosecutor rose. His suit, unpressed; his hair, uncombed and his manner, surly. Rubbing his chin, he finally spoke. "Your Honor, the town asks for a million dollar cash bond, citing the heinous nature of the murder and the defendant's military background and skill set. I believe he will bolt at the first chance."

Astonished, Dash looked over at him saying, "Really! You're serious? If I was going to run, I'd be gone by now."

Judge Pope slammed the gavel down. "Colonel Hammond, quiet!"

Sensing Dash was not finished, Beau clamped his hand over the defendant's mouth. Rising, he apologized for the outburst from his client. He motioned for Livingstone.

The young attorney stood, shoulders back. "Your Honor, like my client, I too find the million dollar cash bond insulting. Colonel Hammond is a respected member of this community. He is co-owner of two businesses and his real estate holdings are considerable. Granted he has several partners, but still the investment in our town speaks to his love of Clover Pointe. The colonel not only has served this town but he has devoted his life to the defense of his country. True, as a highly decorated member of the military, he probably does possess the ability to 'bolt' as Mr. Crownover stated. But, and let me state this emphatically," pausing, he looked down at Dash, *"This colonel does not run."*

Under his breath, Dash looked at Beau, "Who the hell is he talking about?"

Beau uttered one word, "Damn!"

Before the crowd could applaud, a voice, one the colonel knew all too well, shouted, "Damn right, Crownover, you eejit!"

The judge pounded his gavel. "Sit down, Dr. Summers or I'll have you removed from the courtroom."

"So sorry, Your Honor, but it just had to be said." Mae shook her curls, smoothed out her crisp ivory suit and gracefully sat down. She tilted her head as she watched Dash smile, shaking his head.

When quiet was restored, the judge looked from one table to the other. Staring at the defense team, he announced. "Bail will be set at $100,000. Mr. Livingstone, make sure your client lives up to your testimonial." He made eye contact with Dash who nodded.

"Now, gentlemen, we will reconvene in two weeks for the pretrial hearing. Everyone's calendar clear?" When no one objected, Judge Pope slammed the gavel down and rose.

Nine

Dash rounded the corner to his backyard. He watched Grady playing fetch with Charlie Dog. Once the German shepherd spotted Dash, he rushed to him, pouncing, nearly knocking him to the ground. A lot of licking and squirming so the petting would hit the right spots took place. When finished, Dash stopped in his tracks, seeing Mae for the first time. She was leaning against the railing on the steps of the porch. She had changed from her ivory linen suit to a white tee, khaki shorts and sandals. She looked as cool as Dash felt warm.

"Well, if it isn't Clyde Barrow hisself. Come to fetch Bonnie for a run to the border. Gonna rob a few banks on the way?" she asked.

Dash sauntered toward her saying, "Well if it isn't the esteemed Doctor Summers. Come to gloat?

"No, I've come to see if I can help in any way."

"Grady, you call her? We need to talk, sir." Dash yelled over to his good friend.

"No, No, Dolly called, madder than hell. Billy called me, told me to tell you he hopes they hang you." Before Dash could speak, she added, "Elena on the other hand wishes you well; said to tell you she still loves you. I should have asked for particulars but decided, as you would say, it was not relevant."

She stepped down to meet him halfway. "Don't I get a hug and kisses?"

"Charlie Dog showed some enthusiasm that I'm home. He even licked my face."

Leaning forward, she whispered into his ear. "I could lick something else to show you how happy I am to see you. Would that count?"

Dash blushed and pulled back laughing. "I need a shower before we do any hugging, um, and anything else. Does good old Doctor Chandler know you're here making indecent proposals to me?"

"He's at home contemplating his future."

That statement caught her ex-husband's attention. He raised his eyebrows.

"Sooner rather than later I'd like to talk to you," Mae said, adding "in private" when she noticed Dash's defense team hovering.

Looking in their direction, Dash asked Mae if she had met the men. He began to perform introductions. "This is Frederick Caverly, former member of my squad. And this gentleman, so dapperly turned out, is Beau Saylor, formerly of the JAG. And this young man who so eloquently defended me is Matt Livingstone, my attorney."

Dash turned to Mae, "Gentlemen, this is my ex-wife, Doctor Mae Summers."

Beau frowned. "Are you the…"

Beating her ample chest, Mae began. "Mea culpa, mea culpa, mea maxima culpa. I am she, the woman who served the Army's darling divorce papers as he boarded the plane." Turning to Dash, she asked, "Does everyone in the Army know about that? Talk about a gossip grapevine."

Dash shrugged. The men followed Dash into the house.

Mae stopped Grady. "G-man, you look wonderful; please tell me Sharon is coming down. This could turn into a mini-reunion." Glancing at Dash, she added, "Oops, sorry, we know how well reunions turn out for you." She turned back to their old friend.

Grady smiled. "Unfortunately, no, but if we had known you would be here, I'm sure the wife would have tagged along. It would have been like old times, the four of us sitting around shooting the bull." He did a little soft shoe. Continuing he said, "Long road but I made it. Can't do prancing up and down stairs but if I take it easy, I'm almost normal. No morning runs just yet, but hoping one day." He then pointed to Dash. "Mae, what's up with the hippie man? Hair over his ears. Next thing you'll be sporting an earring and a ponytail."

Charlie Dog followed Dash into the kitchen, standing next to him, pushing his snout into Dash's hand for another petting session.

The G-man asked, "Is Charlie Dog after Company C? 'Cause I don't remember that being your favorite company."

"Nah. Charlie's just a good enough name." Dash replied.

Laughing Mae stepped into the conversation. "Like 'Larry'? A good enough name?"

Dash's shoulders slumped and he gave her a side-wise glance. "Please, Mae, let's not go there. Just give me a break, even if it's just for today, okay?"

"Oh no, my good friend," Beau interjected. "Sounds like a story here. Or is...No, better not go in that direction."

Mae smiled broadly, showing all her dimples. "Well, Soldier Boy, what do you think? Story or not?"

"Ah, hell, tell away. But, guys, please listen to this disclaimer. I have no recollection of this so I'm pretty sure she's making it up, just to make me cringe."

"I'd never do that." She said batting her eyes. "Here goes. After the accident, his parents, his brother, Sam, and I waited three long days for him to wake up. When he finally began to open his eyes, he was still pretty groggy. We were so excited, kept saying things like '*Dash*, you're awake. *Dash*, we love you. *Dash*, welcome back.' Then the doc walks in to all this. He leans over and asks Dash if he knows his name. Furrowed brow followed, then this weak little voice says: Call me Larry, that's a good enough name."

She held up her hand adding "God's honest truth. The beginning of many little stories from the hospital bed of the recovering Colonel Dash Hammond." Putting her arms around his waist, she said, "But we still love him!"

Bending down to pet Charlie, Beau asked, "Is he your therapy dog?"

"Nah, he's a stray I found while running one morning. He had been injured, probably hit by a car. I took him to the vet for repairs. Advertised to find his owner but no one came forward so I adopted him. Therapy, yes for me but he's not trained. We just have an understanding." Dash asked the men if they had sleeping arrangements, since the homestead had any number of bedrooms.

"Oh, Dash, I've already sorted that out. Mr. Caverly will stay at the condo. I'm staying here with you. Well, not *with* you, you know, but in the room across from your bedroom." Mae finished with a blush.

"Dash, hope you don't mind but I thought I'd stay in town to meet and greet the locals and get the lay of the land. You know me, Charming Cav. I'll make friends, find clues; sort this out in no time," Cav said.

"Fine with me, but please remember, I'd like to return here once I get out prison. Okay?" Dash pushed past Mae. "I'm going to wash the jail house off. I'll be back in ten. Mae, be the hostess and get the men something to drink. Plenty of water in the fridge but more potent libations available."

"Wait, Dash." Mae called, but he waved her off, headed upstairs to shower and change, saying "I'll be only a few minutes."

Mae stood with one hand on her hip. With the other, she counted out loud. "One, two, three..." Before she could get to five, Dash stood before her, bare-chested, shirt in hand.

"Why do I hear feminine voices coming from my bathroom?"

"I was trying to tell you. I've hired the Tydie Sisters, Irma and Ilene, to get your house in shape for your visitors. They're cleaning the bathrooms and have changed all the linens."

Dash held his hand out. "What? Cleaners? This place is spotless, Army clean." Then motioning to the trio of ex-vets now sitting at his table, he added, "These guys have slept on rocks, in the sand, under the sand. They've gone for weeks without showers. Never changed their underwear. *My* clean, *Army* clean, is their clean. Sorry, Mae, but you shouldn't have spent my money. If there's a place to clean it's your condo. Send them there."

"Don't worry. That's next. I'll ask them to stop so you can take your shower." They headed up the stairs bickering about Army clean vs. the general populace's clean.

The former soldiers sat around the kitchen table having listened to exchange of words. Grady tossed his head back, eyes to the ceiling. "My wife and I always found an evening with them to be *very* entertaining."

"All they need is for Dash to have a brogue and they could be the Irish counterparts to *I Love Lucy*. She has the red hair and all," Cav added.

Upstairs Mae knocked on the bathroom door calling out. Dash kicked off his shoes, emptied his pockets, waiting for the opportunity to strip down.

A big smile lit up his face as two tiny gray-haired ladies exited the bathroom carrying the accoutrements of a cleaning crew. They only came up to his armpits and had matching bowl haircuts.

"Hey, you're twins! And short! Tiny Tydie Sisters. You really *are* sisters. Who's Irma?"

Irma raised her hand. Her big brown eyes filled with laughter. "I'm the guilty one, or shouldn't I use that term, Colonel Hammond? Nice to see you free of the shackles of justice."

She held out her hand, then remembered to take off the plastic glove.

Dash took her hand and then her sister's. Ilene sat on the edge of the bed, her eyes firmly on the bare masculine chest before her. She uttered, "Oh my. Oh my. If I had seen that when I was twenty, I don't think I would have taken the veil."

When she looked as if she was about to touch Dash, he stepped back, quickly slipping back into his shirt. Mae looked at him. Together they shook their heads, saying, "Oh my." Patting his backside, she added, "Still got it, Studly." She winked at the sisters.

"I saw that, Mae. Don't even think about it. I'm accused of one murder; might as well go down for two." Nodding toward the sisters, he excused himself and took a shower. When he was finished, he peeked out the door to make sure his bedroom was empty before he entered to get dressed.

As he walked down the steps he heard laughter coming from the kitchen. Everyone was seated around the table.

"Hey, Dash, the Tydie sisters are not only biological sisters but they were nuns. Convent sisters," Beau announced.

"Oh" was all Dash said, then he asked, "How long have you been in Clover Pointe? I thought I knew everyone, at least by sight. Where have you been hiding?"

"Little Biff's Motel. Biff lets us have a suite in exchange for cleaning and laundry duties. We're trying to expand our business since we didn't leave the convent with a ton of money. Been here about six months, before that we were Lourdites." Irma replied.

Dash leaned forward. "Luddites, you smash machinery. What the hell kind of nun is that?"

Mae punched him in the shoulder. "No! They were Sisters of Our Lady of Lourdes, nickname Lourdites."

"You live at Little Biff's?"

"Yes, we were there when you committed the murder," Ilene answered.

All the color drained from Dash's face. Beau reached across the table to Ilene.

"Say again. You witnessed the murder and Dash committed it?"

Irma jumped up. "No, no. 'Allegedly' committed the murder. Ilene got it wrong. I mean, we were at the motel when it happened. In fact we were the ones who found the body, or what was left of it."

She now had the attention of everyone at the table. Beau and Matt started shuffling the papers received from the prosecutor, looking for their statements. Beau turned to Grady, asking, "G-man what do you have so we can record all this for future reference and accuracy." The G-man pulled out his phone, propping it on the table facing the two ex-nuns.

"Matt, we'll read the statements after we hear what the ladies have to say. Compare notes." Beau motioned toward one of the nuns, saying "Ilene, is it? Would you begin?"

"I'm Ilene Tydie, formerly Sister Mary Regina. I now work as a housekeeper and laundress at Little Biff's Motel. Early Thursday morning my sister and I were hauling some trash bags over to the dumpster which is located behind the motel off to the right if you are facing it. We were coming from the laundry area which is on the left side. This is our normal routine; we each take two bags and walk across the back of the motel."

Irma interrupted to add that there is a sidewalk so it's not like they had to drag the bags across the lawn. She then gestured to her sister to continue.

"We were talking, more like whispering since it was five in the morning. I add this because we weren't really paying any attention or I wouldn't have tripped, literally, over the body of a man. Fortunately I didn't fall onto him since he was covered in blood. Irma pulled out her flashlight and that's when we saw the mess of a man. I did check for his pulse, only to confirm my first visual. I have nursing training so I have seen catastrophic wounds before."

Again Irma interrupted. "We didn't have the flashlight on since we have walked this way numerous times; we felt fairly confident in finding our way in the dark."

A moment of silence followed as Ilene glared at her sister. "Irma, wait your turn." Looking over at Beau, she added, "I'm sorry but she always has to be in charge. Older by minutes you know. Bossy by nature."

Everyone at the table smiled, nodding in agreement about older siblings. Irma snorted, rolling her eyes.

Straightening her back, Ilene continued. "We dropped the bags of trash and, using the flashlight, swept the area. That's when we saw the crowbar and I will say it's the largest one I've ever seen."

Beau raised his hand. "Did either of you touch or move it?"

Both sisters looked at him, tilting their heads, saying simultaneously, "Really!"

He put his hands up, glancing at Dash who just chuckled. "Don't have much experience with nuns do you, Counselor?"

"We retreated to the office where we called 911, explaining about the dead body. They reminded us not to touch anything, like we've never seen a TV show. We were instructed to wait in the office but decided to go back to the body. We wanted another look, wanted to see if we could identify the man."

"Pardon me, Ms. Tydie, but *were* you able to identify the man?" Beau asked.

This time Irma answered. "Yes, at least we felt fairly certain we knew who it was. Jock Hadley, Room 200, located directly above the laundry room."

"How did you recognize him, if I may ask?" Mae joined the conversation.

Ilene nodded to her sister so Irma spoke. "His clothes. We'd seen him the day before arguing with another man. We were housekeeping a few doors down from his when the two men exited the room exchanging heated words. They stopped talking the minute they noticed us so we went back into the room we were cleaning."

"And what did you hear?" Dash asked. When the two women looked appalled at being accused of eavesdropping, he gave them his 'don't kid a kidder look'. "Beau may not know nuns but I do. Never met one who didn't want to know the whole story. I've been on the receiving end of the omniscient nun who really just overheard me babbling about something or other." He looked to Mae for confirmation; she nodded in agreement.

Irma muttered, "Oh for a ruler to smack your hands! Yes, of course, we stopped working and listened. The best we could determine the argument was about money and more money and time or timing. Other guy wanted to 'keep looking' and Hadley was adamant they shouldn't; he wanted to finish what he started and get out of 'Dodge'. Finally, the other man just stormed down the stairs, got in his car and peeled out of the parking area."

"What did the police say when you told them about this?" Beau asked.

"We didn't! We wanted to, but that Chief of Police told us to go to our room and lie down saying 'what a shock you've just had'. Treated us like old fragile ladies."

Both the ex-nuns sat with hands folded on the table, looking very guilty. They looked from one man to another.

Dash licked his lips. "Okay, what happened?"

Ilene spoke first. "Well, we went to a room, just not our room. We decided to check out Hadley's room before the cops did. I guess we were just upset with the way we were being treated."

Being the youngest and least threatening, Matt decided to take the lead. "Ma'am, may I ask what if anything of interest you found?"

Irma shrugged. "He had two suitcases but only one had clothes in them. He was traveling light in the wardrobe department which would explain why he wore the same set of clothes two days in a row. The other had some silver items, candle holders, serving pieces. These were wrapped in towels, monogrammed with "H". A few pawn tickets were clipped together and stuck in the side pocket of the suitcase. Nothing really. No stashes of cash or drugs."

"You didn't remove anything? Leave behind fingerprints?" Cav asked.

Both women sat up straighter, if that was possible. Highly indignant, they answered almost in unison. "We are professional cleaners, not thieves. Nothing was taken and nothing left behind. No dust, no fingerprints."

Beau rapidly read through their statement to the police. "Pardon me, but there's no mention of the argument you witnessed." He held his hands out, "Why not?"

Ilene answered. "We were told to write down everything about that morning. No one asked if we had talked to Hadley at any time. They asked for the master keycard and went off to search his room."

Dash put his head in his hands, sighing. "Nuns. They're still out to get me." He took a deep breath and reached across the table to take one hand from each woman. Holding them tenderly, he quietly said, "Now Sisters" then corrected himself, "Ladies, if you *had* told Rakestraw about the argument, you would have given him another suspect who might have had a reason to kill Hadley." Pulling back he said, "Not that this can't be corrected."

Cav finally spoke up. "Could you describe this man to a sketch artist?" When they nodded in the affirmative, he turned to Dash. "Do you know if the sheriff's department has one on staff? Prefer not to involve the police at this time."

Before Dash could answer, Beau stood up, announcing, "Here's what we're going to do. The good Tydie sisters will continue with their cleaning; no change to the routine. Once we find a sketch artist, we'll get everyone back together. Grady, you see what is coming across about this Hadley guy. I especially want to know when he arrived in town and how. The rest of us are going to the morgue to view what's left of the late Mr. Hadley."

Dash interrupted. "Mae is coming? Whatever for."

"Because I'm a feckin' doctor. I just might spot something you yahoos would miss. I am here to help, remember?" She glared at him.

"What was I thinking? Questioning your participation in all this. Forgive me my sweet." Dash shuddered as he grabbed his truck keys.

Mae waved her hand toward Beau. "After you, Counselor."

As everyone rose from the table, Irma stepped over next to Dash. "Mr. Hammond, Emmysue was very disappointed when you didn't show on Saturday night. She was in tears when she left the motel Sunday morning. I just thought you should know. Not very gentlemanly of you to stand her up."

Joining the twosome, Mae asked, "Excuse me, Colonel, sir, what's this about you and Emmysue on Saturday night? Care to elaborate?"

Ignoring his ex-wife, Dash said to Irma. "I really intended to stop by but circumstances prevented me. Do you know where she went?"

Shaking her head no, Irma turned to climb the stairs to complete her cleaning tasks.

Beau stepped behind Mae and Dash gently moving them toward the door. "Unless this Emmysue could have wielded the crowbar, let's focus on what will help us."

The Lakota County Morgue was located in the basement of the hospital. Mae led the way, stopping at the desk to sign in. Cav shivered, remarking about the cold temperature.

Once inside Mae made introductions. Dr. Everett Brooks, known to all the locals as Brooksie, had the gurney with Hadley's body front and center.

"Gentlemen, Dr. Summers, before I pull back the sheet I want to warn you. Mr. Hadley's head was severely beaten; not much left so if you are at all squeamish now is the time to retreat."

Everyone stood their ground. Dash with arms crossed; Cav, hands in pocket; Matt swallowing rapidly and Beau putting on his glasses while Mae pulled on latex gloves.

"Mr. Hadley died from a single blow to the back of the head. I'm guessing he fell forward so the perpetrator had to turn him over to destroy his face. Have you seen the weapon? Big and heavy. Demolition grade crowbar. What was demolished was Hadley's face!"

"So, deliberate attempt to hide the identity?" Beau asked.

"No question. Other possibility is rage at whatever Hadley did to the perp, but, more likely, to make sure identification would be slowed. Any intelligent person would know that an I.D. would be made some time fairly soon. We have blood type and fingerprints. If he's in the system we should get a match shortly. We've requested dental records even though the front of the mouth is in pretty bad shape. Waiting on those since his dentist's office in Charleston is closed for a vacation."

He pulled the sheet back. Dr. Summers stepped forward while the men retreated. Dash and Cav glanced at each other, thinking of the combat field.

"Did Mrs. Hadley see this?" Beau asked wincing as he view the smashed skull.

Brooksie shook his head no. "No reason. Could you identify someone, even a loved one, from that? No, she glanced at the body, clothes, the wedding ring, and, of course, the wallet, etc. That's how she made the I.D. Very shaken to say the least."

"So she didn't scrutinize the body. Didn't mention any scars, moles, etc." Mae said.

"She didn't want to; said she hadn't been with him for years and could scarcely remember his face much less his body."

Matt stepped forward but avoided looking at the body. "Excuse, Dr. Brooks, but you said something about a wallet. Was it the deceased's?"

"Yes. Found in the back pocket of the pants. Everything is bagged, over on the counter." He said as he pointed.

"Am I the only one who thinks it's odd that the face was obliterated but the wallet left on the body? I'm sorry, but I'm new to all this." Matt said apologetically.

Dash leaned against a counter, looking from Beau to Cav. "Some crackerjack team. The kid's got a point. The killer obliterates the face so we're not sure who this is but leaves the wallet, just in case we can't figure this out. He really just planted the seed of doubt. Smart? Or very stupid?"

Mae picked up the deceased's hands, examining them. She looked over to Dash, gesturing for him to show her his hands. He did.

Pointing to the corpse's hands, she asked, "Brooksie, do these hands look like they were in a fight hours before this man was killed?"

The coroner smiled. "Only if it was a pillow fight."

Beau stepped forward to look at the hands. Turning to Mae, he asked, "So you're thinking this might not be Hadley, even though we have the wallet?"

"Haven't the foggiest. Never met the man. All I am pointing out is that it is unlikely this man was in a fist fight. Dash, did he hit you? Your lip and chin look like they were hit, but is that from the fight with Carter last Saturday?" she asked.

Moving closer to the exit, Dash answered. "Yes, he hit me several times in the face and body. Not very hard but enough to get my attention. I'm not sure but he may have missed me and hit the truck; no idea if that would result in damaged knuckles or not. My hand is bruised since I landed quite a few, mostly on the face but a few body shots. *And I'm pretty sure I hit my truck. Let me amend that: I think that's what happened.* It was all so fast, mostly a blur of flying fists and him yelling at me. Oh, let's not forget the little boxing match with Carter last Saturday."

Mae rolled her eyes. "Another demonstration of the gentlemanly art of fisticuffs. Not a bad word left your mouth."

He shrugged.

Beau asked Brooksie, "Have you definitely stated that this is Jock Hadley? I mean just taking the wife's word. Or do you have some concerns?"

"I always have doubts where murder is concerned....I did caution the chief that he might want to wait for DNA, fingerprints or the dental records. Also requested medical records from Hadley's family physician. Again, that office is closed for vacation. I guess most of Charleston is out of town this week. Other than the obvious lack of a face, I don't have any reason to doubt Mrs. Hadley's identification. Her son stopped by earlier to give a DNA swab but that takes time."

Dash asked, "Why did they act so quickly?"

"Don't know the answer to that; just that you were in the crosshairs immediately. Whatever you've done to piss Rakestraw or Crownover off, well, it's working. Guess you're just gonna have to ask them." Brooksie answered.

Pushing the door open to leave, Dash said, "I might just do that."

Beau motioned to Cav, saying "Stop him."

Dash and Cav stood outside; both were smoking cigarettes. Beau, Matt and Mae joined them. Mae walked over to her ex-husband, holding out her hand. He stepped back, frowning. Shaking his head he said to her, "I'm over 21, old enough to smoke."

Her green eyes met his blue eyes. She continued to hold out her hand.

Dash said, "Mae, you are not my mother. I can smoke if I want."

She pushed her hand forward.

He said forcefully, "You don't know the strain I'm under. Surely that warrants a cigarette."

She reached into her pocket, pulling out a little box. Calming drops. Without saying a word, she extended her other hand, the one with the drops in it.

"Listen, Mae. If I *don't* smoke this cigarette, it's not going to add years to my life. Hell, I'm probably going to get executed for murder. Can I have a cigarette when I'm on death row?"

She took a step forward standing in his space. Her bottom lip began to tremble as she said, "Dash Hammond, don't you ever say that. Don't talk to me about your death." Her eyes glistened with tears.

He sighed, then shrugged. Crushing out the cigarette on the sole of his shoe, he placed the butt in his pocket while reaching for the calming drops. Scowling, he said, "I hate you Maevis Summers. Always did."

She smiled a little as he walked away. "Well, now you will live longer. More time to hate me." She sniffed and walked back toward Beau winking at him.

As she passed him, he whispered to her. "You've got him by the short and curly, don't you, Dr. Summers?" Chuckling he turned to Matt. "I hope you were paying attention, son. Mighty important lesson right there."

When everyone caught up to Dash, he was leaning against Beau's rental car, twirling his phone through the fingers of his hand.

"Question for all you legal eagles. Since I can't talk to Robbie or Crownover, I'd like to chat with Annie. That was not a pretty sight in there. I'd like to make sure she's okay. What's the protocol?"

Beau answered. "Give us some time to go over her statement and whatever else the prosecutor has given us. Is there a place in town to get a decent meal? I'm a bit hungry since all Cav and I have had is coffee. Don't know if y'all got breakfast. Also, I'd like to visit the scene of the crime; get perspective."

While Mae and Dash discussed where they should take the team for brunch/lunch, Matt pulled out his phone and punched in Annie's number. Everyone stopped when they heard him say, "Mrs. Hadley, this is Matthew Livingstone, Dash Hammond's attorney. Mr. Hammond asked me to call you. He is wondering how you are doing?"

Mae leaned into Dash whispering, "And I didn't even see your mouth move." Dash smiled at the reference to his remark about Dr. Chandler Allen.

"Yes, ma'am. I'll relay the message. Ma'am, we should be back at Mr. Hammond's home in a few hours. Would it be convenient for us to meet at that time? I'll give you another call when we're more certain of the time. Yes, ma'am. Thank you."

Matt put his phone away and asked, "Where are we going? I'm starved."

Dash gestured with his hand, "Care to share? How is Annie?"

"Oh, yes, sure. She's fine. Her son is with her." He screwed up his face, "Sorry but she didn't say much more. Didn't ask how you were doing?"

Shrugging Dash turned to Beau. "Listen, why don't we just go back to the house? I have plenty of cold cuts for sandwiches."

Cav spoke up. "Sorry Dash, I mean I eat sandwiches on occasion but would like more food right now."

Mae muttered, "Dash eats other food on occasion. Well, come on guys let's go to Jojo's. The food is good, plentiful and we might be able to commandeer several tables in the back room. We can spread out with all the papers."

Dash shrugged again. "Whatever." So they all piled into the various cars and headed into Clover Pointe.

After the working lunch, the team split up. Beau and Mae headed to Little Biff's, the scene of the crime. Matt and Cav headed to the bookstore to interview Danny Jerome, Dash' partner, and whichever men were at that site. Dash told them Danny could provide names and numbers for anyone who worked this week but was absent today. Dash announced he was going back home where he intended to go for a run and then a swim.

Beau reminded Dash that he was not to talk to Annie without either of his attorneys present. Dash saluted, reiterating his earlier statement of following Beau's orders.

When Mae and Beau arrived at the homestead, Dash was nowhere to be seen. His truck was in the carport so they assumed he made it home. Mae looked out the back door to watch as Dash jogged up the lawn.

"How is your little hamster brain doing now after the run and swim?" Mae asked.

"Much better, thank you. Let me change and I'll be right down."

When he returned to the kitchen, it was empty. He looked outside but no one was there. So he walked out to the vegetable garden. This little plot had been tended over the years by his grandmother, his mother and now his sister-in-law, Marie. Although it was her pride and joy, the whole family benefited from the fresh veggies. Dash did the heavy work and Marie reaped what they had sown. For his efforts, she kept him in frozen dinners, mainly soups and stews. He ate very well for a non-cooking loner, though Marie was teaching him to cook in hopes of varying his menu.

As he walked the rows, stooping to pull a weed or two, he looked up to see Beau coming toward him.

"So Farmer Dash, how does your garden grow?"

"Better than I could have hoped. My sister-in-law is very pleased. I strive to make her happy. She's been very good to me and was a God-send when I came home for recuperation and rehab. She organized my caretakers so I was never left alone until, after months, I could do things on my own without fear of burning down Mae's condo."

He picked a cherry tomato and popped it in his mouth. Motioning to Beau, he gathered a few for sharing. They walked to the back part of the property where Dash had a small orchard of apple and cherry trees.

"Bought this from my cousin about ten years ago, before I moved here. I take the apples and cherries to my neighbor, Mrs. Guzy." Pointing to her house, he said, "Best pie maker in the county. Keeps me happy. Marie gets her fair share and makes applesauce for the family." They wandered around the garden, talking about the differences in technique from northwestern Ohio to the Gulf region.

Dash heard his name being called and looked over to see Annie waving at him. He and Beau walked over to the fence. Introductions were made. Annie informed them her attorney was expected momentarily so they would be over shortly, if that was okay. It was.

Cav and Matt arrived. Cav told Beau they would wait until after this meeting to share their findings, slim as they were.

Dash asked Mae if she wanted to attend the meeting but she declined. She gathered her computer, heading for the back porch to catch up on some emails and classwork.

Annie's team, including her son Timothy, arrived. He was a younger version of Jock but with some of Annie's genes mixed in so his face was more pleasant. His shirt was pressed, short-sleeved but his jeans had the obligatory tears in them. Instead of shoes he wore sandals.

Timothy asked Dash if he could speak to him alone for a minute. Dash shrugged an agreement. They left the porch and walked over to the lawn out of hearing range. Once there, he faced Dash announcing he had been a boxing champ in college. Perplexed, Dash smiled. The next thing he knew the young man sucker punched him and then connected with his chin while Dash was bent over. This did not stop Dash from retaliating. He grabbed the fist, twisted it behind Tim, knocking him off his feet with a well-aimed kick to the back of his knees. The young Mr. Hadley wound up on the ground, face down with Dash's foot on his back. Holding onto the kid's arm, Dash said, "The pain you are about to experience is me dislocating your arm."

Beau jogged over. "Everything okay here, because it looks a bit dicey." The ex-Army officers stood over the boxing champ. Dash glanced over to where Mae sat, shoulders shaking with laughter even though her eyes were cast downwards on her computer.

"He wanted me to know he's a college boxing champ. What do you think of that?"

"Interesting. Never knew a boxer who wanted to fight in sandals. Hmm. Apparently he didn't give you a chance to tell him you went to Uncle Sam's school of combat training. Cheeky kid. You should let him up, given the current trouble you are experiencing."

Annie appeared "Please, Dash, don't hurt him. I hate to say it but he's just young and stupid."

"Takes after his dad, does he?" Dash said as he let go of Timothy's arm. Turning to the young man, he asked, "Is that what you wanted to talk to me about? Your boxing career is foremost on your mind? Let's forget about this and get down to business."

The group started to move back to the porch when Timothy stopped Dash. "Are you in love with my mother?"

Dash stopped. "That is the burning question? Not did you kill my father?" He looked over to Annie, then back to her son. "Junior, my relationship with your mother is none of your damn business. All you need to know is that I wouldn't hurt her. And, just for the record, I did not kill your father."

Annie nodded in acceptance of his statement, then turned to see if Mae had heard this pronouncement. Nothing would indicate any interest in the conversation.

As they walked back to the kitchen, Dash announced to Beau, "You know restraint is my watchword."

To which Beau replied, "Well, I know you understand the definition of the word; and I'm hoping you just aren't going to watch it but also abide by it."

Dash snorted, "Smart ass." Calling out to Cav as they reached the patio, "Cav, frisk the youngster. If he has a weapon, relieve him of it. If he doesn't have a license, throw his ass into the car and present him to Sheriff Sam with my love and affection."

Tim scowled as Cav approached him. Extending his arms and twirling around, he asked, "See any guns?"

Cav shook his head no, adding, "You don't look *that* stupid. Get inside and behave yourself. The colonel seems to be a bit touchy right now."

Everyone gathered in the kitchen. Beau started the exchange of information, inquiring what questions were asked of Annie. Frank Smith, the attorney recommended by Billy Mac, pulled out his notes to fill in the blanks. There was a lively give and take. He did not bring up the possibility that the body wasn't Jock. Annie did admit she was very upset by the corpse. She had asked to see his clothing. When she saw the wedding ring, she knew the body was her husband's.

Cav grilled both Annie and her son about the business affairs of Jock. Timothy admitted his father tried to borrow money from him recently but didn't know the extent of his father's indebtedness. He suggested Cav talk with his older brother, Stephen, who had more business dealings with their father. Both mother and son agreed that Amelia, daughter and sister, would know nothing. She avoided contact with the family after the divorce, blaming that event for her broken engagement and subsequent broken heart.

"Should we check into any health issues? Psychological issues?" Cav asked.

Annie ended that avenue of exploration. "He was an ass, plain and simple. I got the feeling he just needed my money. Another business deal gone wrong or he pissed someone off and needed to get out of town."

When Beau told Annie about the suitcase full of silver items and pawn tickets, she just shrugged.

"Since he asked me for money I'm not surprised he was pawning our possessions. I guess I should say his possessions. Most of the sterling was bequeathed to him by his parents. Nice pieces, sorry to hear the set was broken up." Another shrug.

"Would it be possible for Dash and me to have a few words in private?" she asked.

Beau looked to Cav who looked at Matt. Annie's attorney finally spoke up. "If it would be acceptable, I'll be their chaperone. If they decide to plan a getaway, I'll report back. Surely a word or two can't hurt."

Dash said, "Maybe we could leave notes on the fence post. Come on, a few words. We'll step into the front room, clear view of all of you."

Dash and Annie moved to the front room. They both put their hands behind their backs, nodding to the table full of men.

He lowered his voice. "Annie Bananie! What a mess this is! Jock is in town less than 48 hours or so and slam, bang, I'm arrested for murdering him. Didn't see that one coming by a mile. Seriously, how are you holding up? Tim the gym rat helping or hindering?"

Rolling her eyes, she answered. "Yes and no. It's good to have him here just because I'd be all alone if he hadn't come. No because this is one of the most embarrassing situations ever. I'm waiting for him to ask me if I did it. And, just for whatever record is being kept, no, I did not kill him. If I could be arrested for all the times I either thought about doing away with him or wishing someone else would do the deed, then I'd be serving a life sentence, which is what our marriage felt like."

Dash shrugged.

"Is Billy Mac coming up or were you serious that you've parted ways? Somehow I can't see him missing out on this. And I see your other best friend showed up. Musta burned rubber all the way down from Michigan. Can't believe I'm asking you this, but are you happy she showed up?"

He shuffled his feet. "I'll answer that in a few days. As you might imagine I didn't get much sleep last night and I'm about to fall over. Not thinking clearly at all. Feel like this is some very bad dream, a new very bad dream. I just became accustomed to the recurring combat nightmares. Guess this one will fit into the rotation somehow."

Loudly he announced, "Hey, I'm going to kiss Annie on the cheek so don't jump up and start screaming. Okay." When he got no response from the table committee, he leaned down kissing her cheek tenderly.

Annie said quietly, "Get some rest. I'm sure you'll work something out. You always do. Talk to you when I'm allowed. I don't suppose we can ask for a conjugal visit, can we?"

He laughed out loud. "Not with the red headed lady in the area."

She walked to the kitchen, gathering her son and attorney. "Gentlemen, wish I could say this was a pleasure, but I try not to lie. Afternoon."

As she opened the door to leave, Mae reached for the handle about to enter.

"Sorry, I didn't mean to intrude, but...." She said.

Annie's retort was a snapped, "Sure!"

Glancing back at Annie as she and her son left, Mae raised her eyebrows to the gents still seated at the table. Waving her hand which contained a phone, she walked into the front room.

"Dash, Owen is on the phone. Says he's been trying to reach you and was concerned when he couldn't. You need to turn your phone on." She handed her phone over. Dash nodded a thanks.

Stepping further into the front room, he spoke to his dad asking about the sketch artist. After a few minutes, he said, "Owen, do what you want. Yes, I'll see what everyone eats."

He hung his head. "Hello Marie, no. I don't know what our dinner plans are. No big deal. Why everyone always worries about food...."

Turning to Mae he said, "Oops. Upset Marie." Including the others in the next comment, he almost shouted. "What the hell has happened to my world? My father wants to have a barbeque with all the vets. Says it will be like old times for us. Like we sat around grilling steaks before or after we shot up a town. And, get this, his sketch artist is someone called 'Squiggles' or 'Sketches' or 'Squirrel' Jackson. And Marie hung up on me. What did I do?"

Handing the phone to Mae, he pleaded, "Fix this for me, please. I . . . I . . just . . ."

Mae took the phone and then led Dash to the recliner. "Have a seat. Watch some sports. Close your eyes. Everything will be fine."

Leaving the front room, she pulled the pocket doors closed. Facing the men still seated at the table, she said, "Dash is going to rest for a bit. I'm going to figure out what the devil he was mumbling about, especially the artist. Now, what are your plans for the next few hours?"

Rising, Cav started laughing. "Am I to understand that you just put our Captain, well now Colonel, in time out so he can rest?"

Mae moved to stand in front of him, hands on her hips. "Mr. Caverly, I suggest you adjust your tone." Pointing to the front room, she said, "That man had a serious head injury. If he doesn't get proper rest, his brain starts to shut down. That upsets him. Now..."

Before she could finish, Beau joined her. "Mae, please, we are all on his side. It's just been a long time since we've seen him. Trust me, no one here is judging him. You're the doc. If you say he needs rest, rest he will get."

Turning to the team, he said, "Gentlemen, new assignments. Matt, can you track down this Squiggles man? Talk to the elder sheriff. Cav, back into town. Meet and greet. Grady, see what magic your men can work. Hadley, his associates, etc. Let's reconvene in an hour. Dash should feel better by then."

Two hours later, the pocket doors slid open. Dash looked into the kitchen where Mae sat typing on her laptop on one side of the table; the other side, Beau typed on his. Both turned as he walked to the counter, reaching for a bowl. After filling it with cereal, he sat down.

"I woke up remembering I wanted to run over to Home Depot to get some things for the bookstore remodel. Want to ride along, Beau?"

Mae jumped in. "Don't fall for it Beau. Many's the time I got that invitation wrapped with 'oh, it will only take a few minutes, then we'll stop for a romantic lunch and come home to spend the rest of the day with wine and whipped cream.' Well, what I got was hours of tedium while he looked at every piece of lumber or tool; then, since we didn't have enough time for a nice lunch, got a trip through the drive-thru at Mickey D's. Once home I got to see every tool he bought and a lesson in how it works. You know the one tool I never got to see...."

Looking at Dash, Beau said, "What a terrible way to treat a beautiful woman. Colonel, I'm disappointed in you."

Still crunching on his cereal, Dash replied. "Oh no, don't feel sorry for her. You don't know the very large portion of my life spent outside dressing rooms waiting for her little fashion show. The woman loves to shop. And to buy dresses which she never wears. Must have a thousand. You could be here for a year and never see her in one. I think we're even on the time tolerating each other's shopping peccadillos."

"Hey, it was my money so stop complaining," Mae said.

"Not all of it was yours. What about that very expensive, very sexy green dress I bought for you?"

Mae's throaty laugh burst forth. "I clearly remember you opening your wallet and all the moths flying out. Actually noted the date in my diary."

Ignoring her barb, Dash said, "You're supposedly saving it for some special event and just what would that be?"

Mae closed her laptop. Smiling broadly, she announced, "Your funeral!"

Beau made the time-out sign. "Dash, before I leave I want to see the divorce papers, 'cause you two are the most married *divorced* couple I've ever encountered. And, as to your invite, as much as the thought of wine and whipped cream with you sounds intriguing, I must decline. I have some work for other clients that I need to do. Rain check old pal?"

Leaning back in his chair, Dash said, "Fine. I don't really feel like going. But, and I emphasize this, I don't have anything else to do." Glancing at his watch, he continued, "I guess I could go to the bookstore and do some pounding there."

He felt a gentle nudge on his leg. Charlie Dog wanted some attention. "Or I guess Charlie and I could go outside for a bit." When he got no answer from either Mae or Beau, he stood. "Come along Charlie. The grownups have work to do." He rinsed out the bowl and put it into the dishwasher. No need to vary his routine; neatness first.

Dash glanced at his watch. Five o'clock. His stomach rumbled. Signaling for Charlie Dog to come, they crossed the road and walked through the small gathering of trees and into the backyard. Seeing Cav and Matt rounding the porch, their arms laden with pizza, beer and other junk food, he picked up his pace, trotting up to them.

"Ah pizza and beer. Good choice." He helped them carry the piping hot pizzas and very cold beer into the kitchen. Stacking the boxes neatly on the counter, he pulled open the cabinets for plates and glasses and napkins and anything else he felt was needed for the evening repast.

"Hey G-man, Beau and Mae, food's here. Smell that pizza. Come and get it before it's all gone because this old soldier is starving."

As plates were filled and then their mouths, Cav began reporting on his interviews with the townies. The gist of what he learned was everyone would be happy to provide Dash with a character reference. The problem being the 'characters' were the ones ready to pour their hearts out. According to his notes, Rufus Hill said Dash was a 'good un', never one to start trouble but never backing down. Another Clover Pointe citizen, one Vernon Thomas, proclaimed loudly that Dash would never beat anyone to death. 'Everyone knows his choice of weapon is the gun.' After all, as Jim Nagy pointed out, at the county fair Dash won all the prizes at the shooting booths. And, whatever was Rakestraw thinking? Dash would never leave a body to be found. To a man and woman they all pointed to Lake Erie: The Great Watery Dumping Ground.

Dash muttered, "If everyone who killed or said they killed someone dumped the body into the lake, we could walk to Canada."

"And, my friend, why is Little Biff called 'little'? If anything he should be called 'Gigantic Biff'. What is he? Six eight, four hundred pounds? Cav asked Dash.

"I know, I know. And he is the gentlest of giants. Every time he opens his mouth I look around to see who is talking; he has the softest voice of anyone I've ever met. And his heart is as big as he is. Very generous to every charitable cause in town." Dash answered.

Mae finished her beer and jumped into the conversation. "Dash, remember his parents? Two of the smallest people in town. His dad was known as 'Big Biff', supposedly so named by his classmates since he was just a peanut. Rumor had it that 'little Biff' is a junior and so nicknamed 'little'. Well, *little* did anyone know he would turn out to be a giant?"

Laughing, Matt said, "Passes for small town humor!"

Mae asked him if he had any luck locating the mysterious Squiggles or whatever.

"Everything is set for tomorrow afternoon. The man's name is Brent Yarborough, ex-cop. 'Squiggles' to all his friends because of his propensity to doodle or draw all the time. Once the Tydie Sisters are finished at Biff's they will call Sheriff Owen. He's going to hook the two parties up. I've offered them your place, Mae. When he has the sketch, he'll call us for further instructions." Turing to Dash, he added, "I have to say your father is chomping at the bit to help us. I suggest we assign more duties to him."

Dash shrugged, nodding to Beau. "He's the man in charge now."

The men and Mae sat back in their chairs. G-man reported on Jock Hadley. No known arrests, one traffic ticket in the last ten years.

"My feeling, and that's all it is, is Jock constantly maneuvered his way out of trouble. What I learned so far about his business dealings is most of them were above board, but he has, in the past, walked a fine line. This past year he's either lost his touch or some of his previous ventures went south, dragging him down. His bottom lines have bottomed out. Annie said he asked for money; he needs it if what I saw is true."

"Do you think he hid any assets before he got the divorce? Isn't that what happens? The rich party transfers the money to off-shore accounts." Mae asked.

Dash shrugged. "I have no idea. We never discussed finances, either hers or mine. I guess my cousin Franklin paid her handsomely as he has more money than Croesus. She is doing double-duty: garden designer and house-sitter. We never did anything that would strain purse strings." Scowling, he added, "She said he wanted what I would consider big bucks and that she had them. Just a decision whether to pay him off or not."

Matt looked around, but stopped at Dash. "If I put something on the table, will anyone freak out?"

"Go for it kid. I'll protect you from your client." Beau said.

"Is it possible that Mrs. Hadley paid someone to bump off her husband, but they got the fake husband? Maybe that's why the wrong guy is on the slab. Maybe she thought it would be cheaper to get rid of him. I mean it's just a thought."

"Come on, Matt. Where would you find a hit man in Clover Pointe? And don't look at me. I know she wanted Hadley out of her life. Hell, she divorced him, didn't she? I mean, I don't know that much about her background but, nah, that's out of the ballpark." Dash said.

Beau said, "Let's call it for the night. Matt, follow that angle if you want. Ask Dash's dad; if anyone knows the underbelly of this town, it's probably him. Think on these things, my friends, and we'll see what tomorrow brings."

The soldiers put themselves on KP duty offering to clean up. Dash walked Matt to his car thanking him profusely for his help. He came around to the backyard calling for Charlie Dog.

"Where are you going now?" Mae called.

"Oh I don't know, thought maybe I'd go back to Afghanistan. I hear it's lovely this time of year. Or maybe I'll walk to the beach; gotta problem with that?" Dash called back.

"No. I need to talk to you."

Dash looked to the heavens. "The last time you needed to talk to me you told me you weren't ever going to talk to me again. And yet here you are, talking to me. Is this 'need to talk' going to be another, 'sorry but I'm never talking to you again' or 'you're sorry about the last need to talk and now you want to make sure we keep talking.' Huh? Any clue? Just so I can prepare myself."

Bouncing down the stairs, she said, "You'll just have to follow me to find out." She winked at him and started to run.

Turning to G-Man and Beau, Dash asked them to pray for him. "That gal's got something going on in that red head of hers. Always means trouble for me."

As Dash took off jogging after Mae, Beau heard him yell to Mae, "Anytime you want to apologize I'm ready."

"Me? Apologize to you. No, Soldier Boy, you owe me at least one."

Out of earshot, Dash told Mae to slow down. They walked to the beach and onto the pier in silence. They settled for dangling their legs at the end of the pier.

After a few minutes, Dash chuckled. "You know this all started because your buddy Doctor Chandler didn't want us to talk to each other. Well, we've been alone for several minutes now and haven't said a word. Slide over here and tell me what the hell is going on with you and the not-so-good Doctor."

"You remember Richard, the first bastard I married?"

"I never knew him that well but I remember most of what you told me about your marriage. Please tell me Chandler hasn't hit you. Seriously. I can murder only so many people in one summer."

Slapping him in the shoulder, she shook her head. "No, not that. But listen to this. Last Sunday on the drive home, Chandler started talking, I mean nonstop. By the time we were outside of Ann Arbor I found myself plotting ways to kill him. Almost sent you a text asking if this or that would work. Instead I took a few deep breaths and tried to relax. Telling myself he was just excited about our future."

Holding up her hand so Dash couldn't stop her, she continued. "Monday night I come home to *my* place to find he has decided to move in. Now this had been mentioned but nothing agreed upon. Next I find he rearranged all my furniture. Another deep breath. Tuesday I discover he has cleaned out my closet and dresser, messing with my precious nearly-new dresses. Several more deep breaths but now with angry glances his way. Well, on Wednesday he decided to delve into my financial affairs. Once he discovered you and I still had holdings together I was treated to an evening long lecture which I cut short by using some of those good old fashioned Army words you taught me. Man is as thick as a brick wall. Then, and my dearest friend, this is the kicker. He tells me I need to lose weight and tone up, presenting me with a gym membership."

Dash pulled back laughing. "Where'd you hide his body? What an idiot! Messing with your dresses *and* your beautiful body. But, if he's behind the new hairdo, that's an okay thing."

"Umm, he told me *not* to cut my hair. I hadn't planned on it but dammit it's my hair. And, as usual, you're right about the gym thing. Who the hell does he think he's talking to? I gave him a good ass kicking, right out the door."

Mae jumped up, raising her arms above her head. "God, what a good feeling to finally kick some ass. All my life I've had to listen to one man after another tell me what to do, what not to do, how to do it. Well, I told him what he could do with his gym membership."

Dash also stood. "Mae, you *do* know who you're talking to, right? Tall guy, Army uniform. Hell, when I woke up in the hospital I couldn't remember my name, where I was or how I got there. But when I saw you at my bedside, I thought, 'dammit she's going to chew my ass off for something'. Frankly I'm surprised there's anything left after all your chewings."

"Oh, silly. Those don't count. You never fought back. Felt sorry for me; I know you did. Didn't want to hurt my feelings. I could see it in your eyes, 'poor Mae, she's had a hard life. I'll let her win this one.'"

Chuckling, Dash countered, "Oh no. I didn't feel sorry for you, but my dad always said I shouldn't fight with anyone who was not my equal." Holding up his hand, he said, "Yes, I know that physically you're not my equal. I'm talking about intellectually. Again, not equal, sorry, Maevis."

Mae took a step closer to Dash. "Not equal! That's a load of bull!" She shoved him in the chest sending him into the water. He bobbed up sputtering. He grabbed her by the legs and pulled her into the lake. They splashed back and forth, dunking each other, laughing and coughing. Charlie Dog jumped in to join the fray.

After several minutes, they walked out of the water and collapsed on the beach.

She put her head on Dash's shoulder. "Why do I always choose the wrong guys? Everyone except you. You're just vexing beyond reason."

"That's the nicest thing you've said to me in a while. Sure you don't want to remarry? I meant it when I told you it was a standing offer. We can remarry and die blissfully in each other's arms."

"Murder, suicide, you mean?"

"Most likely."

She put her arm across his waist.

"Dashiell, did you have fun at the reunion? Besides panting after Emmysue, I mean. I found the whole thing, seeing everyone, upsetting. Too many memories of how stressed I was studying all the time; worrying about my future."

Pulling her closer, Dash answered. "Actually I rather enjoyed it; reminded me that once we were so excited about the future, the great unknown; everyone sure it would be wonderful. None of us even considered all the things that could go wrong. Sickness, death, divorce."

Propping himself on one elbow, he looked down into her green eyes. "And, if memory serves, I remember the two of us engaged in some delightful stress-reduction exercises. You know we should have eloped back then. We'd be growing weed on some small farm in Kentucky right now with about ten barefoot kiddos running around. We'd both be fat and toothless. Think we'd be happier?"

"Ma and Pa Kettle! I can't even fathom that. You're the silliest soldier I've ever known." Mae said, sitting up.

"Dash, can I ask you a question? About the case I mean? I know you'll say it's none of my business. In the past I've said you were aggravating, irritating and annoying, and you may be all those things but one thing you're not and that is stupid. I understand you practically left a calling card on the body."

He sat up pulling back a bit. "I didn't kill him. I wouldn't kill for Annie or anyone unless the danger was imminent. Hadley never struck me as that dangerous."

"Then why did someone kill him? And frame you? Wonder if it was just an accident or maybe opportunity that he was bludgeoned to death with your crowbar. Any idea where the crowbar was before someone used it on the Hadley-would-be?" Mae asked.

Dash shook his head. "Yes, as a matter of fact, I just found out that Joey and Johnny were the last ones to have it. One of my dumber moves was leaving town after the picnic. If I had just gone to work instead, I'm pretty sure I would have rounded up and secured all the tools. That's what I usually do since I paid for all of them. Yes, dearie, I am frugal or a tightwad or any other names that mean I watch my pennies closely."

"And what about that son of Annie's? He's a piece of work. What was he trying to prove by punching you? I hoped you'd put the little prick in the hospital. I know I would have."

"Remember Owen's rule: don't pick on the disadvantaged and he's one of them, no brains. So you really did come to help."

"Depends. Do I look fat to you? Gym membership fat?"

Dash pulled back a bit to consider Mae's physique. "I don't think so but if you were to get naked and let me feel around a bit, I could give you a better assessment."

"Like that's going to happen. Let's rinse off and head home; make an early night of it."

Sloshing their way home and onto the porch, they paused to drop their shoes on the porch. Beau greeted them at the door. Dash started to pull off his shirt. Mae stood back. "Another 'Oh My' moment."

Dash looked from Mae to Beau. "Don't you dare! I mean it, Maevis."

"If I outlive you I'm telling that story at your funeral. To lighten the mood."

"Well *now* I've got to know. Come on. Promise not to laugh or repeat it." Beau pleaded.

Dash glared at him as he walked by. Mae winked, mouthing later.

Inside they found the guys organizing a poker game. Dash declined to join, saying he was too tired to concentrate. Mae headed up the stairs to take a shower. Dash yelled to her. "Leave the wet clothes outside the door. I'm going to soak them to get the lake dirt out."

Turning he saw the guys staring at him. Cav spoke first. "That whack on the head really did some damage. Turned you into Martha fucking Stewart."

"Don't dis my woman Martha! Learned a lot watching her show while I was recovering. Do you know how to fold a fitted sheet? I do. Life is not all rifles and warfare." Waving his arm around the room, Dash asked, "Do you see anyone to do this for me? No wife, no partner, no paid help. A man's gotta do what a man's gotta do. A modicum of order and cleanliness is required." Dash started up the stairs

Cav yelled at him. "Hey, we're thinking of playing strip poker. Okay if Dr. Mae joins in?"

"I should hope so. I know I couldn't sleep thinking of just you guys taking it off bit by bit. Shatter all my memories of our squad." Dash stopped, returning to the kitchen.

"Fine, have at it." Dash looked at Grady and Cav. He glanced at the clock. "It's eight so you will be sitting in your birthday suits by nine thirty, ten at the latest. Stand up, Beau. Turn around. Wearing an undershirt?"

After giving Beau a good look, Dash pronounced, "Beau, by ten you'll be in your shorts. Mae, she might lose a shoe or two."

"What are you talking about? Is she that good?" Beau asked.

Taking a step up the stairs, Dash shook his head no. "You guys are *that* bad."

He took a few more steps then yelled down. *"Oh, and she cheats!"*

Upstairs Dash filled Mae in on her pending evening. She smiled slyly at him. "What should I do?"

"Go for it girl. But watch out for Beau. He's as cunning as you are and hate to say it but I don't want to go to sleep thinking of the two of you naked in my kitchen. Too much of an 'Oh My' memory."

Stripping out of his clothes, he handed them to her. "Just put them in the washer and pull out the knob. Everything's set to go."

"See how easy this is. I already have one man naked." She kissed him gently then pointed to his dresser. "I left a pill for you if your little hamster brain starts obsessing about everything. Get some sleep. Don't worry. I'll take care of the world-famous team."

She tripped down the stairs, depositing the clothes in the washer and pulling the knob as instructed. Turning she said, "Gentlemen, I understand strip poker is on the agenda for the evening." Rubbing her hands together, she asked who had a fresh deck.

"Dr. Mae, the Captain, I mean Colonel, says you cheat." Cav reported.

"Don't listen to him; he was always a sore loser."

Beau started shuffling the deck. "Dr. Summers, I am appalled. *Do* you cheat?"

Mae blushed. Ignoring his question, she asked. "Remind me. What beats four of a kind?"

Grady threw his hands up. "That's it. Never a good sign when the babe asks how to play the game. Dash was very good so if she beat him... Think I'll check email. Night, gentlemen. Mae."

Cav wiggled in his seat. "I think I'll take a rain check. Might nose around the strip joint down the road. Beau?"

Beau declined. "So, it's just you and me, Dr. Summers. Game?"

Mae motioned with her hands. "Bring it on, counselor."

Ten

The next morning Dash came down dressed for a run. He felt totally refreshed and eager to face the day. Beau and Mae were not in their bedrooms so when Dash arrived in the kitchen to find it empty, he was surprised. Charlie Dog was snoozing contentedly.

Dash checked his office to find Grady on the computer.

"Where is everyone? I was hoping Beau would go for a run with me."

"And good morning to you too, Colonel. Have you looked at a clock recently? It's ten thirty. You've been asleep for fourteen hours. I've been trying to decide if I should climb the steps to see if you were still breathing or not. I thought Beau and Mae would have returned by now."

"Where did they go?"

"Not sure, think they were heading to JoJo's. Mae grabbed the keys to the Vette and off they went. She did add that if you weren't up by noon to dial 911."

Dash leaned against the door jamb, crossing his arms. "So Beau has taken my car and my woman. And here I was thinking this was going to be a good day. Oh well."

Grady laughed. "I haven't had anything but coffee so if you want to treat me to brunch, lunch, whatever at JoJo's we can see if they are lingering and looking longingly at each other. What have we got to lose?"

"I'd say my dignity but I think that was lost years ago. Hey, before we go, anything on Dr. Chandler?" Dash asked.

"Sorry, pal, but he is squeaky clean. You pale in comparison. His first wife left him because he was 'too' dedicated to his work, saving lives. Mae could do worse." G-man cleared his throat, "You want the report on Jock Hadley or should we wait for Beau and Cav."

Sitting down, Dash put his hand out to receive the report. He perused it and then handed it back. "So his need for money could be from either bad investments or gambling debts. Any idea who holds the markers?"

"Not at this time. The agency is digging deeper; might have something later today. They are thorough but I didn't tell them it was a rush job. At the time I had no idea murder would play into this. I can put a rush on it if you'd like." Grady left the ball in Dash's court.

"Let's run this by Beau and Cav later today. For all I know they've solved this and I'm a free man with no Vette and once again sans best female friend." Dash shrugged, then added "Okay with you if I ask Annie and the twerp to join us? I guess I should dress for work. Told the crew I'd join them today."

Grady held up his hand to signal 'halt'. "I'm thinking Beau would not want you to invite Annie anywhere. You do remember yesterday, when the attorneys would only let you talk within their view?"

"Ah, that was just for show. You think I'm going to try to influence Annie, well, brother, you don't know her very well. And besides, what can they do to me? Arrest me? Haven't they done that already?"

Shaking his head, Grady stood. "Arrest you, no. But Beau could drop you like a hot rock and we both know that would be a bad thing. Listen, I followed you to hell and back but asking Annie along would not be good. How about a little you and me time?"

Pointing to his head, Dash said, "You're right. It's the head injury." Putting his arm around Grady, he added, "Just you and me, good friend."

Mae pulled the Corvette to the curb on Washington Street. Turning to Beau, she pointed across the street to the blue house, the one without a porch.

"That was my house. The porch fell down because my father was a drunk and had no money to take care of the house, or us for that matter."

Beau was a bit taken aback but sat silently. He sensed Mae was going down a journey in her mind, a journey that was not pleasant. She got out of the car, motioned for him to follow as they crossed the street to stand in front of 808, the blue porch-less house.

"Welcome to Clover Pointe's Irish neighborhood. It's about three blocks across and five blocks down. Not sure if only the Irish live here now but fifty years ago, if you were Irish, this is where you wanted to live. Among your own kind. Most of the families were either new immigrants or first generation."

Frowning Beau said, "It sounds more like a ghetto than a neighborhood when you put it that way."

"Sorry, it was never a ghetto, just a great place to live if you wanted to hear your own brogue." She stepped over to 810, a white house with the porch, now enclosed. "This was the Hammond house. Owen, Dash's father, isn't Irish but the dreaded English, though many years removed from Britain. The story goes that Owen was dating or courting a woman and he wanted to buy a house to demonstrate his sincerity about marriage and family."

Mae smiled. "That is *so* Owen. Well, he comes to view the house." She pointed to the next house, 812. "Paddy McCafferty lived there. He was an immigrant from County Galway here with his wife and child to start a new life. Now Paddy was a gregarious man so he invited Owen to share a pint with him. He took him into the kitchen where his cousin, one Helene-Marie, newly arrived from Ireland, stood peeling potatoes for Sunday dinner. She turns to greet the young Owen, smiling broadly as was her wont. Her face with those big blue eyes, her head covered in all that black curly hair and herself flashing a warm Irish smile, what chance did he have? Owen fell in love immediately, asked her out, proposed in two weeks, wed her in three months."

She shrugged. "Just saying, that's the tale. And her son Dash inherited all three of those attributes." Pointing to the next house, she said, "Hard to believe as I stand here now, but that tiny McCafferty house was once filled with ten children."

Touching her chest, she said, "My parents were from Ireland, but no relation to the McCaffertys. I'm an only child. Me mam barely survived my birth. The Hammonds had three. Very strange but Dash, Billy and I were all born in the same month, May. Dash wasn't due until June but so like him to arrive early so he could horn in on our birthday month."

"So you literally married the boy next door." Beau said.

"Yes, but not until many years later. Anyway, everyone expected us to marry right out of high school since we seemed joined at the hip. What a shock when I married Richard, a fellow doctor, and then Dash chose a very sweet girl, Judy. If she had lived, he'd probably be a schoolteacher in some small Ohio town with a bunch of kids he could coach in sports. Don't tell, but the Army was never going to be his career. He just wanted a taste of what his Uncle Joe had experienced. After

Judy's death he stayed in; eventually enjoying it and a military career was born."

Mae handed Beau the keys. As they entered the car, Beau said, "Small town upbringing. The only thing New Orleans has in common with Clover Pointe is both bordering a body of water."

"Do you want to see the rest of the town? Promise it won't take long."

After receiving an affirmative nod, she directed Beau around Clover Pointe. The tour of memorable places in Dash's and her lives took less than an hour. Finally, they pulled into St. Mary's parking lot when Mae's phone rang.

She answered listening intently. "We'll be right there. I'm with Beau Saylor. I haven't seen Dash this morning. Let's see what you're talking about and then we can decide if Dash needs to know."

Turning to Beau, she said. "That was Irma. Something upsetting at the motel. She wants to see Dash but will settle for us. We're to park down the street and sneak in the back way." Sighing, she added, "Lord only knows what this means."

They tucked the Vette around the corner from the motel. "We should have taken your car, Mae. This one stands out like a sore thumb. Everyone will think Dash is around here."

"Can't help it. Let's see what's going on." They climbed the stairs to the second floor finding Room 214. Before they could knock, the door opened with Irma peering out. She shooed them inside.

"We haven't called the police yet or let Mr. Biff know. Thought Dash should know first. After all Miss Emmysue said she was supposed to meet him last Saturday night. We figured maybe he should know she's back."

"You called me because Emmysue came back to the motel? Why would that involve the police?" Mae asked.

Irma and Ilene reached for each other's hands. "There is a lot of blood in her room. We saw her yesterday after she arrived. Chatted for a bit. This morning we went to straighten her room, refresh the towels and stuff. But there is blood everywhere. We shut the door and went to our room."

"Did you check to see if this Emmysue was anywhere in the room? In distress?" Beau asked.

Ilene rolled her eyes. "Of course we did. Does everyone under fifty think we're idiots or senile? The room looks like someone cut off a chicken's head and it ran around spewing blood everywhere. No feathers though, so not a chicken. Come on, see for yourselves."

Irma peeked out of the door. "Move quickly and quietly. Room 205."

Doing as they were told, Beau and Mae followed Irma. She pulled out her pass card, swiped it and pushed open the door.

Beau instructed Mae. "Hands in your pockets and just step inside until we see what's what. We should take photos. Irma, Ilene, return to your room. We will only be a minute or two and then you need to call the police."

They stepped inside, closing the door. Mae pulled out her phone and began to take a video, sweeping the room. "I'll also take stills, starting at this side and panning around." She wrinkled her nose. "Smells awful."

"I'm going to check the bathroom. Whatever you do don't get me in the photos. Your guess? Seems like an awful lot of blood." Beau walked by the bed, pointing to a large spot of blood on the mattress.

"An artery, maybe. But he/she must have been flailing about to spray it all around like this. Should have dropped over. We need to check for drops of blood outside." Mae added.

They spent three minutes tops in the room. Glancing at the outside of the door and the concrete walkway, they didn't see any blood.

Irma had the door open so they could scoot inside.

"Ladies, it's time to call the police. Obviously we would prefer if you didn't mention us or that you thought of calling Dash. Straight line story: you went to clean the room and found all the blood. You looked for the guest, didn't find her and bolted to call from the safety of your room."

"Don't worry. We've read enough mysteries to know what to do. Archie always said to keep the lies simple."

"Archie?"

"Goodwin, of course. Nero Wolfe's right hand man. Surely a man of your breeding has read Rex Stout."

Beau shook his head. "Ladies, the idea is not to lie, simple or otherwise. Omission is the sin we are promoting. Nothing about this to Dash even if you run into him. If, God forbid, he shows up here looking for this Emmysue, tell him to go home and stay there. Tell him I said so, if it comes to that. Listen, we need to leave and you need to call the cops. I'll check in with you later. Thank you."

Mae brushed their cheeks with her lips. "Be cautious. You're going to get a nice bonus."

With that, Beau and Mae slipped out, heads down, walking quickly to the back stairs and the Vette. Beau slipped into the driver's seat.

"Shit, Beau, what the hell is going on? Why would someone want to hurt Emmysue? Or why would Emmysue want to hurt someone? Head for Lakota Hospital. We'll check out the ER."

"On it Mae, as soon as you tell me how to get to there." She pointed.

Five o'clock Saturday found Beau in the kitchen helping Owen prep food for the evening barbeque. As he washed lettuce and other salad ingredients, he asked, "So, Sheriff Hammond, or should I call you Mr. Hammond, are you happy to have Dash home?"

"Call me Owen, most everyone does. Hell, Dash has been calling me that since he was five. And, to answer the question, I'm thrilled to have him here, safe and somewhat sound. Not so sure he's thrilled to be back in the bosom of his family, but...."

Turning to Owen, Beau said, "Well, if it matters, he always spoke very highly and fondly of the Hammond clan as he called all of you. Respected you as a father and a man, or so I gleaned from his conversation."

"Really? Surprises me. Helene Marie always said I just didn't understand him but I thought he didn't understand me. Between you and me, I felt like I never lived up to his expectations. Failed him early on."

Beau chuckled. "Most of the time it's the sons who don't feel like they've lived up to the fathers' expectations. I know that was my case. No matter how hard I tried it never seemed to be enough. Don't recall

Dash ever saying anything like that, but then it wasn't often we had the time for soul-searching sessions."

Now it was Owen who laughed. "Let me tell you a story about the little boy Dash. He was different from Sam, night and day. Not bad, just different. Smart as a whip, always thinking about something odd, as far as I was concerned. Too damned independent. Even at five."

Moving to sit at the table, he continued, "Every summer our parish had a picnic on the church grounds down by the lake's shore. Not miles from our house but a decent distance and several busy streets away. Well, the summer he was five we were all at the picnic when he apparently took it in his head to go home for a book, *The Three Musketeers*. Someone mentioned that he, Billy and Mae were just like the Musketeers. Dash had to get the book; he knew Sam had a copy."

"Wait, he could read at five?"

"Yes, one of the McCafferty girls wanted to be a teacher so she constantly played at it. Unbeknownst to us parents, the three kids picked up everything she said. Learned to read at three. Back to the story. I discover Dash is gone. Billy informs me he headed home. We all jump in the car searching the streets as we drove to the house."

Shaking his head remembering that day, he continued, "Inside I find Dash, book in hand, about to head back to the picnic. I really let him have it, yelled until I was blue in the face. He calmly said, 'I walked to the corners, looked all ways round and then ran across the streets. Just like you said I should.' His mother smacked his butt a few times. Hard. He turned to look at her, more surprised than anything. I banished him to his room for the rest of the summer. He nodded a 'yes sir' to me, a 'yes ma'am' to his mother and walked slowly to his room.

Ten minutes later we went to his room, found him curled up in the closet clutching the book. Putting him on the bed, we talked to him about how worried we were, how much we loved him, etc. Those big blue eyes just stared at us. Finally he said, very softly, 'You don't hurt someone you love.' Crushed his mother and me. That was all he said to us for a week, other than 'yes sir', 'yes ma'am'. Didn't call us dad or mom again. I became Owen or Sheriff; his mom, Helene Marie. Stubborn little piece of shite, as his mother would say."

Owen stared off into space. "After the accident, in the hospital, he drifted in and out of consciousness. Once, it was just we two. He slid his hand over to grasp mine. Eyes still closed, I heard him say, 'Daddy, I crossed at the corners.' And he was out again. Never asked him if he remembered saying that."

Beau watched as the elder Hammond stood to gather the salad fixings. Nothing more to be said. They worked silently until they heard the side door slam open. Dash arrived. He dropped his shoes on the mat and stomped into his office.

"Think he's upset?" Owen asked. "Now what?" he added with a sigh.

Mae and Marie came in from the porch. "Anything we can do to help?"

The men nodded toward the office door.

"Dash is in there. Upset about something. Mae, what do you think?" Beau said.

Mae turned toward the porch. "I think I should leave now. Marie, he likes you. See what's wrong."

"Oh no you don't. He's yours, or was yours. I've got my own to handle. Sister, your turn."

The office door opened and Dash looked out. "What?"

"Rumor has it you're upset. Dare I ask about what?" Mae ventured to say.

"Oh, thought I hid it well." Smiling he said, "Sorry but I didn't notice that anyone was here. I'm sorry I'm late, and for the dust and dirt. I'll shower and be down in five."

"Whoa, pardner. Want to tell us what's wrong? Maybe I can help," Mae offered.

"No thanks, I've seen you try to hang a picture. Not a pretty sight, you and a hammer. No. sweets, thanks for the offer but this is a little bigger than that." He started for the stairs.

Owen stopped him. "A burden shared..... What's going on?"

Laughing Dash said, "I stayed to make sure all the tools, especially those with my initials on them were secure; not making that mistake again. Then reviewed the plans for next week's work. Discovered that the guys took down the wrong part of the wall. Gonna take some time and money to fix. That's all. Just another pebble in my shoe on this long march of life."

Beau looked at him. "Where do you get this crap you spout? Listen, oh my colonel, no one died today, did they? No, so straighten up and get ready to smile and be charming. Two things I've seen you do in the past, so bring it on."

Dash snapped a salute and jogged up the stairs.

"That wasn't all that hard, now was it?" Beau asked. "Let's get this party started. Hungry men are cranky men."

Dash stepped onto the porch. Before he had time to survey his backyard, he heard his name being called and the instruction to 'go long'. The Cav had a football and was about to launch down the lawn. Dash took off running but couldn't catch up to it. He picked up the ball and tossed it back to Cav. Yelling for the rest of guys to join in, a game of touch football was soon underway.

Walking over to Owen, Mae put her arms around his waist, pecking his cheek.

"Isn't it nice when his friends come over for a playdate?" she whispered.

Owen smiled. "Don't mess with him Mae. I'm warning you. If you're not here to help the cause, get back to that school up north and leave him be. He's got enough trouble with the little blonde one. Play nicely or this will be your last 'playdate'."

She faced her former father-in-law. "You know I would never intentionally hurt him. Sometimes I just don't know where his mind is. I promise you. All I want is for him to be happy and safe." She again planted a kiss on his cheek then wandered away to greet and kiss Owen's brother, Father Tom.

When the elder Hammonds had the grills fired to the proper temperature, they assigned Sam to get the steak orders from the guests and to remind them about Tony Packo's hot dogs and sausages so the trip to Max Klinger's favorite place would not have been in vain. Marie and Ruthie brought the salads and side dishes from the kitchen to the long serving table. Sam had set up various tables around the patio so everyone could sit and eat in peace. Charlie Dog went from one person to another, checking for fallen food or secretly offered treats.

Dash noticed Annie standing there. "What are you doing here?"

"Good afternoon, Dashiell. So nice to see you." She said batting her eyelashes.

"Sorry, I mean, I thought Beau forbade the two of us being in the same room."

"Dolly invited me, unbeknownst to Clarence Darrow. He conceded to allow my presence as long as we, that's you and me, aren't alone, away from the madding crowd, as it were. Can I stay?"

Dash looked at the women. "Oh what the hell! Is little Timmy with you? Is he going to take another swipe at me? If so, I think I'll retire to the front room and watch ESPN."

Dash waited until everyone had filled their plates. He walked over to the table where Annie, her son and Trigger sat.

"Wondered if you were ever going to sit down? Did you have fun playing football?" she asked.

"Yeah, but I'm going to be sore tomorrow. Long time since I've done that. Tim, Trigger, why didn't you join in? You would have been welcome, you know that."

Trigger replied, "Never one for sports. Too much running. Always liked to sit and watch."

"Good attributes for a sniper, I guess." Dash said.

Tim's eyes grew wide. "I didn't know you were a sniper. Wow, that's exciting. How many kills?"

"Bullshit, that's what that is." Trigger said, screwing up his face. "Don't know where you got that idea, Dash. Guess from the same rumor mill that said you only peeled potatoes and served soup."

"Point well made, Trigger. Honestly don't know where I heard the sniper report. Maybe I made it up while I was making up the rest of my life story after the accident. Still not sure what really happened and what the family has made up for me." Dash said between bites of his hot dog. "So where were you guys?"

Annie jumped in. "They were out at Lulu's. Trigger is thinking of revamping the place and Timothy was providing some pointers on improving the sound system, lights, etc. That's what he does, audio and gaming stuff."

Dash wiped some mustard off his face. "Pray tell, Mr. Trigger. I take it Lulu's not coming back. I thought you would just close up and head back out west, isn't that where you're located now?"

Trigger glanced at Annie then faced Dash. "Just thinking of it, I mean, the revamping. Decided we offer a real service to the men around here. And don't forget the dancers. Maybe it's not the kind of job you put on your resume but they make good money, tips and all."

Dash agreed. "I know the vets would be devastated if you closed. Only one of two spots open most of the night. You know how sleeplessness can get to you. A bit of music and some nice looking gals pick up one's spirits. The apartment for the vets won't be ready for a few more weeks, longer if I can't get out from under this crap. Trig, stop by and see what you think."

Annie piped in. "I'd be happy to give you some decorating tips. I mean I'm right downstairs at the bookstore." Pointing over to Franklin's yard and the garden she redesigned, she said, "My work is pretty much done over there. Just waiting for the plants to fill out. I won't be adding more until the fall." Waving her hands about, she said, "I see camouflage rugs, wallpaper of mountain or desert scenes. A refrigerator full of beer and those c-rations, MRE's, or whatever you call them. Make everyone feel like they never left the military. What do you think?"

"Mom, are you crazy? Those guys want to forget all that, right Dash, Trigger?" Tim said. "Are you planning on installing a sound system or gaming equipment? I'm your guy, get you a great deal."

"Okay, kid. Why don't you and Trigger stop by tomorrow? Give me some prices for whatever it is you were talking about. Not into gaming myself." Standing Dash excused himself saying he wanted to check on the guys. He then grabbed a beer and headed for the front porch, a bit of solitude.

Dash stretched his long legs out in front of him. He picked at the label on his beer bottle, trying to decide how thirsty he was. The party, as his father called it, was going strong in the back yard. The chatter was still very loud but he wanted another beer.

The door popped open and his sister Dolly approached with a cold brew in her hand.

"Everyone is wondering what happened to you. Mr. Saylor keeps watching Mae who is watching Annie who is just watching everyone. Dad is hoping you didn't just hightail it out of here. Said to tell you he's sorry for all the fuss, if I find you."

"Dolly, you are a godsend. I was trying to decide whether I needed to return to the get-together so I could snatch another beer." Holding up his phone so his sister could read the text, he said, "Your kids. Birdie, I mean Kathleen, seems to be enjoying herself in Ireland with Mom's Galway cousins. And Mikey keeps texting me about how could I get into such a mess without him to witness it. Gotta love those kids. Comin' home next week, right?"

Leaning against the railing, Dolly studied her brother's face. "I haven't seen you except for that brief moment after you were arrested. Want to talk?"

Dash drank from the fresh bottle, then pursed his lips. "Answer me this. Has Robbie said why he's jumped the gun and arrested me when I'm pretty sure he knows damn well he might be wrong?"

"He's feeling the pressure."

"Come again. What pressure?"

"Oh, he's heard rumors that the Town Council is re-evaluating the decision to keep the town's police force. After the last chief was fired, there was a considerable amount of discussion about merging the forces with the Sheriff's department, having that be the law in the town and county."

"I don't remember any of this. Was I out of the country?"

"No, just out of your mind. It was during your rehab and town politics were low on our priority list for you. Robbie got hired as the last experiment. He was relatively inexpensive, not having a ton of experience."

"So my life is about to be ruined because he's insecure. Damn!"

"What would you do? A nasty murder to solve and a blunt instrument sitting there, fingerprints and carved initials."

Shaking his head, he glared at his sister. "Please don't try to justify his actions. Dolly, you know I didn't do it, don't you? Please tell me you don't think I did it."

"Hell no. And if I was talking to Robbie, I would give him what for." She paused. "I guess I should add that you aren't high on his list of favorite people anyway. Many's the time he listened to me say 'Dash says this or Dash thinks I should do that'. Sorry."

Her brother reached for her hand. "If you ever do talk to him, tell him I will always take care of you and the kids. If he had been around when Trevor died, things might have been different. Take that back, things would have been weird if he jumped in right after Trev died." Sighing, he added. "I just want to settle this and I don't think we are making any progress. What with dinners and poker parties and Beau and Mae running around the town in *my* car. Hey, did you tell Annie I was a tightwad? Bone to pick with you dearest sister."

"What I might have said was that you were a tightwad when it came to spending money on yourself, except for tools. Really, your wardrobe is pathetic." Dolly answered.

Before Dash could respond, the door opened again. This time the eldest Hammond sibling carried two beers.

"Oh, I see Dolly's already provided fresh libation for you. Dad thinks you should join everyone. What do you think?"

Reaching for a beer, Dash answered. "That he is probably right. I'm sure he'd add that I should adjust my attitude." Taking a swig, he said to his brother, "Sam, have you been poking around? Any progress?"

"Hate to report, no. Have faith. Now, let's get back to the soiree. Mrs. Guzy sent over a couple of pies. I bet Dash that you could use a little sugar and Dolly, you never miss any sugar. Come along, brother and sister."

The trio departed for the back yard.

"You guys go on. I'll join you in a minute. Wanna get something." Dash said.

Eleven

When Sam next saw Dash, his brother walked down to the unlit fire pit carrying a bottle of Irish whiskey and a rifle. Father Tom stepped in front of Sam holding him back.

"Let him go. I think this is something he needs to do." Turning to his brother Owen, he added, "You're the one who wanted to get him together with his former squad."

Dash approached the vets, calling for Trigger to join them. He motioned for the men to stand, glasses in hand. He opened the bottle and passed it around telling the men to pour themselves a generous amount.

"Men, as the ranking officer of this motley crew, I am asking all of you to lift your glasses to our fallen friends."

The glasses were raised. Dash led them in taking a sip. Calling out the name of one of his men who didn't make it back, Dash fired the rifle into the air. Passing it to Grady who added a name, firing another round. Each man saluted a comrade. When the rifle was finally passed to Beau, he again raised his glass.

"To all our brothers, those who have fallen, those who have made it home and those who still fight the good fight. And to our enemies, may you rot in hell." He then emptied the rifle as all the men snapped a salute.

Dash announced, "Thank you my friends. It is an honor to be by your side now and it was an honor to stand by you over there."

He picked up the empty bottle and rifle carrying them back to the house. He glanced at Sam as he passed, saying, "want to arrest us for shooting a weapon within county limits?" Instead of answering verbally, Sam grabbed his brother wrapping his arms around him. Dash pushed him away, scowling.

When he returned to the backyard, he drifted over to where Annie, Tim and Trigger sat eating pie. Tim prattled on and on about this new techie thing and then another. When the last morsel was downed, Dash asked Annie if they might have a word. Trigger said he would handle the clean-up.

Dash led Annie to the fence near the garden. Leaning on it, he asked, "Funeral arrangements? What's going on? I assume you'll bury him in South Carolina. Do you need permission to leave?"

"Nothing has been said. I asked about when the body would be released and they said they couldn't give me a date just yet. Waiting on one thing or another. I talked to number one son, Stephen, and he is arranging everything down there; just waiting for the body, though I might cremate him. Cut down on the costs you know. Stephen might come up here if nothing happens soon. I'll warn you so you can practice boxing."

"Don't tell me he's another champion."

"Naw, just a brawler from way back. Got his pugnacious nature from his dad. Lacks Tim's skill."

They were interrupted by Tim who called Dash's name. "Hey, Dash, either the president is out front waiting for you or some other serious shithead. Black limo, two black SUV's. I think you should come."

Tapping Tim on the back of the head, Dash said. "No American flags, not President Obama. Excuse me Annie. I'm sure more trouble awaits. If you get a chance to get out of town, take it and head for the border. I'll follow when I can." He kissed her cheek, walking away. Dash whistled loudly, then raised one finger making a circle in the air to gather the troops.

Cav, Grady and Beau fell in step with them. When Owen and Tom started to move, Dash held up his hand stopping them. Charlie Dog walked alongside, growling lowly.

"Now what the hell is going on? You guys look like you're about to retake Fallujah," Sam said as he fell in line.

"Don't know but Tim says we have company. My bad vibe-o-meter is off the charts. You got your badge handy? Weapon? I'll need..." Sam grabbed his hand. Turning to the vets, he said, "No, no guns, gentlemen. Keep your cool."

They walked through the house to the front room. The porch was filled with black suited men. An older gentleman wearing a ten gallon hat leaned on a cane as one of his minions knocked on the door.

Dash opened the door. "Yes, may I help you?"

The Texan stepped forward extending his hand. "Colonel Hammond, I'm Emmysue's husband. She spoke very highly of you. I need a word in private."

"Sir, please come in. This is my brother, Sheriff Sam Hammond. You caught us in the middle of a cookout. Can we offer your men some refreshments while you and I step into my office for that private word? Cav, please show these gentlemen where the liquids are being kept."

Dash stepped forward to usher the men in. The room filled rapidly with everyone glaring at each other.

Pointing toward the office door, Dash said, "This way Mr. Tycoon. Pardon me, Emmysue called you Travis Tycoon. She never mentioned her surname. A thousand apologies."

The old man laughed. "Emmysue always calls me that and I call her Baby Boobs. Figured they cost me enough I could name them." Turning to his escorts, he reminded them that they were not thirsty or hungry. He motioned for one man to accompany him. "This is Evan Bush, my secretary. I'd like him to join us."

As his men exited, the Texan turned back to Dash.

"Gentlemen, back to business. To even things out I'm going to join you. I'm Colonel Hammond's attorney." Beau said.

Dash began to perform the introductions. "Beau Saylor, this is Travis....I'm sorry but what *is* your surname?"

"Benedict. Travis Benedict." He extended his hand.

The four gentlemen retreated to the office. Seats were offered but refused.

"Colonel, this shouldn't take too long. Have you seen my wife?"

Dash cocked his head surprised at the question. "No sir, not since the Fourth of July picnic. I understood her to say she was leaving the next morning to meet you in Chicago. She didn't arrive?"

"No, she did not. She told me she was coming to the reunion to see you specifically, that's why I'm here. I'm hoping you know where she is."

Wrinkling his brow, Dash said, "Sorry, Mr. Benedict. I saw her at the picnic. We had talked about meeting after the fireworks but unfortunately I was detained. The next morning I stopped by the motel but she had already checked out. I assumed she was on her way to Chicago."

The tall Texan leaned back against the desk. He narrowed his eyes. "Colonel Hammond, it is imperative that I find Emmysue. Do you have any idea where she might be?"

Dash crossed his arms and shook his head. "No. If she said something to me while at the picnic it didn't stick in my brain. See, last Saturday was not my best day for thinking. I was involved in a fight early on and the rest of the day got a little strange for me."

Evan Bush looked to his boss. "I'm afraid Mrs. Benedict has been suffering from delusions lately. She thinks someone is following her. She told Mr. Benedict she was going to ask for your help. See, we have put several men onto this when she started talking about having a stalker. No one was ever seen following her."

"Let me get this straight. She thought she was in danger yet you let her come here by herself. She doesn't call you all week and you're just now asking about her. What have I missed?" Dash asked.

Mr. Benedict held up his hand. "Colonel, unbeknownst to Emmysue, I did have her under surveillance. She would have been furious, saying I was trying to drive her crazy. She's made that accusation before when this all started. We couldn't figure out if she was seeing my men who were trying to find who was stalking her or there really was someone else. I've had men in town all week looking for her. All we know is she checked out of the motel Sunday morning and disappeared."

"Have your men been discreet as they are now, driving around in those SUV's dressed in black looking like the Feds have landed? Sorry, but I was out of town at the beginning of the week and I now find myself in a serious spot of trouble. All I can tell you is that I haven't seen or heard from Emmysue since she left the pavilion to watch the fireworks. Wish I could help you but my own problems are taking up all of my time." He moved toward the door then stopped to ask, "Have you talked to the police or the sheriff's department? Shall I ask my brother to join us so you can tell him your concerns?"

"Not at this time, but I appreciate your offer. We'll let you get back to your guests."

Bush handed Dash his card. "If you hear from or about Mrs. Benedict, please call me anytime. We are offering a $25,000 reward for information that helps us find her. Thank you. We appreciate your time."

Handshakes were exchanged as Dash showed them out. Watching Benedict get into his car, Dash turned to Beau. "Something's rotten in the state of Texas."

Beau raised his eyebrows.

Dash explained, "The Prom Queen thought I was dead so she wasn't coming to Clover Pointe to see me. Now maybe Tycoon misunderstood her because I remember her saying she was seeking help from Billy. Maybe the husband is confused. What do you think?"

Before Beau could explain, Dash grabbed his arm, pointing to the highway. Together they watched the chief of police pull into the driveway.

Hands in his pockets, Dash walked over to the driver's side. As the chief began to exit, Dash leaned on the door.

"Unless you've come to tell me the charges have been dropped and you want to apologize, don't even think about getting out of the car. Just back out and head home."

Rakestraw lowered the window. "It's not you I've come to see. I need a word with Mr. Saylor and Doctor Summers." He pushed against the door to exit; Dash stepped back, glancing at the porch he saw his father and brother descending the stairs.

Beau, Owen and Sam walked over to the chief of police. Greetings were exchanged. Rakestraw asked Beau if he would step aside for a word. Turning to Sam, he said, "Sam would you mind finding Dr. Summers? I need a word with her as well."

"Sure. Be right back. Dash, why don't you come with me? I'm sure Beau can answer whatever questions Robbie has for him."

Reluctantly Dash joined his brother and father as they went through the house and onto the patio. The Hammond women had gathered there, drinking wine and laughing.

Sam separated Mae from the group. "Mae, Robbie's out front. Wants to talk to you. Care to share?"

Mae whispered to Sam. "Tell Grady to check his email. I've sent him a video." She glanced at Dash who had joined the vets at the fire pit. "It's about the prom queen. Not sure whether Dash should see it or not. Not sure what it means. Beau and I spent the afternoon trying to....Well, you'll see." She walked around the side of the house.

"Grady, can I see you for a minute?" Sam called across the yard. Grady, Dash in tow, headed up to him. Cav followed.

"Mae said for you to check your email. Dash, she's not sure you should see this which means you probably should. Let's go gentlemen."

In Dash's office the men gathered around Grady's laptop. The email contained the video Mae shot at Little Biff's, showing all the blood splatter in the motel room.

Sam said, "I'm going to find Robbie. Think I'll sit in on the questioning. Dash, stay here." Turning to Dash's men, he added, "Do not let him out of your sight. He is not to leave this property. Understood. Don't know what this shit means but going off half-cocked is not a good idea."

"What if I'm fully cocked? Can I leave then?" Dash asked.

His brother just snarled. "Stay put, dammit. Do the dishes or something. I'll call as soon as I can."

Cav said, "Don't worry. G-man and I have this. Get going."

As soon as Sam left the room, Cav looked at Dash who had collapsed in a chair. G-man glanced up at Cav, then they both looked at their former leader.

"Captain, you okay? Any idea what that video means? Any thoughts?" Cav asked.

Taking a deep breath, Dash answered. "First, we need to end this backyard party. As quickly and politely as we can. Then we need to talk to the Tydie Sisters." Standing he brought the men up to speed about the Prom Queen and Travis Tycoon.

The former military men did a bit of policing, gathering cups and plates and then they departed after profusely thanking Owen and Dash.

Dash asked his family to remain for a few minutes while he said goodbye to Annie, Tim and Trigger.

"May I ask what's going on? Something to do with Jock's murder?" Annie asked.

"No, nothing to do with Hadley but everything to do with the Prom queen. Wish I knew what was going on but I only have bits and pieces. Right now nothing makes sense. Listen, if and when I learn something I'll call Trigger and he can relate the details to you. It would be best if there was no record of a phone call between us, or Tim for that matter. Have a good night." He leaned over to peck her cheek.

Nodding to Tim and Trigger, he headed back to his family.

"Okay Hammond clan, as always I need your help. Owen, you're with me. Father Tom, you and Ruthie drive over to her house, then walk up to Little Biff's. See what's going on as quietly and inconspicuously as possible. If you can, make your way to Room 214 and talk to the Tydie sisters. I'd like to talk to them myself but can't. So, any conversation has to be on your phone, Tom."

Father Tom held up his hand. "Want to give us a clue what this is all about? Does this have to do with your murder charge?"

"Sorry, I'm way ahead of myself." Taking a deep breath, he began, "One of my classmates, Emmysue Miller, former prom queen, has gone missing. Last seen at Little Biff's motel, either last Saturday or later in the week. Beau and Mae must have stumbled onto something while at the motel..."

That last statement brought a round of 'What?'

Owen shushed everyone. "Son, Beau and Mae were at the motel? Doing what most people do? And where are they now?"

Dash again said, "Sorry, with Rakestraw, downtown. Sam decided to tag along. I'm sure they're not being questioned about a little hanky-panky at the motel. Pretty sure no one has ever been arrested for that. Right Dad?"

"So, Dash, back to what it is you want us to do. Care to give me my assignment?" Dolly asked.

"You, my sweet sister, head downtown. March into the police department looking for your sister-in-law. Full head of Irish outrage at

Robbie's treatment of Mae. Then, back off and nose around. You report to Dad; he'll report to me."

Marie was next. "And I'm to....?"

"Sam, who else. He told me he'd call as soon as he learned what was going on. If/when he gets home, make sure he's done that or sit him down and make him do it."

Owen looked at the troops. "Let's get everything inside. Dash and I will do the final cleanup while we work on whatever it is we're working on. Good night all. Drive safely."

The head of the clan made the rounds, pecking the cheeks of his daughter, his daughter-in-law and Miss Ruthie. Dash winked at her which set her blushing. She lightly punched his arm as she left, trailing behind Father Tom.

Owen sat down in front of Grady's laptop to watch the video sent by Mae. He studied it carefully. Cav and Grady voiced their thoughts.

"Well?" Dash asked. "What's your take?"

"I agree with Cav. Blood spatter, though there is a lot of it for no body to be found on the premises." Swiveling around to where Dash was leaning against the kitchen counter, he asked his son. "Why are you concentrating on this rather than figuring out who killed Hadley? Unless I'm mistaken, the only connection is that both this Emmysue and Hadley stayed at Little Biff's."

Dash shrugged. "You're mostly right. Hadley was on the run; ended up here trying to get money from Annie. Emmysue was running from her husband; she came here hoping Billy Mac could help her but stumbled over me instead. And I was absolutely no help. So she disappeared. Now it's possible both have been murdered."

The men looked around the table, nodding to each other.

"Or were they?" Grady voiced what all were thinking.

Glancing at his watch, Owen said, "Son, I'd like to head home. A good night's rest and I'm sure we can all come up with some answers. Oh, I need a lift home."

Cav jumped up. "I'll do the honors." To Dash, he added, "Call me when you hear something."

As if on cue, Dash's phone rang. Father Tom reporting in. One room at Little Biff's secured by the police. No sign of the Tydie sisters. Over and out.

Dash stopped Cav as he was about to leave. "Give me a second. I want to see if I have a photo of Emmysue."

Chewing on his thumb, he pulled out his phone and scrolled through to see if he had a picture of the prom queen.

"On the Fourth of July we had a bit of a class reunion and Emmysue Miller, now Benedict showed up. Her husband was the old man who visited us earlier with his cadre of tough guys. Long story short, he says she's missing; might have mental health issues or, I'm a fan of *this* theory, in a lot of danger. Sit tight for a minute."

He punched Elena's number into his phone.

"Hey, Elena it's your favorite felon. Yeah, my life is shit. Billy can rejoice. Listen, by any chance did you snap a photo of the prom queen last weekend? I'm not sure what's going on but she might be missing and I need a photo to show some friends who are willing to look for her. Thanks, sweetheart. Tell Billy to watch his back. Having allegedly killed one husband I might just take him out so I can run away with you. Love you, Elena."

A few seconds later his phone pinged. Elena sent a photo of the prom queen in the famous bikini. Dash then sent it to Cav for easy reference.

Cav whistled as he studied the photo. He nodded to Owen and they bid Dash and Grady a good night.

Dash started cleaning the kitchen while Grady began an internet search on Emmysue and her husband. Remembering the prom queen telling him about a friend who kept her informed of the Clover Pointe news, Dash racked his brain to recall her name. Finally remembering it, he got online to see if he could find where she might be.

Sam called. Beau and Mae were on their way back to the old homestead. His summation contained nothing useful. All speculation.

Grady said good night while his friend retired to the front porch, beer in hand. Dash watched as Annie and her son drove toward town while

Trigger headed out to Lulu's. A few minutes later he watched as Mae's car pulled into the drive.

Beau approached his client. "Apologies all around, Dash. I meant to take you aside for a quiet word about Emmysue. Never found that moment. Then Rakestraw showed up. Can you forgive us?"

Mae joined the men. "It's all my fault, Dash. I told Beau not to say anything until we knew what all this meant. I figured you already had enough on your mind." She sat down in the chair next to Dash. She took his hand. "Forgiven?"

Dash nodded and then stood. "How about we all head to bed? Let our minds relax and reconvene in the morning. Rested, I'm sure it will all make sense tomorrow."

After letting Charlie Dog have one last run, Dash made his nightly security rounds. Lost in thought he climbed the stairs to his bedroom. Pushing the door open, he stopped in surprise. There on his bed was Mae, lovely in a silk negligee.

He leaned against the door jam, waiting for her to speak.

She didn't, just tilted her head a bit and patted the bed space beside her.

Dash smiled. "This is unexpected, Dr. Summers. To what do I owe this visit?"

"I just need a hug." She purred, meeting his eyes.

Shutting the door, he said to her, "Well, you've come to the right man. I'm *very* good at giving late night hugs."

Twelve

The next morning a weary Sam knocked on the back door and then let himself in. Beau and Grady sat at the kitchen table drinking coffee and scanning the local paper.

"Good morning, gentlemen." He looked around. "No Dash. It's kinda late for him to be in bed."

"Well, his door was shut as was the door to Mae's room. I can't say for certain but if I were a betting man, I'd say only one bed was slept in last night. If you need to talk to him, feel free to knock on his door. It's not worth my life to do that but you're his brother. Have at it," Beau said.

Sam scratched his head. "Damn. I don't really want to sit here waiting for their passion to die out. Guess I'll have to interrupt no matter how awkward it will be." Sam rose from his chair just as Dash came through the back door."

"What's awkward? Good morning all." He began to peel off his wet tee shirt.

Beau and Grady both tilted their heads, eyes on Sam who mumbled "Well, nothing now. Have a seat."

Dash looked around, then smiled. "Oh, I bet you thought Mae and I were upstairs together and you were trying to decide whether to knock on the door. Shame on you, Sam. On a Sunday morning too. Wait 'til I tell Mae." Shaking his finger at his brother, he bounded up the stairs.

Sam sighed.

A few minutes later Mae came bouncing down the stairs wearing a very mischievous smile. She hummed a song about getting it on as she walked over to her former brother-in-law. Sitting next to him, she trilled, "Good morning, Samuel. Dash told me what you have on your mind this beautiful Sunday morning. Should I ask how Marie is doing?"

"Honestly, Mae. Ninety-nine times out of a hundred I would have been right. Oh, I forgot about Annie and Chandler entering the picture. My apologies, dearest *former* sister-in-law."

Mae stuck her tongue out at him. Standing, she kissed him on the top of his head. "You're forgiven because you are the best brother-in-law

I've ever had. What brings you to our table? I'm sure you weren't just checking on the sleeping arrangements."

Yawning Dash entered the kitchen. He had changed into dry clothes. Getting himself and Mae a cup of coffee he joined the gentlemen seated at the table while Mae leaned against the counter.

Sam studied his brother until Dash asked "What? What changed from last night?"

"Gentlemen, Mae, I'm here in an official capacity. I have some questions to ask all of you. We'll do this informally then I'll ask you to come downtown for a formal statement."

"Spit it out, Sam, who's died this time?" Dash asked.

Instead of answering, Sam asked, "All of you have spent the last two nights here, correct?"

All four nodded in ascent.

"Dash, have you set the security system both nights, like you usually do? And am I right in thinking you, Mae and Grady know the codes?"

"Yes, to both questions. Do you want the security feeds? We can send the tapes to your office, won't take but a minute. Hopefully you'll believe them, not like Robbie the rat."

"Let's start with Friday. Dash, did you leave the house or grounds anytime Friday evening or night?"

Dash shrugged. "Mae and I went down to the beach probably around seven. We got back about eight. Each of us took a shower, separately. I went to bed shortly after eight. Took the pill Mae left for me. Dead to the world all night."

Mae answered next. "I stayed up talking to Beau until a bit after eleven. I let Charlie Dog out and back in, then went upstairs. I checked in on Dash; he was sound asleep. I went to bed, leaving the door to my room and his room open. Wanted to hear if he woke up, if he was having a bad night."

"And?" Sam asked.

"He slept all night. I didn't. Up and down to check on him." She smiled weakly at Dash knowing how he resented her motherly concerns.

Beau went next. "Talked with Mae, stayed with her while Charlie Dog went outside. We went up the stairs together. I watched as Mae did her first check on Dash; we parted to our separate bedrooms. I checked email and did a bit of work on my laptop. Turned off the light about twelve thirty and slept like a baby. Heard nothing, since I'm thinking you are fishing for something to do with anyone leaving the house."

Sam turned to Grady. "And you, sir?"

"Our little party in the kitchen broke up a few minutes after Dash went upstairs. Cav decided to head back to town or to that place called Lulu's. Don't know which way he went. I went into Dash's office to check emails from my guys and gals. Headed to bed around ten; saw Mae and Beau playing cards. Dozed a bit but, since the car wreck, I have trouble sleeping, especially in strange beds. Got up a little after midnight and spent the rest of the night in the recliner, dozing and then conversing with Charlie Dog who makes the rounds several times during the night." Shrugging, Grady said, "Sheriff, I will swear no one left this house during the night. Unless you think I could have done whatever was done. If only Charlie Dog could talk, he'd swear we spent most of the night together."

Sam nodded. "Okay, that's Friday night. Same thing on Saturday? I mean after we returned from Rakestraw's office."

Dash said, "That's easier. Mae and I spent the night in bed together, and before you smirk, we were talking about some personal issues. Then we fell asleep in each other's arms."

Beau finally spoke. "Sheriff, how about you get to the real reason you're here?"

"No easy way to say this." Sam finally said.

Dash's shoulders slumped. "Crap. You found Emmysue's body. Man that sucks."

"Well, maybe this won't be so bad after all. Not hers."

The last word caught their attention. He continued, "Mae, please have a seat." When she was seated, Sam took a photo out of his pocket and slid it face up across the table. He watched his brother pick it up. A look of confusion crossed Dash's face.

"This is Jock Hadley without his bad goatee, but with glasses and a bullet hole in his head. Pretty good disguise if you want someone to think you're dead. More correctly, I guess I should say this is the guy who introduced himself to me as Jock Hadley the other day. Is this the old bus station?"

Sam slid two more pictures over. One of Jock Hadley, still dead, but without the glasses and moustache. The other of the deceased sitting on a bench waiting for the bus to that station in the sky.

"Did you show these to Annie? What did she say?" Dash asked.

"Nothing, just fainted dead away." Holding up his hand as Dash started to rise from his chair, Sam continued. "She's okay. Very shaken, but did say it was her husband. I've asked the son to come downtown to make an identification. I'd like you to come as well. Beau, I suppose you might want to tag along. I'd like a statement saying this is Jock Hadley. Of course we'll check the fingerprints, DNA and dental records just to make sure."

"Of course you will. Don't follow in Robbie's footsteps!" Dash snorted.

Mae's hand covered Dash's. "Does this mean the murder charge will be dropped? Dash is free?"

Beau jumped in, "Yes and no. Out from under the charge of murdering the mistaken Jock Hadley but Dash still might be considered for the murder of the as-yet unidentified man. Sam, do you have a time of death? The case is getting slimmer and slimmer. Rakestraw and Crownover surely will reconsider a new warrant. I'll start drafting our brief requesting the charges be dropped." Looking at Sam, he added, "Yes, I'll come along. Dash get dressed."

"Beau, hold it. The time of death has not yet been established. Could be anywhere from the same time John Doe was killed to Friday night. Now, Dash, I have a question for you. At any time in your relationship with Annie did you take her out to the old bus depot? Wondering how Hadley ended up there, that's all."

"Samuel."

"Yes, Dashiell."

"I may not be the most sophisticated of lovers, nor am I a rich man, but do you honestly think I would take a woman out there among the cigarette butts, used condoms, beer bottles and general run of the mill debris that usually defines abandoned buildings? How low I have sunk? Is the old depot our Disneyland, not to be missed? Clover Pointe's main historical attraction?"

Shaking his head, Dash looked at Sam. "I really should go over to Annie's or at least call her. Do I have time?"

"No. I'd prefer you didn't talk with her until after the identification and statement." Sam put his hand on Mae's shoulder. "You're the doctor. Make sure she's okay."

"Aw crap! I get all the good jobs." Looking at Dash, she added. "Sweetie, I'll be professional. Can't be easy to lose your husband twice in a few days, down right careless if you ask me. I'll tell her of your concern. Honestly, I'll be kind and reassuring." As she walked away, she tossed over her shoulder, "If I happen to call Trigger to hold her hand in your absence, so be it."

Dash started to rise when Sam asked, "Another question. Where is your Beretta?"

His brother stopped in his tracks. "So, Columbo, he was killed by a small caliber gun?" He puffed his cheeks out, slowly letting out the air. "Honestly, the last time I saw the gun was a few months ago when Annie shot me."

Beau put his hand up. "Wait, what did I miss? Annie shot you and still you, um, slept with her. Supposedly killed her husband for her." Slapping his forehead, he said. "Insanity plea. Why didn't I think of that in the first place? Let's go, Colonel. I have a lot of work to do. Move it, Colonel, double time."

Trotting up the stairs behind Mae, Dash mumbled all the way. He returned in less than five minutes wearing his Army tee, camouflage pants, sunglasses and his Army ball cap. Mae followed him down carrying her black bag. They parted with a quick kiss.

Mae tentatively knocked on the back door to Franklin's house, the house where Annie lived while she reworked the garden, the garden where Dash rescued her from the woman-eating rose bush. Like Mae believed all that gibberish.

"Annie! Hey Annie!" Mae called.

No answer so Mae walked on in, thinking Annie might be in distress, reasoning that fainting at the news of your husband's, okay, ex-husband's, demise constitutes reasonable concern for her safety. Glancing around at the shiny stainless steel kitchen, Mae grimaced. The warm wooden kitchen next door may not be modern but it wrapped her in long remembered love from the Hammond family.

She moved into the front room, again a scalpel had been taken to the old Victorian wooden features to scrape it into an overly bright stark room. There danced Annie, head phones on, wine glass in hand. Mae listened, astounded when she realized that Annie was singing about the wicked witch being dead. Nothing about this morning was making sense.

Shouting Annie's name, Mae cautiously approached the woman, not wanting to scare her into another fainting spell. Though Mae suspected the first faint was a fake one.

Annie turned in her dance and dropped the wine glass when she spotted Mae. A blush crept up Annie's neck.

"Oh, I didn't hear you come in. Sorry." She said as she swayed a little. Brushing at the wine running down her chest, she added, "What brings you barging into my house, oh great Dr. Mae?"

Picking up the wine glass Mae answered, "Sam said you fainted at the news of your husband's second death. He asked me to check to see if you were okay." Looking around she shook her head, "Okay doesn't seem to cover it."

"Oh, don't be so self-righteous. I suppose Dash doesn't care if I'm alive or dead. He's a bastard just like the rest of them."

"Them being all men?" Mae asked. "Here let's get you some coffee. I mean, it's only nine in the morning. When did you start drinking or have you been guzzling since Sam left?"

Annie waved her hand about. "No, no coffee! I'm drunk and I want to get drunker. I want to stay drunk the rest of my life. My life *alone*." She toddled over to the low table in front of the couch and grabbed the almost empty bottle of champagne.

"Come on, Annie. Give it up. Your life isn't so bad, probably never was. You want bad? I'll give you bad. My bastard of a first husband only married me because he wanted to use me to get to the right people so he could climb the medical ladder. When I turned out to not be the right ticket, he decided to use me as a punching bag." Mae waved off the offer of a drink from Annie who was not going to deprive herself of another toast to the newly departed Jock.

Annie raised her glass. "To your bastard of a husband, may he rot in hell next to Jock." Downing the last of the champagne, she walked into the kitchen to return with two bottles of wine.

"No more champagne but this wine ain't bad. Still good for toasting our freedom from bastards." Annie declared as she struggled to open a bottle.

Mae reached over to help her, wondering why she was cooperating and not stopping this weird jubilee. As she poured herself a generous helping, she realized that she had never 'celebrated' her escape from a hellish marriage, one where slap and tickle meant bruises and a bloody lip.

Raising her glass, she said, "To ex-husbands living and dead, though dead is definitely better." She downed the liquid in one gulp.

Annie wobbled to Mae's side. "All men are bastards, even the tall good-looking impish ones."

The women unceremoniously flopped onto the couch. Mae poured more wine into the glasses, saying, "I think technically that a tall person can't be impish which implies a certain lack of height. Or is it they can't be leprechaunish? Imp, leprechaun, one of them isn't very tall."

Turning to Annie, she asked, "And why were you singing about the wicked witch being dead? A witch is a woman. Am I missing something?"

"Cuz bastard doesn't fit in the song. Witch, bitch, bastard, warlock. Just went with the lyrics as written." She put her head on Mae's shoulder. "But you're right. Dash isn't a bad one, not most of the time anyway."

Mae nodded in agreement. "Yeah, most of the time he's wonderful but when he's bad, he's very, very bad." Laughing she said, "But when he's good, damn he's good."

Both ladies raised their glasses. "To Dash!" Both down the contents.

Mae reached for the bottles, passing one to Annie. "Let's skip the pouring. Hate to miss the glass and lose the vino."

"To those beautiful blue eyes!" Annie said as she took a swig. Mae joined her.

"To that dimple in his right cheek!" Mae said. Another swig.

"To that little crease at the corner of his eyes when he smiles!" Annie shouted. Another swig.

"To that sweet little tush of his." Mae raised the bottle and downed the remaining wine. Annie followed suit.

Both ladies turned their bottles upside down. Mae said, "Don't get up. I'll get some more."

Annie replied, "Good, cuz I don't think I can get up." She hiccupped.

"Don't go away. We're just getting to his good parts." Mae walked slowly, deliberately to the kitchen's wine rack. "Hey you want some Jameson's to go with the wine? I do better with whiskey. I'm Irish you see. Don't think I ever told you that?"

"Bring it all. I think I want to drink all day. Hey aren't the Irish the ones with the long drinking parties in hope the dead don't wake up?" Annie yelled.

Mae gathered two glasses for the whiskey. She stumbled back into the front room, arms laden with more bottles of wine and whiskey.

"Now we don't have to get up again unless we have to pee. Which I have to, where is the john?"

Annie waved in the direction of staircase, "Little girls' room is next to the steps. And it doubles as a big girls' room as well. Dual purpose. Clever isn't it?"

Mae set the glasses and bottles down. "Don't start without me. I have some catching up to do." She headed unsteadily toward the bathroom.

Annie called out. "You're much bigger than I am so you hold your liquor better than I do. Wonder if we need snacks." She pushed herself off the couch and stumbled into the kitchen. Tearing the cabinet doors open, she rummaged around to find some chips, crackers and pretzels. The refrigerator yielded cheese and dip.

By the time Mae returned, Annie had set the cocktail table with snacks. She artfully lined up on the table, a mound of chips, then crackers, then pretzels, interspersed with the cheese and dip. Proud of herself, she announced to Mae, "See a virtual smorgasbord."

Mae giggled. "I think you mean verichable, not virtual. But you got smorgasbord right! Go you!"

Annie tried to bow but fell on her face into the couch. Mae helped to right her adding, "Hey, don't quit on me now. I'm just getting started."

The two ladies started toasting again, working their way from Dash's head to his other parts. They laughed and hugged.

"Hey, Annie, you're a good 'un, you know. I'm glad I left Dash in your good hands." Mae said.

"To his hands! They deserve another toast. He's very good with his hands." Annie slurred. "And, as for you Doctor Summers, I see now why he loves you like he does."

"Well, he's the father of my baby girl. Poor Gracie. My one chance." Mae said. Looking at Annie, she added, "I can't have babies. Can't carry 'em more than a couple of months."

Annie grasped her and both women began to cry. Wiping away their tears with their blouses, they raised their glasses again to 'poor Dash' and his lousy luck with women, children and friends.

Annie looked blurredly at Mae. "Maevis, as he calls you, we should work together to make his life happier. You still love him, don't you?"

Mae nodded her head. "And you love him too, don't you, Banana Annie as he calls you?"

Annie nodded her head. "We'll do it. We'll live together with him and he'll be soooo happy."

Both women stood to hug again. Annie excused herself but got lost in the living room, bouncing off furniture until she announced she would just sit here for a bit and collapsed on the floor behind the couch.

Mae peered over the couch. "Amateur." She slid slowly down to sit on the floor. She smiled. "Wait 'til Dash sees you. He hates women who can't hold their liquor. Ha. Got the last laugh on you, Banana fana go anna." And she laid her head down amongst the chips and dip.

For the second time in three days Dash found himself in the morgue leaning over a table. This time he felt confident in identifying the body as that of one Jock Hadley. The caveat being he believed the man who gave that as his name, but wanted to be clear he had no substantive knowledge that the man spoke the truth.

A very pale Timothy, on the other hand, was certain this was his father. He asked to see the first body but was dissuaded by the coroner, Dash and Sam.

Walking to a room set aside for use by the coroner's office, they found Ruthie inside with a tray filled with cups of coffee. Dash refused on the grounds of a previous drugging experience. Before anyone could question that statement, Sam asked everyone to sit. "Begin by stating that you have just identified Jock Hadley's body. Then explain your relationship to him or, in Dash's case, when you met him and what was said. Mention Annie in this portion to give context."

After the statements were written and collected, Dash stepped outside to join his brother who was holding up the building. To help, Dash also leaned against it. He fished a cigarette out of one of his cavernous pockets and offered one to Sam.

The usual banter began. "I thought you gave up smoking."

"I did. Thought *you* gave it up."

Sam sighed, "Marie will have a fit when she smells smoke on me, but I'm too damn tired to care. Been up most of the night." Taking a drag, he asked, "Come on, honestly, what's with you and Mae sharing a bed last night? What's going on?"

"Little bit of this and maybe a little more of that. We did talk about all sorts of things. Pretty much all night if you must know. For once no shouting match, but then again we had guests in the house so we did whisper. Think we're maturing?"

"Possibly. If Mae's parents' marriage had been less volatile and her dad less of a brute, *and* her first husband not such a bastard, maybe Mae would be less confrontational. I doubt the shouting was ever all on your side, and to be fair, you guys always argued about most things ever since you were children. But hopefully all that's in the past, little brother. What does the future hold? What about Annie?"

"Uncertain at this moment. Honestly I'd just like Mae and me to get back to being friends who don't constantly argue. When this is over, we'll talk some more. Got plenty to think about in the meantime. Just as a point of information, do you and Marie get into these intense matches when you argue, or is this a Dash and Mae thing?"

Sam started chuckling. "Hell, Dash, Marie is *Italian*! All I get to say is 'yes ma'am' and back slowly out of the room. I'm not going to win any argument so why even start?"

A moment of silence while both brothers considered the state of marriage, whether theirs or those of their friends.

"Hey, little bro, if you *do* decide to tie the knot again, Mae or Annie, don't care. Can I be your best man? I mean this would be number four for you and I have yet to stand by your side."

"Oh, why the hell not? Just don't get that good suit out any time soon. Annie made it clear from the start that marriage wasn't what she wanted and Mae has problems with change. Tough to overcome." The little brother glanced at the older brother.

Sam's eyes opened wide. "Did you just say *Mae* has problems with change? This coming from the man who got upset when the coffee maker was moved from the right side of the stove to the left. And don't try to say it has to do with the head injury; you organized your toys in the crib."

Dash crushed the cigarette out on the sole of his boot and field stripped it, pocketing the filter. When his brother just threw his cigarette butt down, Dash shook his finger at him and picked up the offending butt. "Never leave anything behind, bro, could be deadly."

"So you've never really left the war zone? You *do* realize you're in Clover Pointe. *This* is a safe place," Sam said.

"Tell that to Hadley and John Doe in there. Hell, tell it to Emmysue wherever she is. Chamber of Commerce won't be happy about losing all these visitors."

Beau opened the outside exit to the hospital where the morgue was located. "Oh there you are. Matt is here now and we are heading to his office to start on the briefs/appeals. I'm pretty sure Tim would like to be with his mom. Dash, would you give him a ride? He promises not to take a poke at you."

Sam patted his brother's back, saying "Later."

Dash collected Tim. As they walked to the truck, Dash asked the young man.

"Tim, what say we drop by the apartment before heading back to the house? This way you can take a look and give me some suggestions about the video equipment we might fit into the space. Your idea about games and stuff could work. Might give the guys something else to do rather than just watching T.V."

"I don't know. I'm not so sure any violent games might not trigger the wrong response in the 'guys' as you call them." Tim said.

Dash shook his head back and forth. "Probably volumes will be written, if they haven't already, about that topic. Most of these guys have seen the real thing so they might not be as affected as someone else. But, who knows, I could be wrong. I'm not into gaming myself. I go fishing to unwind."

They parked in the alley behind the bookstore. Dash led Tim to the adjoining building where he took out the keys and unlocked the back door leading to the steps. The upstairs room was a real work in progress. Dash gave Tim a two minute guided tour: two small bedrooms, a bath to be renovated, small kitchenette and a large room for entertainment, meetings and what not.

"Want something to drink? All I might have to offer right now is some pop or water if there is any left in the cooler," Dash said, pointing to the container next to the wall. "I wish I could keep beer but not while we're working. Most are amateurs and have enough problems driving a nail into the wall when sober."

Tim meandered around the room. When he stopped he asked, "You got a budget? One big screen T.V. or several?" Seeing Dash's confusion, he explained, "One big screen, one game played or station to watch. Several T.V.'s; multiple games, shows."

"Hadn't even thought of that. Sounds very noisy if you ask me. Shit, should have thought of that; soundproofing so we don't disturb the bookstore downstairs or any of the neighbors. Well, hopefully not too late. My partner will be thrilled with the changes." Dash said.

The two stood in silence; each visualizing something different for the space in front of them. Finally, with a sigh, Dash asked, "Tim, do you mind a few questions? About all that's been going on. Annie has said that she kept in touch with you. Did you tell your father where she was? Any idea he would come looking for her? I mean, you got here in record time. D.C., wasn't that where you said you were when she called you?"

"What! Am a suspect? Just because I punched you?"

"Don't you know that there aren't any suspects anymore? Person of interest, perhaps to me only. And the punch means nothing as you say." Sighing, Dash added, "Checked you out, as a matter of routine. Found that you weren't in D.C. when you said you were but already in Cleveland when your mom called you. Were you coming to visit?"

"What gives you the right to check up on me? I ought to sue you, invasion of privacy or something." Tim glared, starting for the door.

Holding his hands out, Dash continued, "Just saying, why lie to your mom? Cleveland, D.C., no big deal so why cover it up? You suspected your dad was either here or on his way, right? Natural for a son to be worried about his mom, I totally understand. And your mom's probably thrilled that you care so much. So, Timmy boy, 'fess up. I doubt the truth will kill you."

Gritting his teeth, Timothy starting prowling the room. When he stopped he turned to Dash. "Stupid, stupid, me. Okay, I told Dad where Mom was staying. He just kept pounding me for the information. At first I figured no big deal. He'll call her and scream at her like always and she'll give him what for and hang up. Then I discovered he had left Charleston. So I hightailed it up north. I was outside of Cleveland when she texted that Dad was dead. I didn't want her to know I gave her up to Dad so I pretended I was in D.C. and would catch the next plane, hoping to arrive later that night." He turned to face Dash. "She was really scared. Not sure if she was going to be arrested. When I got here, she told me to stay where she was housesitting. We talked briefly about raising bail if she did get arrested. We had everything arranged to drop into place Friday morning."

"When you opened the safe to get the money, did you happen to notice a small gun in there?"

Timothy looked surprised. "What safe?"

"Don't bullshit me, kid. Crazy cousin Franklin installed two small safes at the same time I had similar work done at my house. He had one for himself and one for the wife. When he decided to travel for a year he cleaned out one to give to Annie for her use." Shaking his head, he continued, "Your mom told me my eccentric cousin paid her in cash, her wages for the whole year. So she always has cash; never has to stop at the bank. Was this the money you were going to use for bail if she was arrested? If yes, just answer me: was there a small gun in the safe with the cash?"

Sighing, he said, "Kid, I'm just trying to find out where the gun I gave her last spring is. The sheriff's department returned it to her thinking it was registered to her but it's really mine. I didn't ask for it back then, thinking she would keep it under a pillow for self-defense. Well, it's not under any pillow or in any drawer in her bedroom. I checked."

"You're a nosy son of bitch you know." Timothy growled. "You're no better than my father. Always spying."

"Now *that* hurts. I wasn't spying, just being cautious. She's not the best shot in the world; thankfully as my arm can attest and not my head or chest. Well, that's settled at least. If it isn't in the safe, only your mom knows what happened to it. Probably threw it out by accident." Crushing his empty can, Dash tossed it into the trash. "Come on kid. Let's go home and see how your mom is doing."

As they went down the stairs, Dash tossed over his shoulder, "I'm still interested in your ideas for upstairs, if you're still interested in the project."

"Yeah, sure, whatever." Tim said.

It was nearly noon when Dash and Tim arrived back at the old homestead. Dash checked in with Grady to learn that Mae had not returned. He hurried over to Annie's house to find Tim standing dazed within a foot of the door.

Looking at Dash, Tim mumbled, "Do you think someone killed my mom while I was gone?"

Taking a sniff in the air, Dash answered, "No, but I think someone might just die while I'm here. You smell all that alcohol? What the hell happened?"

Glancing at all the open cupboard doors and the overturned wine rack, Tim said, "I think someone was looking for something, if I had to guess." He started forward but Dash put out his hand signaling for him to wait here.

Dash cautiously entered the front room. Mae sat on the floor, leaning on the couch. Bits of chips and dip decorated her hair like expensive clips.

"Hey, Sailor, want a drink?" She held up the mostly empty whiskey bottle. "We've had a bit of a party. Celebrating the demise of good, I mean, rotten old Jock. Fare thee well, you bastard."

Squatting down in front of Mae, Dash brushed back the hair/chips/dip from Mae's face. "Sweetie, where is Annie?"

Motioning with her head, Mae indicated back of the couch.

Standing, Dash peered over it to find Annie curled up in a fetal position, drooling onto the floor. He walked around to kneel next to the still female. After taking her pulse to determine she had not drifted over the line to join her deceased ex-husband, he picked her up and started for the stairs, calling out, "Timothy, your mom is okay, out cold though."

Mae offered this statement to Tim as he walked over to Dash. "She's drunk as a skunk who'd rather be a monk." Giggling she reached for a chip slathering it in dip and popping it into her mouth.

Dash handed Annie to Tim. "Put her on the bed, recovery position. Prepare for her to vomit upon re-entry to the land of the living. Make sure she can't choke on it. I'll start the clean up and see if I can get Mae next door and into bed."

Sitting down next to Mae, he took her hand. "Precious, why are you crying?"

"Oh Dash, Annie is such a lovely lady. You know she is truly sorry that our baby died and all those other wives and friends of yours. We both drank many toasts to the wonderful you. But we also cursed our ex-husbands, dead 'n' alive."

Putting her head on his shoulder, she smiled. "You know what, Dash? We think the three of us should live together. I mean we both love you and you love both of us. What do you think?"

Dash closed his eyes, rubbing his temples with his fingers. "I can't even begin to fathom that arrangement."

Mae handed him a piece of the chip bag. On it she had scribbled a bunch of M's and a few H's. "See I worked out the sleeping arrangements. M means you sleep with me and H is her. Based on the calendar month that's how it works."

Laughing, Dash asked, "Why are there many more M's than there are H's? Not exactly fair."

Pulling herself up straight, Mae answered succinctly, "You snooze." She nodded toward the back of the couch, "you lose." She leaned into Dash, pinching his cheek. "I just love you!"

"And I love you too, my crazy Mae-Bea." Pulling her up, he said, "Let's get you home and to bed, alone. Doubt you'll be heading north today. Come on, sweetie. Up and at 'em."

Leaning heavily on Dash, Mae negotiated the walk home.

Grady met them at the door shaking his head and clucking over her condition. "Dare I ask what condition Annie is in?"

Mae leaned into Grady putting a finger to her lips. "She can't hold her booze but don't tell her that. I love you Grady. Why didn't you bring Sharon with you? I love Sharon; she's my best friend in the whole world."

"That's all we would need to complete this fiasco. My wife!" G-man held the door open. "Anything I can do beside not fall over laughing."

Dash sent him a scathing look. "I'm going to put her to bed. Locate all the car keys and lock them up. She's daft enough to try driving north since she obviously can 'hold her booze' or so she thinks."

After he got Mae undressed and settled into the bed, he returned to the kitchen. "G-man, you would not believe what nonsense she uttered. She and Annie are now 'best friends'. They think the three of us should live together. Mae even has a calendar of who gets to sleep with me and when; heavily weighted in favor of the red-headed she devil. Can you imagine what Owen would say to that?"

The back door opened. Owen walked in asking, "What am I to imagine?"

"Owen, Owen. You don't want to know. Mae and Annie got dead drunk this morning. Mae's upstairs sleeping it off. I'm afraid she'll want to drive home this evening. Do you have your handcuffs so I can keep her here?"

His father cast his eyes to heaven muttering, "Dear Lord, give me strength."

"Dash, Dash! Where are you? Where are my clothes? What happened?" Mae shouted from the top of the stairs.

Taking the stairs three at a time, he bounded up to meet her. She stood at the top. One hand and her head rested on the wall; the other hand held onto the sheet wrapped around her.

Mae's eyes were half-closed. "I'm afraid to find out what I've done to make myself feel like this. Hangover right? Last thing I remember is your neighbor sitting on her sofa whining on and on."

Dash shook his head. "How quickly the times have changed. Just a few hours ago you were telling me how lovely Annie is. You even wanted all of us to live together in peace and harmony. I've been downstairs drawing up plans to remodel the upstairs into one large bedroom to accommodate a bigger bed and all sorts of quirky sex toys."

Mae put a hand over her mouth and ran to the bathroom, leaving the sheet behind.

"If that is your response, I'm guessing you're not a fan of my new plan. Oh well, it was fun to dream while it lasted." He picked up the sheet and followed Mae into the bathroom. She sat on the floor holding her head.

"Do you have, how do you say it, your weapon? This is the perfect chance to use it. Put me out of my misery." She held out her hand so he could pull her up. She stumbled back to the bed, flopping backwards.

"Dash, what happened? Did I do this to myself? And I really want to know how Annie is. I didn't kill her, did I? Wouldn't that be something? The room needs to stop spinning, Dash."

She lay there naked on the bed. Opening her eyes, she looked at Dash and asked, "What are you staring at?"

He tilted his head slightly. "I'm trying to decide if Doc Chandler is right, whether you've gained weight or not." He extended his hand toward her but stopped when she growled. "Touch me and I'll kill you." She rolled over, one hand searching for something to cover herself. Dash obligingly placed the sheet over her.

"Not like I haven't heard that a few times in our sorry life."

She buried her head in the pillow. "Dash, make this stop. My head is killing me."

Sitting on the bed, picking soggy chips out of her hair, he began to stroke her hair.

She purred, then announced. "Did I tell you I called Billy? Told him since he was class president it was his responsibility to help us find Emmysue. Said he had to discreetly call or text all the kids and see if anyone knew where she was. Want to know what he said?"

"No, but you're going to tell me anyway."

"Said I was a traitor to be canoodling, or contriving, or con...something or other with you, the dreaded enemy. I told him to do something physically impossible to himself. Fortunately Elena was there and she is going to help us. Remind me why we were we ever friends with him?"

"Well, our mothers kept us in the same playpen together as infants and Billy *is* my cousin. But you're right. We will vow to never ever con-whatever with him. Conspire, connect, consent, console, connive and conquer. But good idea asking him to get in touch with the class. Now my dear heart, you go back to sleep so you will be presentable when the guys show up to report on the day's activities." He kissed her gently as she snuggled into the pillow.

Just as he reached the door, she sat up quickly then grabbed her head. "I'm supposed to leave today. I have classes to teach tomorrow. Oh crap."

"Sorry. Forgot to tell you. I called in to report a sudden bout of food poisoning. Didn't tell them it was the liquid kind. You're off the hook for tomorrow's classes. Now to sleep."

Hearing Annie's voice coming from the kitchen, Mae sat up, looking at the clock. Her nap lasted only a few hours. She dragged herself out of bed and slipped into one of Dash's oversized tee shirts. She dared not look in the mirror but hoped splashing some water on her face would make her presentable *and* wake her up. She made her way cautiously down the stairs, leaning on the wall for support. Not only was Annie present but also Sam, Owen and Beau and the young lawyer, Matt. Dash and Grady stood over the sink wolfing down watermelon. The juice ran down their chins.

She stepped cautiously into the room realizing everyone was staring at her, male eyes open wide.

"I do have clothes on, don't I? I couldn't find mine but this is fine, right?"

"Let's just say you have your important bit barely covered. I'm afraid the tee shirt shrank, sweetie. Don't move and whatever you do, don't raise your arms." Dash rinsed his hands and walked to the laundry nook. He opened the door to the dryer and took out a pair of her shorts. He guided her into the powder room adjacent to the kitchen.

"Put these on and let's rinse the chips and dip out of your hair." He turned on the faucet and pushed her head under the cold water. He rubbed her hair while she squirmed around, swatting at his hands.

Mae pulled back, shaking her head. "How dare you?"

"Me? How dare you come down here all 'I'm here to help'? Is that what you call playing strip poker with Beau, riding around town with Beau, getting dragged off to the police station, again with Beau? And let's top this performance off by getting stupid drunk. Sober up, baby doll, or that ass you wanted to flash around will be on the receiving end of my combat boot."

There was a pounding on the door. Sam yelled, "Come out or take it upstairs. We have work to do here."

Mae pushed the door open so fast Sam didn't have time to draw his head back. As he rubbed his nose, ready to curse her, Mae fired the first volley. "Samuel Owen Hammond, you're a prick and a prude. Now sit down and shut up."

She slammed the door. Looking at Dash, daggers shooting from her eyes, she said, "Don't you ever talk to me like that again! Help? You *always* need help and I've *always* been there. Now kiss me and let's get to work."

He did as ordered and they exited the powder room, wearing sober, in all senses of the word, faces to the table.

"Owen, everyone. I'm so sorry for the distraction. I either need to stop drinking or get more practice. What were you talking about before I interrupted?" Mae asked sweetly.

Beau started, "Annie was explaining why she identified John Doe as her husband. The wedding ring and the clothes. She never saw his face; was told it was a wreck."

Mae worked her way to the coffee machine and poured a cup. After a sip she jumped right in asking Annie. "Did you look at his body? Surely you could have told from that. Scars, tattoos, birthmarks. Right?"

Annoyed, Annie pointed at Dash and countered. "If his face was gone, would you be able to say for certain the body was his?"

"You mean other than the corpse would be taller than average, even with no head. Seriously, no problem. First, I'm a doctor and we are trained to look closely at our patients. In Dash's case it would be easy. He has burn scars, faded, from the ambush; at least two scars from his good old football days. His left pinkie finger is crooked; broke it as a child and never told his parents so it healed with a bit of a hitch. Let's see." She closed her eyes, started with his head and went to his feet listing twenty or so identifying marks.

Beau started laughing. "So that's how you cheat at poker. You have an eidetic memory. You just read his medical chart to us."

Mae shrugged as Owen and Sam said in unison, "You cheat! You'd better pay us back all that money you've won over the years."

Ignoring the Hammond men, Annie turned to Dash. "How would you identify Mae?"

"You mean if her head was missing, silencing that mouth? Well, probably the tattoo."

"Wait a minute. She doesn't have any tattoos. I've seen her in a bikini," Sam spouted.

Dash leaned against the sink. "Brother, I'm not sure I would have said that out loud. What the hell are you doing scrutinizing my wife's body? And don't give me any of that bullshit about recognizing your constituency."

Annie chimed in. "You mean your ex-wife, don't you?"

Mae scratched her head. Looking coyly at Dash she said, "Dashiell, did *you* read the papers? Maybe we're not really divorced."

"Maevis, low blow. Either play nicely or you'll get sent to your room."

"Dash, sorry to tell you, but Sam is right. I don't have any tattoos. Want to try again?" Mae sighed.

He looked over to Annie asking, "Is it you? Do you have a tat?"

Annie shook her head no.

"Damn, wonder who it is, with the tat, I mean? Nice looking, excellent placement." Dash sat down, eyes on the table. He pulled out his notebook jotting down that he needed to remember who had the tat.

Mae sat down next to him, looking over his shoulder. She finally said, "Don't bust your brain. It's really not that important." Turning back to Annie, she asked, "Did you look closely at the body? I mean even for old times' sake. Okay, if" gesturing toward Dash with her head, "his head was missing, could you have identified his body?"

Frowning, Dash said, "I'm beginning to resent all this 'if his head was missing' crap."

"Well, I don't have access to his medical chart. I'd have to go from my very recent memory, something you may not have had..." Annie smirked.

Mae asked, "What about memories of the dearly departed Jock?"

"Jock and I shared the house but hadn't lived 'together' in twenty years. The last time I saw him buck naked was when he ran from the house trailed by his likewise naked secretary as I stood at the top of the stairs waving a gun." Her voice rose. "One rule! I had only one rule: Don't bring your sluts into my house. He thought I was out of town but I came home early, feeling unwell. As soon as he skedaddled, I filed for divorce. Got everything I wanted. He was feeling grateful that I didn't shoot him and the secretary."

Owen turned to Dash who sat with his mouth open, a dazed look on his face. "Son, did you know this woman almost killed her husband?"

Annie slapped at Owen's hand. "Nonsense. The gun wasn't loaded. I never bought bullets for fear I *would* kill the son of a bitch." Laughing, she said, "I never asked where they went or how they got out of the car. Both being naked as the day they were born and all."

Silence reigned as everyone imagined the scenario presented by Annie. Beau finally turned to Owen and asked, "What do you have for us, sir? Please say you have something, anything."

Dash moved to stand by the counter, arms crossed, staring at the back of Annie's head.

Owen flipped over several pieces of paper. He passed them around, sliding one into the middle of the table.

Mae pulled the sketch toward her. "Who is he when he's at home?"

"That's the man the Tydie sisters saw coming down the stairs at the motel. The guy who had the argument with Hadley. I've stared at it all morning hoping he will start talking and divulge his name." Owen said.

"Any chance of getting a refill?" Mae asked as she handed her cup to Dash. She continued to stare at the sketch. Wrinkling her brow, she looked at Sam, then motioned to him to retrieve her phone from the charging station on the counter. She scrolled down to find the photo of the man who accosted her at the picnic. She passed the phone to Sam saying, "This man was at the picnic on the Fourth. We had a close encounter of the groping kind. He tried to cop a feel as I passed him so I elbowed him. Told him to keep his hands to himself if he wanted to keep them. Then I went on my way; I looked back and he was watching me so I snapped the photo."

Beau shook his head. "Expand. Height, weight, color of his eyes. Come on Doc, strut your stuff."

She closed her eyes. "My height, maybe an inch taller. Probably 190, stocky build. Eyes, medium brown, as was his hair. Clean-shaven, but could grow a heavy beard. His complexion was mottled, like too much sun or drink. Plaid short-sleeved shirt, unbuttoned, over a wife-beater undershirt. Green shorts, brown sandals."

"Boxers or briefs?" Her ex-husband asked.

Mae shot back, "Didn't stick around to check."

Annie shivered. "You just described my ex-husband, mottled skin and all, except his clothes. Right, Dash?" She reached for the sketch, studying it then reached for Mae's photo.

Looking over her shoulder, Dash shrugged. "Your ex-husband and the faceless man in the morgue. Two ugly peas in a pod. "

Turning to Mae, he asked, "Why the hell didn't you say anything at the picnic? Dammit, you were practically assaulted."

Sam and Owen both voiced the same opinion.

This time it was Mae who shrugged. "Not saying this like I'm proud or anything, but this happens to me a lot. I told Chandler and he went looking for him but came back empty-handed." To Dash she added, "I didn't say anything to you because I didn't want to interrupt your playtime with Emmysue."

Hoping to steer the discussion back to the photo, Matt pulled it toward him. "Well, that puts him in town before Jock turns up. Or does it? Do we know when Jock arrived? Maybe the two men arrived together, then split up to look for Annie. Did you see him?" He asked Annie.

"No. If I had, I probably would have thought he was Jock unless he stood right in front of me. Sorry, I was distracted." She answered by looking at Dash.

"Are we sure this guy was looking for Annie?" Matt asked.

Dash sat down, chewing on his lip. "Well, hell. Why else would Jock and his buddy come here? If you're on the run, you don't necessarily head for Clover Pointe, Ohio? Not exactly the Hole-in-the-Wall of northwestern Ohio. We know for certain Jock was looking for Annie; we know Jock and John Doe had an argument. And we know they both ended up dead here, our small town. Pretty soon the Chamber of Commerce sign will read, 'Be careful when visiting Clover Pointe'."

Annie put a hand to her mouth. "So you're saying that this could be the man without a face? The man who died in Jock's place. Does this have anything to do with Emmysue?"

"Only connection to Emmysue is she was at Little Biff's over the Fourth. Days after she split, Jock ends up there. No big surprise since there are only a few places in town to stay." Sam reached for the sketch, turning to Mae. "Would you send that photo to our office so we can print and distribute? That photo and the sketch should ring a bell or two with someone. We'll start the search of motels and B&B's around. Work our way out. Still doesn't explain how John Doe ended up in Hadley's clothes and wearing his wedding ring. But one thing at a time."

He stood and turned to Dash. "Since you think I'm Columbo, I do have one more question for you. Join me on the porch."

Beau spoke up. "Sorry, Sheriff, but my client answers no questions without me present." He stood to follow the brothers out. Sam pulled two small evidence bags out of his shirt pocket. They contained a wallet-sized photo and a business card. Handing them to Dash, he asked, "Anything?"

Glancing at Beau, Dash answered, "Yes. This is Emmysue, though from several years back. And the card is one of her husband's." Flipping the card over, he saw the phone number written on the back. He stepped back to the screen door. "G-man, run this phone number."

Sam grabbed the bag. "You think I haven't tried calling it or tracing it? Anything else you want to add to this very unofficial statement."

"Yes. Mr. Travis Benedict is or was offering a twenty-five grand reward for information on the whereabouts of Mrs. Benedict, aka Emmysue. Mr. Benedict's secretary offered a similar card to us last night; no number on the back, though." Beau volunteered.

Trigger started up the porch stairs as Sam started down them. "Sam, Dash, you were looking for me? Sorry I'm late but some idiot left his car in the parking lot near the woods. No one noticed it until the bright light of morning. Been searching the area in case the owner is passed out somewhere. What can I do for you?"

Sam motioned toward the back door. "Come inside. Got a sketch I want you to see." Handing a copy to Trigger, he asked, "Seen this guy around town. Maybe at the Lounge?"

"Nah. But I haven't been out to there much this week. Get me a copy and I'll ask the dancers and crew. This the John Doe?"

Taking back the sketch, Sam asked, "Where did you hear that? Didn't think it was announced yet. The mix-up I mean. Guess I better get back to the station. Robbie's probably having a fit as we speak. Later, guys and gals."

He opened the door, stopped and turned around. "Trigger, what did you say about a car being left at Lulu's? Don't touch it. I'll send a deputy out there. Wonder if it belongs to Jock." Again, Sam headed for the door. "Nice *seeing* you, Mae." He winked.

Annie rose, announcing she planned to take a nap hoping to rid herself of the headache. She glanced at Dash who nodded. "Get some rest. I'll call you later," he said.

Dash wandered the kitchen, straightening things that were already straight.

Mae raised her head from the table. "Spit it out, Soldier Boy. What has the hamster running at double time?"

"I can't figure this whole thing out or any of its parts. *Why* the body double? And how the hell do you pull something like this off?"

Beau interjected, "I know what you mean. With today's forensics, you have to know that this would be disproved in short notice. So what does this maneuver gain?"

Matt joined in. "Time, not a lot but enough for whatever needs doing. It's a stall tactic, pure and simple. He, the perpetrator, knows he gets *maybe* 48 hours. So the question becomes what do you do in those hours?"

Dash said to Mae, "Well, sweetheart, you said you came to help. So start helping."

Mae got up to pour another cup of coffee. "Okay, the thing that really bothers me is how the hell one finds someone who resembles you enough to pass off as you. This has to have been premeditated. You don't just show up in a small town and hope you can find a doppelganger."

"And how do you rope someone into standing still so you can clobber him with a crowbar? What's the con?" Matt asked.

With that last question, everyone except Beau and Grady turned to look at Trigger.

"What? Why are you assuming I'm familiar with all the criminal elements and activities? If I didn't know you really valued my friendship, I'd be hurt." Trigger lowered his eyes trying hard to look dejected.

Beau asked, "What am I missing? Trigger, are you the local miscreant? Or a mythological creature of the night?"

Dash laughed. "A bit of both. When your mama runs the strip joint, occasional brothel, you become a person of envy, at least for all your male peers. Then you disappear into the military to supposedly become a lethal weapon and hero. When you reappear you have the trappings of ill-gotten-gains, plenty of them. Being tight-lipped, you let everyone assume the best and the worst. That's our Trigger."

Taking a sip of her coffee, Mae returned to the topic at hand. "Focus gentlemen!"

Matt said, "Excuse me, Doctor Summers, but that is rich coming from you."

She gave him her 'watch it little man' stare and continued, "Okay, Hadley and John Doe were, as you said Dash, two peas in a pod. What we don't know is why both were here. Hadley obviously was after money from his ex-wife. I wonder if Hadley recruited John Doe in South Carolina and brought him north for the express purpose of killing him to establish his own death. Opens more questions than answers any."

"Bottom line is they were here to extort money from Ms. Dewitt. Why did they need it? Any number of reasons. If they were searching for Annie, why didn't they approach her at the picnic? Too many people around; they wanted her alone. I mean we now know at least John Doe was there from his close encounter with Doctor Summers. Besides money, did they need Ms. Dewitt for anything else?" Matt asked and answered his own questions.

Looking in Trigger's direction, Dash said. "What has Annie said to you about all this? I hate to put it this bluntly, but I'm sure she is fucking lying to *me*. Exactly about what I don't know but she didn't need me to save her little ass. Sam visited earlier that day and everything was fine, a veritable tea party. Trigger?"

He pursed his lips. "Dash, you'll need to ask her why she wanted you to come running." He glanced at Mae. "The answer might not be as complex as you think."

Mae made the time-out gesture. "Gentlemen, let's table, so to speak, that piece of the discussion. As Dash would point out, not relevant to the murders. Or is it? Any proof your little neighbor called Jock, begging him to come north so she could call you to 'save' her. Just a bit of feminine insight, but my vote is no. She, like all women, has other skills to entice a man to do her bidding. I can't see her bringing a piece of shit back into her life just to upset you. And," turning to Dash, "just why are you the center of attention AGAIN?"

Beau nodded. "She's right. Forget about that aspect. Here goes. Annie is surprised by Jock. Whether he tells her the real reason, if it's other than money, is still open. She doesn't strike me as the type to be cowed by him; apprehensive, yes. But not in mortal fear. She would have gone to Sam or Trigger rather than wait for you to arrive. A lot can happen in the two-three-four hours it took you to get back home."

"Let's agree that Jock comes north to find Annie, either to get money from her or for a place to hide, or both. I remember her saying none of the family knew where to find her, so how did Jock? Is her son, Timothy, the weak link? He breaks down and tells the father, then discovers his dad acted on the information. Fearing for her safety or sanity, Timothy flies up here, in time to help his mom out," Trigger speculated.

Dash held up his hands, calling for a time-out. "Let me end one speculation. Jock was here solely for money, or at least that's what Annie told me. A goodly sum. And Tim admitted to me he gave his mother's location to Jock."

Matt jumped in again. "So Jock knew Annie's hidey hole, and we know his agenda. Now the question is: did he bring John Doe with him or find him here? Until we know where he was staying, if he indeed stayed here in town, and why was he here, we could speculate 'til the cows come home."

Dash said, "We've got to run with some assumptions or we'll go crazy. Get Cav on the phone and let's see what he has found out, if anything useful. We need to focus on finding out who is this John Doe and where he was staying. And was Hadley staying with him until he moved into Little Biff's?"

Grady dialed up Cav and then put him on speaker phone. "Hey, whatcha got for us? Dash, Beau, Matt, a miscreant named Trigger and the always delightful Doctor Summers are awaiting whatever shred you can offer up."

"I got nothing. Nada. Sorry to report but I'm out at the Blue Belle B&B. No bikini queen now or ever. About the other matter at hand, there's a car in the parking lot. South Carolina plates. I did the old 'sorry but I tapped the car, do you know the name of the owner' routine. I even batted my eye lashes and everything at the sweet young thing behind the desk but all she would say is she hasn't seen the owner for several days. Is the sheriff there?"

"No, he isn't but I'll call him and tell him to get over there." Dash said, pulling out his phone and punching the button for Sam. Beau looked around the table and then asked for the license plate of the car in question. Grady copied it down and headed for the office. Dash turned to Beau asking, "G-man on it?"

"Yeah, his little 'I Spy with my Little Eye' agency; he has a branch down south so they're helping with the Charleston connection. Pretty sure we'll get the information about the same time as your brother."

Dash groaned, "How much is this costing me? Damn, if I don't go to jail for murder, I'll end up in debtor's prison."

"Dash, what has happened to you? Whining like a little girl. Trust me, you will not be out one red cent. *Now* your little town might be bankrupt but you'll be able to lend them money to stay open." Beau winked at his old buddy.

Thirteen

The folks at the table waited for instructions. "Anyone?" asked Matt. "If not, I'm going to the office to get all this into the file. Call me if there is something I should be doing."

Mae announced she was going back to bed to finish her nap.

Trigger looked at Dash, nodding in the direction of Annie's house. Dash shook his head, "No, go if you want. I think I'll go for a run, clear my head." Swiveling his head toward Beau, he asked, "Should I be doing something else? I mean besides pray."

Chuckling Beau said class was dismissed. "Get some rest. Some exercise. Eat, don't drink too much but be merry. We just might be rounding that corner of 'case dismissed'."

As Dash stood to leave, Beau reached for his arm. "Hey, you okay? Seem to be on a roller coaster of emotion. Calm then crazy. I'm afraid your PTSD is showing. Should we talk?"

Dash sat back down. "You mean my PTTTTSD. Sat down one day and listed all the traumas I've endured. Hey, not trying for sympathy because I've had a lot of help to work through most of it; not recovered, but able to cope." Standing, he turned away. "I know this will sound ungrateful but I didn't realize how having the guys here would take me to places I never wanted to revisit. Cav calling me Captain just reminded me of our last mission, the one that didn't go well, which is putting it mildly." He shuffled his feet and continued. "Mae, Annie. Feel like a ping pong ball. Not a good summer."

Leaning back in his chair, Beau said, "I know this is none of my business but I'm going to ask; you don't have to answer. But what the hell happened between you and Mae? I mean, when you're together, you really seem like you *belong* together. And the divorce was a long time ago if I remember correctly."

Dash had the good grace to blush. Shaking his head he said, "Man, when I mess things up, I do a good job." He stood. "The divorce was years ago and we ended up friends. Right before the accident, if my journals are correct, I had purchased a ring and was going to propose that Christmas.

"Then wham bang, some drunk plowed into our car and life as I knew it, as Grady knew it, changed forever. Not to mention the two officers whose lives were snuffed out immediately! Fast forward a year and I was drummed out of the service...."

Beau held up his hand. "No, you weren't. You were given the option of extending your medical leave. Just because you tried to return once and failed didn't mean the Army wasn't going to wait for you."

Smirking, Dash said, "Yeah, like forever! Anyway, the pension and crap was a long time coming and I panicked, as was my wont at that time. Not thinking straight, I decided to attend that conference you mentioned earlier. A shitload of money coming my way, didn't think I could *not* go. Mae and I had a doozy of a fight over it. I wanted her to come; she couldn't, some damn medical thing. So I stomped off like the petulant child I was at the time. As you know I got reacquainted with Jamillah aka Millie. To say this choir boy dipped his wick where he shouldn't have is putting it crassly but accurately."

Rolling his eyes, Beau began to laugh. "And I bet the choir boy confessed his sins upon returning home. And the Lady Mae was none too happy about that. Give you the boot, did she?"

"Did she ever! So I moved out here and have spent a good deal of time doing penance. Confession might be good for the soul, but not so good for relationships. Luckily Millie didn't get pregnant nor did I get some horrible disease, so Mae relented. I suspect she had a few encounters of her own on the side and she is nothing if not fair so we became friends again. Then she decided to accept this teaching position and *told* me I was to move with her. Sorry, I had just started building my business. So I said no; still friendly. And then along came Annie. We had a bit of an escapade last spring and I was intrigued by her. Mae acted like it was no big deal until apparently it became a big deal. Murder and all. My life in several paragraphs."

"When this is over, my man, a trip to New Orleans is mandatory. Relax. I've got all this in hand, except the Mae and Annie thing, but that will work itself out. I'm almost positive. Now go for a run, a walk, a swim."

"The beach it is. Brain works better when I'm there. I'm sure there are things we are missing, but what are they? Back in a bit, full of new ideas and leads." Dash smiled and headed out the back door, Charlie Dog wagging his tail as he followed.

Sitting on the beach, Dash put on his glasses, pulled out his ever-present notebook and started recording questions unanswered in his mind. Phone in hand he called Sam. "Hey big brother, just wondering about a few things. Okay, John Doe has a car but how does Jock get around? Bicycle? No car that I know about. How did he get out to Annie's? Or did I just miss his car? Did he walk out to the bus depot? And don't you have the shells from the Beretta from last spring? Can't you compare those with the one in Hadley's skull? If you have a match, Miss Annie will have to rack her little brain until she remembers what she did with the gun. Finally, for now, certain Annie said Jock wanted money from her. Begs the question, did she give him any but is afraid to admit to it now? And, if she did, where is it?"

Sam laughed. "What brought on this burst of energy resulting in a ton of questions? You guys must had one helluva skull session after I left. Oh, the car is registered to one Roger Scott, formerly of Charleston. The P.D. down there is faxing a copy of his driver's license. Maybe that photo will match the sketch and Mae's photo. One question answered." He sighed. "And I wasn't going to tell you this but, those questions you posed, I've been receiving texts from a cousin who shall remain nameless but who is following all this with a great deal of interest. You two are on the same page, though he is one page ahead of you."

"That rat bastard! If I wasn't so busy I'd drive to Columbus and kick some ass." Dash could almost see his brother rolling his eyes when Sam said, "Still working on that maturity thing, are you?"

"Back to business, leaves us about ten thousand questions to answer. Grady is leaving soon so I guess I should head back to the house, though the quiet out here is very nice. Talk to you later. Signing off." Dash said.

"Roger that little brother." Sam replied.

Fourteen

As the sun nestled down on the horizon, Dash sat on his back porch with his long legs extended, resting them on the porch rail. Charlie Dog sat next to him and all was right with the world. He breathed in the humid lake air remembering his conversation with Mae last evening. She had asked if he ever got homesick while on deployment. It didn't take him a moment to answer: Yes, I missed the smell of the lake, the aroma of Helene-Marie's Irish stew and Grandma Hammond's Christmas turkey in the oven. Tonight, one out of three was just fine.

The back door opened and Mae walked into his view. He glanced up at her.

"Why so glum? Not feelin' better? Did the nap make you groggier than before?"

He pulled his legs down and patted his lap. "Come here my Mae-Bea and tell your Uncle Dash all about it, little girl."

Mae accepted the invitation and nestled into his arms.

"I have to go back tomorrow. And, truth be told, I don't want to. You never thought to ask me if *I* ever got homesick."

Pulling back a bit, Dash peered into her face. "Pardon me, but you only live two or three hours away. And I'm pretty sure you talk to someone here every day, plus the texting and, before Doc Chandler, we even skyped once or twice. Not seeing the relationship between your job in Ann Arbor and my months/years in Afghanistan. I am sooo sorry I didn't pick up on it."

She gave him one of her big sighs and her bottom lip began its journey out. He kissed her on the cheek.

"A sigh and the pout. Poor Maevis, life is so hard. Come on, snuggle up. Now this reminds me of the other thing I missed: you in my arms."

She started to nibble on his ear and he kissed her neck. Eyes closed, hands roaming. Buttons were undone; hands slipped in to touch skin. She reached down to undo his belt, saying, "Feeling a little tight down there, Soldier Boy."

"In about two minutes we are either going to embarrass ourselves here on the porch or I'll carry you inside and tell Beau to close his eyes and ears."

They clasped each other, their breathing heavy.

The back door banged open as Beau came out onto the porch. He put his hands over his eyes. "Dash, Mae. Oh God, I'm so sorry."

Dash and Mae jumped, immediately pulling back from each other. "Jesus Christ, Beau. Damn! I had a flashback to when I was fifteen and my Dad came through that door hellfire and brimstone. What the fuck do you want?"

Beau held his hands up. "So sorry but that Trigger guy keeps calling you. Figure it might be important." He was about to hand Dash his phone when Trigger walked into the line of vision.

Mae rubbed her head. "I know why our relationship never works. We never get a feckin' minute to ourselves. Also never get a minute to, well you know. Trigger, this better be damn good!"

"Dash, I'm sorry but Annie has gone missing. We need your help to find her."

Mumbling a bunch of expletives under his breath, Dash finally said. "Well, Trigger, I'll tell you where she's not and that is on my lap. Go, take Beau with you. Dammit, did she leave the house?"

"Don't know. Don't think so. I just went upstairs to check on her and the bed is empty."

Mae swiveled around, "Gentlemen, if you would be so kind as to give us a minute to get ourselves presentable, Dash and his bloodhound Charlie Dog will join you in the search for the elusive neighbor. Me, I'm going to take a bubble bath."

Dash finally found the cleverly disguised door to the dormer. He quietly climbed the steps, stopping when he could peer into the room without revealing his presence. Annie sat Buddha-style in front of the back window. There were candles lit through the room, throwing shadows on the wall.

"Come on in." Annie said when she spotted him. "Quite the retreat isn't it?"

He looked around. The room was serene, a place of meditation. Japanese simplicity. Admiringly, he said, "Franklin's wife Keiko put this together. I wonder if she did it for him so he could relax. Got the feeling his job is stressful. How did you find this?"

"Same way you did just now. I looked for it. I remembered you saying the houses were identical and you talked about the dormer at your place where all you kids slept during those summer vacations. Took me a while but I managed. Haven't come up here enough but felt the need for it tonight. Join me. I'll be quiet so you get the full effect."

Dash walked over to her and sat down, crossing his legs as she had. They sat in silence for minutes.

"Annie, Trigger and Tim are looking for you. They're worried. Should I tell them you're safe or do you want to come down?"

"They're worried, but not you?"

"Didn't know you were missing until minutes ago. I came, as usual, as always." He shifted positions.

"Mind if I ask you something and I'd appreciate an honest answer," he said.

Annie looked in his direction. "You're not going to add 'for once' because that's what I'm hearing."

"Add it. Why *did* you want *me* to come when Jock showed up?"

She stood up, walking away from him. He rose as well.

"At the picnic Mae mentioned you have this thing about damsels in distress. Thought I would test it and bang you came running. I felt the 'power of Mae'. She snaps her fingers and you're there." Letting out a deep breath, Annie continued. "But trust me, had I known what happened would happen, never in a million years would I have asked you to come. Please believe me when I say I never intended any harm. The flowers were a nice apology; just wanted more."

Dash walked away. "Fair enough. Shall I tell them you'll be down shortly or not at all?"

"Where are you going, if I may ask?"

"To find my white steed, ride off into the sunset or more accurately into the sunrise. I'll tell them you'll be down. Don't forget to blow out the candles. Burning down the house would be the capstone for the week, and not in a good way."

Dash passed Trigger and Timothy, telling them she'd be there in a minute.

Beau sat on the porch as he cut through his backyard, Charlie Dog in tow. Pointing to the lake, he walked on.

Fifteen

At 9:30 Monday morning the prosecutors and Dash's defense team assembled in Judge Pope's chambers to hear his pronouncement regarding the dismissal of charges against Dash for the murder of Jock Hadley, since it wasn't his body lying on the slab.

Before anyone could speak, Judge Pope said, "I've reviewed your motion and have decided to dismiss the charges against Colonel Hammond without prejudice. Now, if it is proven that he had a hand in the death of John Doe and/or subsequently Jock Hadley, he will be arrested. Whole new ballgame. Any questions."

Then he added, "Chief, Sheriff, anything you bring to me regarding these murders had better be rock solid. Enough wasting my time and the taxpayers' money. Thank you."

As everyone rose to leave, the judge asked Colonel Hammond's team to remain behind for a word. He included Mae, Owen and Sam in that request.

Beau began, "Your Honor, I want to apologize on behalf of my client for his absence. I..."

Pope held up his hand. "No need for an apology. He gave me one by himself not forty-five minutes ago, standing just about where you are. Gentlemen, Dr. Summers, he is the subject I want to address. Have a seat please."

"I'm sorry, Your Honor, but Dash was here? Where is he now? Do you know?" Mae asked.

Settling back into his chair, he answered, "I came into my chambers this morning to review the briefs and, as usual, have some breakfast. I nearly shit my robe. Dozing in that chair was what I assumed to be a homeless man. He woke up and, lo and behold, it was Colonel Hammond, apologizing for his appearance both sartorially and in my chambers uninvited. For reasons he did not explain he spent the night on the beach and, also unexplained, decided the best course of action would be to present himself to me in this state. It was very odd. His speech was very lucid but coming out of a man who looked deranged."

He threw his hands open. "I'm not a psychologist but thought maybe he was having some PTSD episode so I listened; we talked a bit and then he excused himself because of some unfinished business. Anything from his nearest and dearest?"

Owen answered through clenched teeth, "Sorry, Martin, but this is the first I'm hearing that my son didn't sleep in his own bed, or anyone else's. Mae, Beau?"

Beau jumped in. "Without a lot of detail, last evening Trigger came over to the homestead to say Annie was missing and would Dash please help look for her. Not sure what specific powers of detection Dash possesses but he wouldn't take no for an answer. Mae graciously allowed the interruption and off Dash went. Last I saw him he was walking toward the lake. I figured he'd come home. Mae and I went to our respective beds. This morning I, we, just assumed that he went back to Annie's or came here. It's hard to tell if he was home or not. Neat freak."

Mae added, "I took a sleeping pill. Upset about all of this. Didn't realize he hadn't come home; I figured he was with Annie. Another reason for my current headache. He's a big boy, or so he thinks."

"Speaking of big boy, Sheriff, I'd like to address security in this building. When I asked Dash how he got in he said through a door, not caring to elaborate. I'm beginning to understand Rakestraw's concern for Dash's skill sets. When, if, you see your brother, bring this up and then correct it."

"Excuse me again, Your Honor, but did Dash give any indication as to where he might be heading when he left here?" Mae implored.

"Said he was going to get cleaned up and go to work. Something about someone effing up something and he was a bit pissed about having to fix it. That's all I have for you, Dr. Summers. Sorry it is so little. And now I think I'm going to go to JoJo's for another attempt at breakfast. Dash ate all of mine and drank most of my coffee. I was waiting for him to leave me a tip, but sadly he did not. Now go. Find him, make sure he is alright and, if not, get him some help. Dismissed."

The team split up. Beau and Matt headed to the bookstore work site. Mae, Owen and Sam drove to the condo, closest point for Dash to clean up and get some fresh clothes.

When they entered the condo, Charlie Dog greeted them with wagging tail. They could hear Dash moving about in one of the bedrooms. Owen called out, "Dashiell!"

He walked out of the bedroom, towel drying his hair. He had on jeans, an OSU tee shirt and work boots. Everyone just stood there, glancing back and forth. Finally, Mae stepped forward to confront him.

But Dash spoke first, looking at Mae. "You still here. I thought you were going back early this morning." His tone less than friendly.

"Oh, so you weren't going to say goodbye. Is that why you decided to sleep on the beach last night? Missed the sand so much?"

He wrapped the towel around his neck, shrugging. "Figured if you wanted me you'd wave your little wand, or maybe I should say wiggle your little ass, and I'd come running. You know 'the power of Mae' and all that. Maybe you should have fainted so you'd once again be the damsel in distress I've come to know and love."

Owen looked at Sam who looked at Mae and asked, "Do you know what he is talking about?"

"Damned if I know." She answered. "Hey, Beau is a little upset with you. Skipping the meeting with the judge only to learn you decided to do a solo act. Speaking of someone whining about needing help, you win that prize. Next time you're on your own."

"Judge Pope and I had a nice conversation. I got the impression, since he didn't call for anyone to lock me up, that I was free to go."

Owen shook his head. "No, son. He was afraid you were having a PTSD moment and didn't want to upset you. Pretty sure the only thing he got from your little talk was that an insanity plea would be entertained."

He stepped forward to take his son's arm but Dash pulled away.

"Back away old man." Then looking in his brother's direction, he added, "That goes for you too big brother. I'm fine; more than a little pissed with Mae but what's new? She's spent a lifetime using me so why not share her secrets so every woman in town can get teary eyed and I'd melt. Selling my soul or killing their husband or lover. Maybe my business should be 'Gun for Hire'. What do you think?"

"I think you should keep your mouth shut, brother. Let's go. I'm pretty sure your therapist can fit you in when I tell her of your latest escapade." Sam moved forward again.

Dash held up his hands, stepping back. "No, Sam. Since there is already a doctor in the house, I'll have a few words with her and then be on my way to work. Owen, Sam, I'll probably see you later."

"Oh for God's sake, do as he asks. I'm very curious to hear what he has to say. Then I will leave," Mae said.

Owen countered, "We'll wait in the other room." Looking at Dash he added, "If I hear raised voices or anything that sounds untoward, Sam and I *will* intervene." They exited the room, pulling the door close but not shut.

Dash stood silently, looking Mae up and down. A smile crept onto his face. Shaking his head, he said, "I can't do this, Mae. You, I can try to save; have been doing it all our lives only to have you throw your life away with the likes of Richard. But for you to talk about me like I'm some puppet of yours or any female. 'Let's watch Dash dance to this tune or that'. Not good Mae."

Mae stepped closer. "Dashiell, I mean this sincerely. I'm not sure what you think I said about you or to whom I blabbed, but I'm more confused than ever. Yes, at the picnic I did refer to your jumping in to distract Carter as saving a damsel in distress. But that's a good thing, sweetheart. And, hell, you were all over Emmysue at the picnic; if we are to believe you, she wanted you to save her from some stalker. You can't pick and choose."

"At least she had the good grace to ask for help. I guess Annie is very disappointed in me that I didn't kill her husband for her. She intimated that if you asked me, I would kill for you. And, no, I did not kill her husband and for the record I doubt I would kill for you."

He turned away, then turned back. "Please notice that I did not say I wouldn't kill *you!*"

She ran her finger along his cheek, staring into his very sad blue eyes. "Fair enough. Is this another goodbye? We really are cowards, you know. We should have tried all those years ago to make this work." She stood on her tiptoes and gently kissed him.

Picking up her purse, she left the room, the condo, with only a quick nod at Owen and Sam.

Dash stood staring out the window for a few minutes, then shook himself. "Get it together Hammond. There's work to be done."

He walked into the living room to face his father and brother. He looked back and forth from one to the other. "Okay, spit it out. Think of all this as just another screw-up by little ole Dash."

Owen said, "I really don't know what to say. Always thought you two would eventually get back together. Now I'm not so sure that's a good idea. Why don't you clear out your stuff? Consider this place as a stranger's, not Mae's."

"No, no. She can get her own place. This was mine long before it was ours, then hers." Dash said.

Sam chimed in. "Let the attorneys fight this out. Come on. I'll give you and Charlie a lift out to the homestead. I'm assuming you want to get your truck and let Charlie snooze in his bed."

The men rode in silence. Sam kept glancing over at his brother who stared out the window. When they arrived at the house, rather than just dropping Dash off, Sam followed him into the kitchen. He watched as his brother stomped around the room, finally grabbing a chair about to toss it across the room.

Sam stopped him. "Hey, that is not yours to destroy. Calm down will you."

"Thanks for reminding me that I own nothing. Glad I worked all those years."

Sam leaned against the counter. "Want to talk. I'm always ready to listen. Hey, if you want to just sit and have a beer, I can do that as well."

Dash shook his head. "Thanks but no. I really do need to get back to the bookstore. And, truth be told, you have some murder solving to do. Can you let me know if I should make a run for it?"

Seeing the quizzical look on Sam's face, he added, "In case it looks like I'm going to be arrested for Hadley's murder. Again. This time I'm not sticking around."

"As you pointed out, I do need to get back to work. Yes, I'll keep you updated. Listen, dinner tonight, six o'clock. Then we'll talk."

Dash shrugged.

When he arrived at the worksite Dash found Beau and Matt loitering. Sensing the tension between the two military men, Matt said, "Listen, good to see you're okay. I'm going to leave now but, Dash, if you ever need me, please call. I'm all yours."

"Thanks, kid. You done good. I'll be talking to you in the next few days."

Turning to Beau, Dash held out his hands. "What can I say? Not a good excuse in sight for my behavior. Part jealousy, part weariness, a lot of stupidity. I'm sorry, Beau, I should never have called you and the guys into this mess. Right now I'm thinking a padded cell might be best for me."

"You chose the damp beach over a warm bed with Mae in it. Yes, I'll agree that something is definitely wrong with you. I can move my flight back if you want to go somewhere and talk." He watched his friend as he tried to decide what to do.

"Thanks for the offer but I need to get things settled here." Dash pointed to the work site.

"Rather than getting your life in order. A little off on the prioritization of things."

Dash shook his head. "There was a time when this was going to be my life. Now I need to finish things here. Gotta settle one thing, something, in my life so I can move on. I'll never get everything tied up but some of the physical tasks can be completed."

"Listen, Dash, I'll give you two weeks and then I want you and Charlie Dog standing on my doorstep. A little R & R is what you need and I don't mean the usual 'rest and recreation'. I mean recuperation and redirection. Time away from all your wonderful friends and family is definitely needed before you end up in that padded cell. Some jazz and good jambalaya and you'll be good as new. Sound like a plan?"

"A good one for sure." Holding out his hand, Dash said, "Thanks."

Beau not only shook Dash's hand but pulled him close in a bear hug. He whispered into Dash's ear, "Should I plant a big kiss on you? The guys are watching. Want to give them something to talk about, as they say."

Pulling back and laughing, Dash said, "That's all I need. I'm pretty sure I don't want to live here anymore but I might like to visit. Beau, you are a nasty, nasty man. See you in two weeks. Thanks doesn't quite cover it."

Beau circulated the room, shaking hands and thanking the crew for their help. He told them to watch over Dash, make sure he doesn't overwork and to get these jobs done within two weeks.

Then it was back to work.

At 5:30 Dash's phone pinged. A text from Sam: Dinner at six!

At 5:45 the phone pinged again. This text was from Marie: 15 minutes and counting.

Dash replied: Have to feed Charlie Dog and clean up.

Marie answered: Joey fed CD. Soap and water here. Now!

Mumbling Dash packed up his tools and secured the work site. He arrived at Sam's with a few minutes to spare. He splashed a bit of water on his face and washed his hands.

The whole Hammond family sat around the table enjoying Marie's chicken cacciatore. Everyone that is except Dash who was struggling to keep his eyes open. He hadn't even taken a sip of the glass of wine in front of him when he lost the battle to stay awake. Sitting upright, eyes closed, he slept.

Marie glanced at her brother-in-law, then nudged her husband, motioning with her head toward Dash. Conversation slowed, then stopped as they all watched him sleep.

It was the silence that woke him. He jerked himself awake to see his family smiling at him.

Owen spoke first, "I guess sleeping in the sand wasn't as restful as you thought. I'm sure Sam and Marie wouldn't mind if you want to spend the night."

Embarrassed, Dash said, "Thanks but no thanks. Need to get back to my routine. Thanks again, but I'll skip dessert and head home." He pushed back from the table, stretching out his back.

Nephew Joey also stood. "Dash, let me drive you home. I've already messed up your life enough; would hate to have you fall asleep on the way home. I'll spend the night and mow the lawn in the morning. Deal?"

"Thanks Joey, not a bad plan. Remember to mow Mrs. Guzy's place as well." Standing, he added, "Everyone, thanks again. Sorry to be such poor company. Next time I promise to be sparkling. Sam, can I touch base with you tomorrow about the case and stuff?"

Sam nodded. "Talk to you then. Get some sleep."

As they drove across town, Dash asked Joey to stop at Little Biff's. He wanted to talk to the Tydie sisters about cleaning the old homestead and a few other small jobs.

He knocked on their door, heard some scrambling going on inside.

Irma cracked the door open. "Dash, what a surprise. Can I help you?"

"Mind if I come in for a minute. Have something confidential to say."

Irma looked back into the room and then swung the door open wide. Dash stepped into the small studio suite. He glanced around.

"This is bigger than it looks from the outside. Two bedrooms, small kitchenette and sitting room. Cozy and comfy. Sorry about interrupting your dinner."

Ilene picked up the two plates and silverware from the table, moving them to the sink. She said, "We just finished. About to wash the dishes. How can we help you?"

Dash explained what he wanted them to do and the timeline. And how it was all to be in confidence. He walked over to the common wall between 214 and 213. He noticed the old connecting door.

"You don't see these very often in the newer motels. Does the door open into the next room?"

"Yes, Biff said he kept them on this floor since there have been the occasional large party where the people want to drift from room to room. So far we haven't had any and, truth told, I'm dreading finding out that these are orgies he's talking about." Ilene continued, "Don't know why I think that way. Okay, yes I do. Most of the clientele here are not top of anyone's list, except the most wanted."

Laughing Dash said, "Wish I could say my presence here would change that but, coming off an arrest for murder, my slate isn't the shiniest. Ladies, thank you for taking on my tasks. I'll talk to you tomorrow when I collect the boxes. Do you want me to drop them off here or I should leave them at the homestead and Mae's condo? Remember my stuff only. And, before I forget, what is your phone number? I musta put it in my phone incorrectly since I've been trying to reach you all day. Or maybe I'm just too tired."

After numbers were exchanged and entered properly this time, good nights were exchanged.

Sixteen

The next morning Joey sat at the kitchen table eating cereal when Dash came down the stairs. He looked up from the book he was reading to say good morning to his uncle.

"Sorry I'm so late. I just can't seem to get enough sleep. I hate it when I start the day behind. Let me grab some coffee and some cereal and we'll be off. We're going by the 4B. I want to see what you and Johnny did, or didn't do, so we might be able to close that job. What'cha reading?"

"Oh I grabbed one off your bookcase. *American Sniper*. Can I ask you? Since you were there why do you want to read about it? I mean I would have thought you'd had enough."

Shrugging Dash answered. "My experience was just one small piece of the puzzle. Reading other accounts gives me a wider perspective. Take it all with a grain of salt."

Joey said, "I think it's funny that this guy writes a best-selling book and you wrote the Sgt. Spikey Mikey misadventures for us kids. I saved every one you sent to me and I'm pretty sure Johnny did too. We're thinking of publishing them for you. Would you care?"

"If you published them? Nah, though I doubt there's much market. Good project for the two of you."

"You mean since we've screwed up almost everything else you asked us to do this summer. Guess the handyman gene skipped us. Cutting grass is about as technical as we can get. Do you hate us?"

Dash walked up to tap Joey on the head. "Hell no. You just need more supervision that's all. If I had you working right next to me, your performance would have been stellar. Now, take the book if you want but no reading on the job. Safety first, knucklehead."

En route to the Blue Belle B&B, Dash called Johnny telling him to report immediately. While waiting for twin number two to arrive, Dash and Joey walked the site. The porch, steps and railings had been replaced and were sturdy. The paint job was good, not perfect but for a back entrance, acceptable.

Dash met with the owners and got their approval to call the job 'finished, well-done'. He then sat down with the twins.

"Mr. and Mrs. Handke are happy with the work, saying it was timely and neat. So, my dear nephews, anything you'd like to add?" When neither twin opened his mouth, Dash continued. "Johnny, want to tell me where you were from late Tuesday until Friday because I understand that you weren't here working with your brother."

Johnny turned to Joey. Frowning he said, "I never expected you to rat on your own brother. Thanks a lot."

Shaking his head, Dash said, "No, no. Joey never opened his mouth which I will address in a moment. Do you think Danny doesn't keep track of who's on a site and who's not? It saddens me to tell you, Johnny, but you're fired. Your behavior was unacceptable. In the Army you would have been AWOL, facing a court-martial and prison time."

"You and your stupid Army. So I took a few days off, so did you. You can't fire me, I'm your nephew. What will Dad and Owen say? Turning your back on family, but that's what you've always done. You're just sore because you got arrested."

Joey reached over to grab his brother's arm. "I'd shut up right now."

Dash stood, flexing his back. "I'm not firing you as my nephew; I'm firing you as my employee. Any one of the men who cut work, no call, nothing, would be out on the street same as you. And, just for the record, I don't give a shit what the rest of the family thinks. They'll probably agree with me that you need to grow up and start acting like you're ready to enter the real world."

He reached into his pocket and pulled out a check. Handing it to Johnny, he said, "Last wages. I suggest you spend them wisely. This conversation is over."

Dash started to walk away when Joey ran after him. "Wait up. How much trouble am I in?"

"Enough but still employed, unless you want to quit in solidarity with Johnny. Otherwise, hop in the truck and we will discuss covering for him. You never lied, just skirted the truth. Let's not do that again, okay?"

After another full day of tearing down and redoing what had been done, the crew decided to end at six p.m. Dash ordered two pizzas and grabbed a six pack of beer. Six thirty found him knocking at the Tydie Sisters' door.

"Pizza man!" he yelled.

Once again Irma opened the door. "Thought that was you through the peep hole. What's with the pizza? Don't remember ordering any."

"Thought it would be neighborly if I came bearing gifts. Didn't feel like eating on my own. Mind if I come in? I've got half pepperoni, half cheese, half veggie, half sausage. Hope I covered everyone's likes."

Ilene came out of the back bedroom. "Company, how nice."

Dash proceeded to set the table, four places. When he saw the puzzled look on their faces, he announced, "Just thought Emmysue would want to join us. I mean her no harm. Come out, come out, wherever you are!"

No one moved. Then the door to the front bedroom opened and Emmysue came slowly out.

"Lucky guess?" she asked.

"Pretty much. Last night I noticed a third place setting in the sink. In itself no proof of a third resident but then I caught a whiff of your perfume."

"Don't kid a kidder. You remembered my perfume?"

"Well, Mae wore it for a while and I really liked it. Noticed it at the picnic; just didn't say anything. Filed it away in my little hamster brain as Mae says."

He walked around her, looking up and down. "Don't seem the worse for wear, losing all that blood. Though I'm not a fan of your new look. Hopefully that black crap on your head is a wig and you didn't cut off all that beautiful blonde hair. You guys want to 'fess up. What's going on?"

Emmysue sat down at the table and pulled a piece of pizza toward her. After taking a few bites, she wiped her hands.

"Well, Mr. 'I'll see you after the fireworks', when you didn't show I ran for the hills the next morning, trying to regroup. You were my best hope and you failed me. Just for the record; not that I'm keeping track."

"You're the only female I know who isn't. Disappointment is my first name; failure being the middle name. Extenuating circumstances, decent length story for another time, or I would have been here."

"Decent length story, as you say, for another time, but I hopped about like a Mexican jumping bean and finally decided to throw my fate in with the good sisters. We sorta bonded when I was last here, you know, sisterhood and all."

Dash spoke up. "Yeah, I can see it. You in your bikini and the good sisters in their cover-all habits. But underneath all that, sisters united."

Ilene reached over and slapped his hand. "Behave or you'll sit in the corner."

"What did you think of our idea for the blood spatter? Are they still working on it?" Irma asked.

"Wish I could answer that definitively but I'm so far out of the loop where the townies are concerned. Good brother Sam is supposed to keep me informed but I sorta screwed things up with the family and all. Back to that neighborly comment when I first arrived, I've moved out of the homestead and into the room next door."

"So that's why you had us clean and pack everything up. Your family seem like very nice people. Want us to intervene/intercede?"

"No, it's all part of a masterplan. Now that I've confirmed Emmysue is living here, I feel it is my duty to protect her." Turning, he asked, "Have you been cooped up in here all this time? I guess I should start with 'why the blood spattered room?' Reason? Result?"

The three women glanced at each other. Ilene took the lead. "Let me begin by saying we are amateurs at all this. Reading a bunch of mysteries does not make for solid training."

Dash snorted at that remark, mumbling, "Tell me something I don't know."

Irma said, "The blood was my idea. I used my nursing skills for nefarious ways. Drew blood from the three of us and added two pints of pig blood. Told the butcher I was going to make blood sausage. Ever had any?"

"No, but sounds delightful. Wait, do you mean black pudding? My mom used make that. Thought it was good until I found her making it. Turned me off all pudding but tapioca. Okay, so you had a regular blood bath going on in the room. Again, why?"

"I wanted everyone to think I was dead or mortally injured. Needed time to figure out how to deal with the criminal element surrounding me," Emmysue offered.

Dash nodded in agreement. "Criminal element being Travis Tycoon?"

Sighing, Emmysue said, "I totally underestimated his 'empire' so to speak. I really thought he made his money in the oil fields. Maybe he did to start but I uncovered information that he is also dealing in dope and I think illegal immigrants and human trafficking. It took me years to piece this together and more time to suss out the right documents, so to speak, to copy for proof. I put them on a flash drive and brought it with me from Texas. Dash, I know I'm not smart like you or Billy or Mae. I was hoping I could get one of you to help me. Hate to say it but once I saw that you were alive, you seemed the most logical and, sorry to say, susceptible. And, rumor has it, your military experience taught you how to help people disappear."

Dash pushed back from the table. He paced the small room several times, occasionally glancing at the seated women.

"I really *must* find out who starts rumors like that. Hell, I spent most of my military career in charge of the kitchen. I have no idea how to make someone disappear, other than throw them into the lake,"he said slyly.

Finally he walked over to Emmysue, placing his hands on the back of her chair. She turned to look up at him. He said, "Unfortunately for you *I* don't know how to do that; fortunately for you, I *do* know people who do it for fun on a Sunday afternoon."

He grabbed a cold beer from the under-the-counter fridge, popped the cap. After taking a healthy swig, he sat down.

"Okay ladies, top to bottom. Spill."

Emmysue started and then the sisters took over when the story wound its way into Clover Pointe.

"Where's your computer? Let me see what's on the flash drive."

"Oh, the drive isn't here. We hid it."

Holding the now-lukewarm beer bottle to his forehead, he cautiously asked, "Of course you did. Where?"

"At the old bus depot. On top of a mud dauber's nest. Unlikely place for anyone to look."

He covered his face with his hands. "Go ahead, tell me. You saw Jock Hadley being murdered while you were hiding the drive. Christ, all we need is a bow and we can wrap up two murders and your disappearance."

Ilene snorted. "Of course she didn't go out there during the murder, but afterwards. Once the place had been thoroughly searched and all that stupid crime scene tape slapped up, then she hid the drive. We figured no one would look there, not after all the cops had combed through all the debris. We waited until the cop guarding the scene was pulled. I guess it was Monday morning, early hours."

"How did you get there?"

"We drove her, parked down the road at LuLu's. The lounge was still open so the parking lot was fairly crowded for a Monday."

"You took your pink rust-bucket out to a strip joint and sat there while Emmysue cut through the woods to the old depot. Anyone see you?"

"No, and if they did, they would have seen three old nuns with car trouble."

"Nuns? How would they know you were nuns?"

Emmysue answered. "We wore old habits, Dash. The black ones, veils and all."

It took Dash a second for the 'we' to register. He leaned toward Emmysue. "We, meaning all three of you; meaning you have a nuns' habit." His grin grew. "Do you still have it? Want to model it for me?"

Ilene rapped his hand again. "Colonel Hammond, wipe that filthy smile off your face. And the answer is no. She will not model it for you."

"My sixth grade teacher. Young woman, the most beautiful woman I had ever seen up to that point. Well, all I saw was her face but I would spend my youthful nights dreaming of what might be under all those robes. Not that I was sure what *should* be there." He shivered. "Another piece of kindling on that fire in hell with my name on it."

Shaking his head, he continued, "Sorry, sorry. Need to refocus on the task at hand. Question: why aren't you taking this information to the authorities? Why just disappear?"

"Leverage. Once I turn the info over, I have nothing to keep him from killing me."

The discussion over what should be done and how it might get done continued for a few more hours. Dash became more and more adamant that the flash drive be turned over to authorities so the criminal activity, mainly human trafficking, could be stopped.

Glancing at the clock, Dash said. "Look, it's one a.m. I need to get some sleep. We can continue this again tomorrow evening, but remember, if I find that the drive does contain information about trafficking, it goes to the authorities. No argument. That's what you get when you invite me to the party. Emmysue, do not leave this place dressed as Sister Mary whatever or Emmysue the stripper queen. Ilene, can you unlock the adjoining doors? I'd like to have quick access to your room if I need. Don't worry, I will keep my carnal desires in check. Listen, I brought Charlie Dog and he'll stay in the room while I'm at work. If you open that door, he would be available to help guard. I'll start making phone calls."

He got up, kissed the cheeks of all three women. His final words to them were, "No more reading mystery novels until this is over. No thrillers, no espionage. Get back to your religious tracts; meditate, contemplate. Okay?"

Seventeen

"Dammit." Dash hit his hand for the fourth time. Shaking it and making a fist over and over, he slumped to the floor. His nephew came over to him.

"Bit of a rough day, Dash? Anything I can do to help? Like take away your hammer? Send you out for coffee?"

"Smart ass," Dash replied. "I think you're right. I need a break anyway. Hafta make a few phone calls in private. If something catches fire, I'll be in Dolly's office." He pulled himself up, handed Joey his hammer and exited through the sheets of plastic hung to keep the dust from invading the bookstore.

"Hey, grab Dolly's sketches for us, okay?" His partner Danny yelled.

"Will do."

His sister Dolly and Tracy were shelving some new books. Dash pointed to the office saying, "Private phone calls. Knock before entering, okay?"

The two women nodded. Dash grabbed a cup of coffee from the sidebar before he went into the office. Tempted as he was to straighten Dolly's desk, he settled in, gathering his thoughts. If he knew for certain what was on the flash drive, he would know exactly where to take it, but the uncertainty made him leery of going too far up the food chain with only a tease of 'maybe I've got something'.

Deciding he was in no mood to listen to Billy raking him over the coals, he went back to his ace in the hole: Beau.

Beau's first response to seeing Dash's name pop-up on his phone was to answer with "Don't tell me something has come up and you won't be heading south."

"And hello to you too, Beauregard. As usual you are correct but this time only fifty percent. Something has come up but I am still planning on invading your home and eating all your food. Do you have a minute to listen to what may turn out to be a fairy tale? Remember Emmysue and Travis Tycoon Benedict? Here is chapter two or three."

Dash brought Beau up to speed: The prom queen on the run, the flash drive hidden behind a mud dauber's nest at the bus depot and what may or may not be on the drive. He also mentioned her wish to disappear and his desire to help her.

"What the hell is a mud dauber?" Beau asked.

"*That's* your only question?"

"No, my first question was going to be what in the hell are you smoking or drinking and save some for me. Seriously, how do you get involved in crap like this? I didn't see a sign saying 'Need help, call Dash at 1-800-sucker'."

Dash leaned back in the chair. "So you're not only a wonderful attorney but also a comedian. Listen I'm having a less than grand day, which is becoming very common for me, so cut to the chase. I figure I get the drive, see what's on it and then decide which higher authority gets it. Emmysue can disappear after she gives her side of the story to a D.A. Am I right in thinking I can go to any fed for this, especially if human trafficking does appear on the drive?"

"Precisely. But you can turn it over to Sam and he can move it up the chain if you want. First, get a look at the drive. Maybe the prom queen, as you call her, is bonkers like her old man says. Don't build up the hopes of the federalis and then end up with some of the dauber's mud on your face. Let me see if I know anyone who might work out of the Cleveland office, that's fairly close to you, right?"

"About an hour and change away."

"How soon can you retrieve the drive? Crime scene tape still up, not that that is much of a deterrent for you. Oh, what the hell is going on with the murders, if I may inquire?"

"Sam hasn't reported back to me on anything. Haven't spoken to Annie recently; don't know if she is still in town or went south for the funeral. I'm guessing I should ask questions so someone thinks I give a rat's ass. About the recovery of the drive, might try tonight if all is quiet out there. For all I know the depot has become a partying spot for the local teens. 'Dance with the dead' and all. I'll call you as soon as I have reviewed it. Emmysue stays put, right?"

"Right. Who are you thinking about for the new papers, ...? The guy in Montana? Is he still in business? I really shouldn't know things like that."

"I'll keep it under my hat. Beau, remember you said something about suing my little town. Well, after careful consideration, I'd like you to begin writing something up. I've asked Matt to research the cost of law enforcement in the city and county. Thinking of slapping the city with an enormous lawsuit, say fifty million. But offering to withdraw it if they merge the departments with county personnel being in charge. Your thoughts?"

Beau whistled, "I doubt if you can blackmail the powers that be in your town/county into the merger. But what do I know? Why fifty million? For what?"

"Defamation of a war hero's character. They're painting me as a killing machine."

"Hate to point this out, but isn't that what you are/were? A very efficient one if rumors are correct. Fifty million, huh? Always did think highly of yourself."

Dash shook his head and answered, "Hey, if you're going to do a job, do it well."

"Well, there's that. Okay, I'll write something up and get with young Matthew. But remember I'm booked solid for the next few months, so tread carefully, my friend. Give my love to the darling Dr. Summers when next you talk to her."

"Call her yourself. Haven't heard from her since the blow-up. You've got her number, call her and see what's going on." Then hesitating, he added, "Then call me back and tell me."

Beau signed off with a chuckle.

Closing his eyes, Dash rested for a minute. He opened the store's computer and began searching for the names of U. S. Attorneys in the Ohio area. He jotted down several names and numbers, filing the paper in his wallet for future reference. He sat silently then flexed his injured hand. Noting that it had swollen to the size of a baseball mitt, he went in search of ice. Filling a pitcher, he stuck his hand in it, wincing at the temperature.

He searched Dolly's desk for her sketches of the new children's book room his crew was creating. Carrying the pitcher and the sketches he wandered back to the work site.

The afternoon was spent reviewing, recalculating the sketches and then the architectural plans. Dash put aside the pitcher and just favored his hand. After having a late lunch/early dinner, he returned to the site to make notes on the proposed or necessary changes. After rewriting the daily task sheet for the next day, he slid to the floor to rest his eyes and his hand.

"Dash, Dash, wake up." Sam said, gently shaking his brother.

Jerking himself awake, Dash peered at the sheriff. "Sorry, didn't realize I had fallen asleep. Didn't sleep well last night. Too much on my mind."

Sam sat down next to Dash. "I went by the house to return your guns. No ballistic match. I put them in the safe, the safe in your very empty office. And, speaking of not sleeping well, what the hell happened to your custom-made-to-die for bed that once resided in your bedroom? Sleeping on the floor here is more comfortable than your bed?"

"I'm going to do some painting so I decided to move a few things out, to make it easier, you know."

"Curious that the only things moved were *your* things. Sure nothing else is going on?"

"Seems a bit irrational doesn't it, but rational to an irrational mind. Do you have any ibuprofen? I took several a while ago but musta worn off. My hand is killing me." He held up his damaged hand.

"Yeah, Joey told me you were having a bad day. Reason I came looking for you." Sam reached out to help his brother up, saying "I believe a trip to the ER is in order. Get that hand x-rayed. Then we can get a bite to eat at the place of your choosing. We might as well get caught up 'cause I'm sure at least one of us has some things to get out in the open. Capisce?"

They found themselves trolling the cafeteria line at the hospital. As soon as Sam saw that roast beef with mashed potatoes was on the menu he reneged on his 'you get to choose'. Watching Sam wolf down the food and listening to him rave about it, Dash put down his fork.

"How many times have you been a patient in a hospital? I mean really eaten what is called hospital food, not this gourmet meal crap."

Patting his stomach, Sam answered. "Never. What about you? I mean other than the auto accident. Really never knew much about where you were or what you did. Remember the meltdown after the ambush but then you were in the psych ward, right?"

Dash moved to cover his face with his left hand when he remembered it was encased in a plastic splint to immobilize the broken bones. So he just leaned back sighing. "To answer your question, I've been in and out a few times, short stays, minor wounds, nothing serious. And I was not in the psych ward. Grady and I had luxury accommodations in 'let's hope we don't have to move you into the psych ward' area, right outside. A few feet, lot of difference."

Sam shook his head. "You really should have been inside the ward."

Holding up his right hand, Dash pleaded with his brother. "Please. Let's not talk about that. Incredibly painful period for me. Suffice it to say, the food as a patient is never as tasty as this." Pushing aside the leftovers from his meal of roast chicken and stuffing, he grimaced.

"Sam, any other news about the murders? Care to share, if you can."

"Might as well tell you. Maybe you can settle down a bit if you know. Right now forensics have pegged Hadley for the murder of John Doe/Roger Scott. Blood residue on his socks matches Scott's. Still open who shot Hadley. You are pretty much in the clear as the time of death looks like Thursday night/Friday morning while you were sawing logs as a guest of Clover Pointe. As for Emmysue, did I get her name right, the blood in the room is half human, half pig. Go figure."

Sam looked over at his brother waiting for some reaction.

Instead Dash changed topics by saying, "I'm leaving town as soon as I get a few more things settled. That's why my stuff is packed. Need to regroup."

"Where are you going and for how long?"

"I'm heading to Beau's for a bit. He's letting me crash there until I can at least start to think clearly." Seeing the reaction of his brother, Dash continued, "I'll tell Owen face to face before I leave. I will keep in touch with him and you, if you want. I just need to sort things out and I can't seem to think straight here."

"Have you told Mae? Billy?"

"No, two more threads to cut. If they call me, I'll talk but I'm not initiating anything at this point."

"Annie?"

"She has her hands full. Doesn't need me, probably never did. And I could be wrong but I think she has good old Trigger panting after her. Not upsetting that applecart for any number of reasons."

He looked down at his wrist. No watch. "Did I drive? Thinking maybe you should give me a ride to Little Biff's. Whatever that guy shot me up with is really kicking in and, once again, I'm about to fall asleep sitting up."

Sam dropped his brother off at Room 213 then knocked on the door of 214. Irma peeked out.

"Yes sheriff."

"I just put him to bed; injured his hand, shot up with pain killers. I'm guessing you have access to all the rooms. Would you please check on him? Call me if necessary. Good night ladies."

Eighteen

The next morning Sam pounded on the door of 213. "Open this goddamn door! Now!"

Dash yelled back, "Just a minute. I'm not dressed."

"Hell, I've seen your bare ass plenty of times. Open this or I will kick it and that ass as well."

Dash opened the door and Sam pushed him and the door into the room. The adjoining door was open into the Tydie sisters' room. Walking through it, Sam told Irma and Ilene to get into Dash's room.

Dash pulled on his jeans. Sam pointed to the mussed second bed. "Who slept there?"

"Charlie Dog, it it's any of your business," Dash answered.

"All of you sit down. And listen up. I don't know what game the three of you are playing but it has to stop." Looking at Dash, he said, "You know who Portia Henderson is, right? She's the woman you sent Cav to question about Emmysue. Correct?"

Dash nodded his head, muttering dammit.

"Well, hot shot, she was found severely beaten, in a coma, early this morning. A co-worker was concerned and went to her house. Found a bloody mess. The Vermillion police found one of your business cards in her wallet. They called me. Well, Dash, did you learn what you needed from this woman 'cause you ain't learning anymore any time soon."

Sam stomped over to a chair and sat down. "So anything any one of you want to tell me?"

"First, Irma and Ilene have nothing to do with Emmysue's…"

"Bullshit, try again before I call the Vermillion cops and hand you over, telling them to throw away the key? Where is Emmysue?"

Before Dash could answer, Emmysue stepped into the room, tears streaming down her face. Looking at Dash, she said, "Believe me now? Travis is a mean son of a bitch."

Dash walked over to her, putting his arms around her.

"Jesus, another fucking damsel in distress. I take it this is this the infamous Emmysue. You don't look like your picture." Turning to Dash, he asked, "Do you give off pheromones to attract the needy?"

"Real cute, Sam. You do one job and I do another." He walked over to give a hug to Ilene who was crying. "You happy? Now that you've made a nun cry?"

Sam was about to release another tirade when Dash held up his good hand. He walked over to his brother, standing over him.

"Now listen, closely, Samuel, as I'm going to say this once. You can help or you can hinder. If you help you will be a bona fide hero; if you hinder, you will either end up in the hospital by my one good hand or in the same boat as Robbie 'I can't find my own dick with the lights on' Rakestraw. If you want, I can stick around and run against every one, sheriff, chief of police and mayor all at once. I'm that mean when prodded."

Irma said, "So much for brotherly love. Gentlemen, calm down. Ilene, Emmysue, stop crying. That isn't helping anyone."

The tiny ex-nun straightened up and began to tell the tale with one big omission: the flash drive. When she was finished, all eyes were on Sam. He leaned forward in the chair, his big hands covering his knees.

"Nice beginning. Now let's expand it to include what the hell you, Miss Emmysue, have that your delightful husband is willing to kill for. Portia's house was trashed. Someone was looking for something and it wasn't darling Dash's business card. I get most of this. You want out; divorce isn't an option because you are a) still alive and could talk; b) in possession of something that could do professional harm to your hubby and I don't mean professional in the good sense, more like the criminal sense."

Nodding toward Dash, he said, "See, I'm not as stupid as I look." Turning his gaze to Emmysue he added, "What is it and where is it? And, why the hell didn't you just keep going once you got out of Houston?"

He held up his hand, "On second thought, don't answer that last part. Don't want to part with my breakfast when you tell me you just couldn't run away without seeing the old heartthrob over there."

Emmysue rose from the edge of the bed. She had on an oversized long Ohio State shirt. She walked slowly over to Sam, knowing he was inspecting every inch of her body. Standing in front of the seated sheriff, her sculpted breasts thrust forward, hands on her hips, she leaned down so she was eye to eye with him. Tossing her head back toward Dash, she pronounced, "When my mama moved us from the hills of Tennessee to this crap hole by the lake, the only person who treated me with respect was that man over there. No, Sheriff, I didn't come to see him since I had been told he was dead. I came to pay my respects at his graveside, one time, before I ran or was killed. See, I didn't take this to any lawman because as far as I'm concerned you're all in somebody's pocket. In Texas it was my husband's. If Dash tells me you're the one honest sheriff in the country, I'll tell you what I have and where it is."

After a moment of silence, Dash got up. "Ladies, it's time for all of you to retreat to your room. The sheriff and I have a few things to discuss."

Once they were alone, Sam shook his head at Dash. "One helluva glowing recommendation. Didn't know you were such a treasure."

Smiling shyly, Dash said, "Well, you know me. I try to be wonderful at least once a day."

Sam glanced at the second bed in the room. Dash shook his finger, "No, no. She did sleep there last night but Charlie was her pillow, not me. I'm in desperate need of a cup of coffee. Give me a second to brew some. Yes, I did bring one thing with me from the homestead. Makes great coffee. Then sit down and prepare to listen."

After two cups each, Sam said, "So you don't know what's on the drive. Why haven't you retrieved it yet?"

"Trying to figure out how to do that without being obvious. Was going tonight at dusk so I wouldn't need a flashlight and the wasps would be less aggressive, or so the internet says. I have an appointment at the VA in Cleveland tomorrow afternoon. Figured I'd review the drive tonight and, if there was something of use on it, take it to the Feds tomorrow after my appointment."

"Is Emmysue going with you?"

"No." When Sam didn't follow up, Dash added, "Listen, let me shower and make a few phone calls. Danny is going to kill me; I've missed so much. I'll meet you in your office in say forty-five minutes. We can get the drive and check it out. Okay?"

Sam rose, shaking his head in agreement. He left.

Dash knocked on the door jamb and walked into the sisters' room. The three women sat around the table.

"What are you going to do? What should we do?" Ilene asked.

"Sam and I are going for the flash drive. Once we review it we'll decide where to take it. For now you just sit tight. Emmysue, you might have to come with us to provide background. Then I'll get you out of the picture. Everyone okay with that?" Dash asked.

Ilene answered for the all of them. "We're good. You take care of what you need to do. Don't worry about us."

Dash walked over to them and gave each woman a peck on the cheek. Emmysue pulled him back and gave him a full kiss. "Thanks for sticking your neck out for me."

"The least a knight can do for his Prom queen. I'll call or text as soon as I can. Be good, be quiet and keep the faith."

Ilene followed him to the adjoining door, locking it after him. She turned to Irma and Emmysue. "Be good, be quiet. That man can spout the crap can't he? Well, ladies, I think it is time for plan A. Let's get changed. As soon as he pulls out, we'll make our move. Start packing."

She walked over to the little refrigerator/freezer, opening the top compartment. She pulled out the pistol which was wrapped tightly in plastic then covered with aluminum foil so it looked like a piece of meat. The gun was the reason Irma had been kicked out of the community. A gun-toting nun was not the image the Sisters of Our Lady of Lourdes were espousing. But Irma was a practical woman. She was principal at an inner city school and the three nuns who taught there lived in a small house next to the school. After several break-ins in the neighborhood, a parishioner offered to teach her to handle a firearm and she agreed. Then he kindly bought her this Glock, reminding her that was James Bond's weapon of choice. She never thought she might have to use it, but, since Emmysue's appearance in her life, she was glad she had this particular skill.

The ladies worked methodically and quickly. Irma checked to make sure Dash's truck was gone. All were dressed in the religious habit; each carried a small duffel bag. Ilene had the pistol tucked under her scapular, the long piece that covered her tunic.

The three women crept down the stairs. They got into their little pink car saying a prayer to Our Lady of the Highways to protect them as they travelled down the perilous road. Ilene put the key into the ignition and turned it. Nothing. Everyone wiggled in their seats. Taking a deep breath, Ilene tried again. Nothing. Perplexed, Ilene got out and raised the hood of the car.

While she was peering over the engine tapping this and that, Dash walked up behind her. He joined her in inspecting the engine, breathing down her neck. She jumped up almost smacking him in the face.

"Looking for this?" he asked, holding out the distributor cap for their little pink vintage machine.

Emmysue and Irma got out of the car.

"Really Dash! How dare you?"

"How dare I? Whatever happened to staying inside? Letting me handle this? Or did I hear you incorrectly that you came up here from Texas so I could help you?" Pointing to the staircase, he finished by saying, "Upstairs, double time."

The three women sat around the table listening to Dash berate them. Their eyes were downcast, their fingers crossed as they promised him to stay put, let him handle things.

Sam and Dash drove out to the old bus depot in silence. They exchanged glances but not words. The wasps' nest was easily spotted.

"That look like a mud dauber's nest to you? I'm thinking more hornet than friendly wasp. Anyway, you should go first, oldest and all. Sheriff and all," Dash suggested.

"Should we knock it down with a stick? What do you think?" Sam asked.

"Well, that always works in the cartoons I've seen. Listen, I'll find the stick and you knock it down. Division of labor and all."

Sam shook his head. "Nah, you have to knock it down. You can run and I can't. You do see the logic, don't you?"

"Wait, I've got an idea. Why don't we just stand here and see if they bring it to us?"

Dash flexed a bit and walked over to the nest built around the station light. He checked it from all the angles then looked over at Sam. Shrugging, he pulled the bench away from the building and climbed on it. From this vantage point he could see the flash drive. Easy peasy. He reached for it, grabbed it and accidentally knocked the nest off its mooring, releasing a bunch of angry hornets. He lost his footing, falling off the bench and landing on his broken hand. Swatting as best he could, he got himself upright, cursing Sam, Emmysue and anyone he could.

When he caught up with Sam, he still had a few hangers-on stinging him. Sam helped to smack them dead. When they got back into the squad car, Dash held his arm, rocking back and forth.

"Just drop me at the ER. Did something to my arm and I feel like my face is swelling to gigantic proportions."

Sam put the siren on.

Two hours later Dash was sitting on the bench outside the hospital. He had pulled his ball cap down over his face. He heard his name being called. Nephew Joey had arrived. He sauntered over to the car.

"Crap. Dash, have you looked in a mirror? Dad kinda explained what happened but..."

"Just drive, Joey. Did 'Dad' tell you I'm leaving town? That is, if I live long enough to get out. At least my arm isn't broken just bruised. And supposedly the swelling and redness will go down in a few hours. I guess you need to take me to the station."

Joey nodded. "Danny wanted me to tell you we're doing fine at the bookstore. Not to worry. The plumbers will be there tomorrow to install the bathroom stuff, both upstairs and downstairs. Does your face hurt?"

"No, I've had much worse pain. All relative I guess. Thanks for the ride. Later."

Dash found Sam and Ruthie in the Sheriff's office. They were making back-up copies of the flash drive.

"Interesting stuff on this. I've talked to the U.S. District Attorney in Cleveland and he wants to see this a.s.a.p. Ready to roll. We'll swing by and pick up Emmysue. She can shed some light on a few things."

"How about you go on ahead and I'll bring Emmysue in a little bit; make that a long bit. Give me a chance to put something on my face. Okay?"

Sam pursed his lips. "She's gone, right? Do you know where she is?"

Dash shrugged. He laid the distributor cap on the desk. "I foiled one attempt by the Tydie Trio to leave town. After our fiasco with the hornets and my trip to the hospital, well, when I got back, the rusty pink-mobile was sitting stone cold in front of Biff's and the desperadoes were gone. This is about the most embarrassing thing that has happened to me in years."

Ruthie chuckled. "That's' saying something 'cause I'm still laughing about your 'Oh My' moment."

Putting his head in his hands, he mumbled. "Someone just shoot me." He looked up at Sam. "You know I used to make people disappear as part of my job over there. Spirit folks out the country to safety. Hell, I could outsmart the Taliban but two little old nuns have beaten me soundly."

Sam interrupted. "I thought you said you were in charge of the kitchen. Just what did you do?"

Waving his hand, Dash said, "Whatever needed doing. I ticked off my C.O. so I did six months in charge of the mess. You wouldn't believe how hard that is; everyone griping about the food." Sighing, he continued, "I just hope the Tydie Sisters have her well-hidden and safe. Any luck, deep deep underground by now."

Sighing Sam said, "Well, we can ask the good Sisters when/if they return to pick up their car. The good women won't lie to me for long."

The brothers looked at each other, then burst out laughing. "Yeah, right!"

Nineteen

Annie opened the back door to her house. She carried the brown plastic box containing her husband's ashes to the kitchen table. Then she sensed Dash's presence.

Without turning around, she said, "Let yourself in I see. Going to make yourself at home? Maybe I should serve tea. No, whiskey is more to your liking. Come to say goodbye?"

Dash stepped into the kitchen. "Wasn't sure you were still here, but yes, I guess I'm here to say goodbye. Though I think I'm really here hoping you'll answer a few questions for me. This time truthfully."

She looked him up and down. "You look like, is it 'shite', you would-be Irish say? What happened to your hand? Your face? One of Emmysue's protectors take offense at you touching her? Oh, how is the prom queen?"

He shrugged. "Missing again. Though I think this time she might actually be somewhere safe. Mind if I sit down?"

Annie waved her hand toward the kitchen chairs.

He looked toward the box and said, "Rest in peace, if you can do that in hell."

She leaned against the counter, smiling. "You realize our positions are reversed. Usually I'm the one seated and you're doing the manly arms-crossed menacing stance. Spit it out, Colonel. I have packing to do. Leaving this evening for Charleston. Funeral's the day after tomorrow."

"Where's Timothy? You're not traveling by yourself are you?"

"Tim left yesterday. Said he had things to do now that his father is dead." Pursing her lips, she asked, "Do you care if I have to travel alone? Would you come?"

"Yes and no."

She looked perplexed.

He gestured with his injured hand. "Yes, I care if you had to make the journey alone. I know you and Jock had your problems. Yours that you didn't leave him long ago and his that you didn't leave him long ago. But, no, Annie, I'm not going with you. I've got a sneaking suspicion that Trigger will be by your side. Good man. Don't abuse him."

Annie looked surprised. "Should I take that to mean *I* abused *you*?"

Shaking his head, he answered. "No, if you abused me and I'm not saying you did, it was because I was being an ass and deserved it. And, if you feel I abused you, I truly apologize for that. Basically you're a decent woman."

She moved to the table and sat down. "Basically? Really opens a can of worms. What did I do or what do you think I did?"

"You lied, Annie. From the minute you sent that text to me to, I don't know, the last time I saw you."

"I'm listening. Explain yourself. If you're going to be an ass, go all the way."

"You didn't need me to come home. You've admitted that. Okay, fine. But why in hell did you identify John Doe as your husband? What really was going on with Jock?"

"Do you think I killed him, I mean, at the bus depot?"

"No, well, maybe. Not completely off the hook though. Got a sniggling little feeling you arranged his murder." He held up his hand. "Before you object I know you didn't hire Trigger to kill him. He's not for hire, too good a man to kill for money."

She studied him. She could almost feel his weariness.

"Most of what I said was true. He surprised me. He wanted money. He wanted me to help him disappear. But, honestly, I had no idea he planned to kill John Doe/Roger Scott. Never met the man; didn't know of their relationship or debts. Jock needed a substantial amount of money, most of what I received in the divorce settlement I still had, not being a spendthrift like him."

"Did you know the first body wasn't his?"

"Suspected it from the get-go but figured I was doing him a favor having him declared dead and me a favor getting him out of my life. I planned to give him some money, no large amount, so he could get out of town, the country. Told him I'd get him more once he was gone. I thought identifying the body as his would seal the deal. Having him declared dead would surely help get whoever was after him off his back."

Shaking her head, she added, "Actually I was too shocked about it all to think clearly, believe me on that."

Dash rubbed his face. "Go on. Why didn't you tell Robbie you changed your mind and weren't sure?"

"*Why?* I'll tell you why. He let me stew for a few hours and then came in, threatening to arrest me as an accessory to murder for withholding evidence. Was that the right time to say: Just kidding! Body wasn't Jock's so take off the cuffs. Credible, right?"

She got up and walked back to the counter, crossing her arms. "And then I find out they've arrested you as well. Again, perfect moment to say, 'hey guys, I'm recanting my I.D. Dash and I had nothing but love for Jock, really!' Think even a dolt like Robbie would have gone for that? And, I mean this sincerely, I believed you would find a way out the mess. That's what you do."

He shrugged. "So you really were surprised when Jock's body turned up at the depot. Still don't understand what he was doing out there."

She held up her hand. "My bad, as the kids say. Once, in Jojo's, I overheard a conversation between some geezers talking about the good old days when the bus brought all kinds of characters to the town. Like there aren't enough here already. I listened carefully and figured out where the depot had been. I drove out there one day on a lark. Being a mystery aficionado, my first thought was 'what a great place to hide a body'. Obviously never really thinking of acting on it but when I needed a place to stash the money for Jock, I immediately thought of the depot."

"Did you take money out there? When? Can I ask how much?"

"Fifteen grand, pal. Not nearly what Jock wanted, but…"

"I wonder didn't the cops find it?" Dash asked.

"I don't know. I sent Tim out there to look for it but he came home empty-handed. Guess I should have given it to Jock when he first showed up. Maybe all this could have been avoided, but I was too shocked to see him. Definitely not thinking straight."

She shrugged and then continued. "When Jock showed up at the store, I told him I would get the money and leave it at the depot. He wasn't happy but you walked in, ending all discussion. Anyway, I borrowed Tracy's car, drove out to the house and then to the depot where I hid the money. I figured we were done. Bang, he jumps us in the parking lot. After that I didn't know what was going on with him. I didn't think I could ask him if he picked up the money, not with you there. Next thing I know there's this body, you're arrested, released and then, as if out of a magician's hat, there's Jock's body. Wonder why no one has said anything about finding an envelope of money."

"Really? Cash? Chances are the killer took it. This is really screwed up."

Dash looked off into the air and then back at Annie. "What kind of a hitman kills with a small caliber gun? And whoever was chasing Jock, why kill him if more money was involved? Jock must have been intimidated to let the killer get that close to him *or* he knew his killer. Did Jock have a gun? Ever?" Dash asked, then added. "I told Sam to see how many guys in suits leave town now that Emmysue is officially missing again."

He sat there staring at the floor. Tapping his toe, he looked up at her. "You know what really hurts. You didn't trust me enough to tell me the truth. You said you believed I would take care of things. Well, if you really thought that, you would have told me what was going on."

Annie made a face. "What was I supposed to do? Get myself arrested so I could slip you a note between the bars while we were in jail?" She snorted, then sighed.

"Now who's being stupid? Annie, you had a million opportunities to whisper in my ear what you were doing. That way I could have directed things better."

She tilted her head, giving him her 'oh really' stare. "Just when would that happen? With Mae glued to one ear and Beau hanging off the other? And the 'you can't talk to a witness' malarkey." Shaking her head, she continued, "I'm truly sorry for not trusting as you think, but, honestly, I've always had total faith in your ability to do anything *I* directed you to do."

Dash looked over at her, then shook his head. "Putty in your hands, am I?" He smiled, "Annie, Annie, Annie. I think I should put you back under the rose bush, but that's kinda like putting the genie back into the bottle." He chuckled again. "Never had a chance. Not with you, not with Mae. Maybe I should become a recluse, a monk somewhere."

"Rumor has it you're leaving town. For a vacation or for good?" She asked.

He shrugged again. "All I know is I have to get out of this place. You, Mae, Owen, Sam. I can't think straight. I ..."

"Dolly said Mae is really pissed at you and that's why you're going. She thinks you're going to see her, try to patch it up."

He shook his head. "No, Mae is pissed at *you* and *I'm* pissed at her. No, I'm heading south not north."

"What did Owen say? This has to break his heart. You're finally safe at home and now you're leaving again. How much time can he have left?"

"Oh he's fine, seems to be the only one who understands why I have to go. He just asked that I keep in touch and try to make it back for Christmas. Hell, for all I know I'll be back in two days begging for a roof over my head. I wouldn't have chosen to come here after the accident but, when you are totally out of your head, you don't get to make decisions. I don't know. Ask me in six months; maybe the answer will be different."

He stood, walking to Annie. He took her in his arms, kissing her. "It was a helluva ride, Annie Bananie. Take care and think fondly of me. Another time, place, maybe another ending."

She pulled back just enough to look into his face. "Call, text, whistle, snap your fingers. I'll come running. You owe me a trip to Paris and several dances. "

"Hey, want to do the 'let's meet under the Eifel Tower' thing. We can keep that option open. Might be fun. I guess I should get going so you can take care of the things in your life."

"Please take care and get some rest. I'm sure things will be fine, for both of us. It *was* a helluva ride, Colonel. Might just put it in a book."

He shrugged, saluted and headed toward the door.

His next stop, the bookstore. Dash shuffled papers around the desk.

His sister's idea of filing consisted of stacks of papers, usually in categories known only to Dolly.

There was a soft knock on the door and his niece, Kathleen aka Birdie, slowly opened it. She stood there with a tiny kitten mewing in her arms.

"Hey Dasher, look what I found in the alley. I've decided to call him Bernie the Burglar. He'll be our bookstore cat. Every bookstore worth its name has one, a cat that is."

Smiling Dash asked, "Why? Why do bookstores have cats? And are you sure he doesn't belong to someone?"

Birdie handed the kitten to her uncle causing Charlie Dog to growl. She told the dog to hush. "I've seen him outside foraging for food for two days now. I bought a can of kitten food for him. He can sleep in the office. If it's okay with you, that is. Can we keep him, please?"

Dash tilted his head. "Have I ever denied you anything?" Handing the kitten back to Birdie, he added, "I suppose you heard that I'm leaving Clover Pointe."

Birdie sat down. "Were you going to say goodbye or slink out of town? I thought you told me you would always be here for me and Mikey. I thought *here* meant here not somewhere else. You can leave if you take me with you. Please don't leave me to the mercy of Mom and Aunt Marie. One doesn't ever look up from her books and the other won't let me be a teenager."

"Listen, little one. Both love you dearly. I'm leaving you here because I need someone to take charge of the store so, if/when, I return there is still a bookstore. You are in charge of overseeing your mother's book orders so our stock isn't all fiction. Add whatever teen books you think will sell; start with small quantities. Make sure you keep up the history books for me. I'll text you when I hear about a book we need. Help Tracy manage things. Your mom won't notice unless you two set the place on fire."

She reached over for a piece of paper. She scribbled a date, October 1st, on it. Rounding the desk she stuffed the note into her uncle's shirt pocket saying, "You know what day that is?"

He pulled out the note and nodded. "October 1st. Your birthday. Your fifteenth birthday. And, yes, I remember my promise to teach you to drive. Fifteen and a half before you can get behind the wheel. If Sammy or Owen haven't taught you by then, I will slip back into town and give you a whirl in the hot red Corvette."

Smiling she put out her hand. "Why don't you give me the keys and I'll have that cute quarterback teach me?"

Dash narrowed his eyes. "I'll swallow them first." Standing he came around the desk to wrap Birdie and Bernie in his arms. "If I could, I would take you with me. But I'm just the substitute dad. Pretend it's another deployment. I'll probably be home before you miss me."

She looked up into his eyes. "Promise me you'll send me postcards and texts and buy me stupid little trinkets like you did for all those years. And I'll promise to watch over Mom and the bookstore. And Auntie Mae. You know she won't last long without you."

"You make her sound like a fish out of water, but it would be very nice if you could keep in touch with her. She loves you like a daughter."

He kissed her forehead and little Bernie's as well. One last hug and Dash stepped through the door, Charlie Dog at his heels.

Twenty

Dash stood at the end of the pier. Charlie Dog sat at his feet. Breathing in the aroma of the lake, Dash felt tears beginning to form in his eyes. Shaking off the black feeling, he said to the dog, "Well, this is it old buddy. Take a good look and have a good sniff. We're off to parts unknown."

The only sound was the lapping of the waves against the pylons. Then Dash heard footsteps coming his way. Familiar footsteps.

"Hello, sweet cheeks."

"Hello, Billy. Come to say goodbye?"

Neither man looked at the other; both stood facing the lake with their hands in their pockets.

"Actually I've come to apologize for what I said at the picnic. I'm not sure you'll accept it but I am sincere. You're not crazy nor are your friends. I guess I'm a bit jealous because you guys are heroes, braver than I'd ever be. Don't know why I should begrudge you some credit after all you've been through. Sorry you saved my life?" Turning to Dash, he held out his hand. "Friends again. And I won't be insulted if you punch me in the face. I deserve at least that."

Dash looked at his cousin. "Come here you big load of shite. The only reason I don't pummel you is that Elena would have my head. And that hurts too much already." He enveloped Billy Mac in his arms. "And no, not sorry about saving you. You're a good man. We've had too many good, great times to let one evening spoil it all. We all say and do stupid things once in a while. Fourth of July was a bad day for a lot of people. Why should we be different?"

Reaching down to pet Charlie Dog, he asked his cousin. "Can I ask you to do a few things for me? Sort of a penance."

Billy Mac rolled his eyes, shaking his head. "I should have known. What can I do?"

"First, you of the large bag of money, would you donate a big screen television, best you can afford, to the vets for our, well, their, new meeting room. And," putting up his hands, he added, "Second, some of them could use some legal advice, free of charge. What say you my ginger-headed man?"

Chuckling, Billy replied, "Is that all? I really thought you'd assign me something along the lines of the labors of Hercules. Done. I will make it my mission to help the guys and the gals out. Will you do something for me in return?"

Dash scratched his head. "You are the goddam silver-tongued lawyer, aren't you? Well, what do you want because I'm pretty sure you don't *need* anything?"

"Keep in touch. Let me know where you are and how you are. You know I was kinda hurt that you didn't ask me to help you with this murder charge." Seeing the look on his cousin's face, Billy continued. "It sounded like fun. Very selfish of you not to include me, especially since I could have shown off for my prom queen."

Looking back to the lake, Dash said quietly, "I guess I should get going. Long drive to New Orleans. If you come up for Christmas, might see you then. Promised Dad I would try to come home."

Patting his thigh, Dash signaled for Charlie Dog and the twosome strolled up the pier. Billy watched as they climbed into the truck and drove away.

Dash sat dozing on the chaise lounge in Beau's courtyard. Postcards lay scattered on his chest and lap. He dreamed of his home town, missing his family. He felt a tap on his leg and opened his eyes to see the outline of Beau standing in front of him, blocking out the sun.

Shading his eyes, he sat up. "Hey, are you home early or have I slept that long?"

Beau pulled up a chair and sat down. "Home early. Wanted to see how you were doing. Landon called to report you got good news from the doctor, that being nothing's wrong. Did he really say 'battle fatigue'?"

Smiling, Dash shook his head. "No, not in so many words. He thinks my headaches, as severe as they were, are from stress or anxiety. All the tests showed fairly normal activity. No swelling, no bleeding and no stroke. He suggests I take it easy. Try meditation or relaxation exercises, just calm strolls through the beautiful neighborhoods of New Orleans. Unfortunately, he also said no alcohol. He wants me back in two weeks if I'm still here. If not, he suggests I visit my doctor in Ohio."

"Beau, I can't thank you enough for not calling Owen or Mae when I collapsed and you rushed me to the hospital. I'm pretty sure they would have carted me off to some unknown hideout where I'd be held captive for years, chained to a bed."

Seeing Beau's reaction, he held up his hand, "For the record I called Owen today and told him I was fine, had had a few bad headaches but relaxing, feeling tip top right now."

"For what it's worth, I had a fleeting moment of guilt, thinking I should call your Dad. But sanity prevailed. I figured if you dropped dead, I'd just tell Owen 'oh he was here a day ago, you just missed him' sending him on a wild goose chase until I could liquidate my assets and disappear." Beau rolled his eyes. "This might be a vacation for you but it is turning rather stressful for me."

Seeing the look of horror on Dash's face, he added, "Just kidding you. What kind of Southern host would I be if I kicked you out because you were troublesome? Besides, Landon has grown quite fond of you. And Mrs. Garcia wants to fuss over you like you're one of her grandkids."

Pulling himself up into a seated positon, Dash started laughing. "Landon is a gem. He decided we should celebrate my good news so he took me to this quaint little restaurant and then gave me his personal guided tour of the *interesting,* or so he called them, parts of New Orleans. I never laughed so hard. Thought I might wet myself. I can see why you love him. Hell, I'm half in love with him myself."

Beau waved a finger at his guest. "Careful, Dash, I have one house rule: no falling in love with my partner. Now, get up or at least turn over. I think that side is done. Mrs. Garcia and Landon are whipping up something spectacular for dinner so fireproof your stomach. They never met a spice they didn't like." He bent to pick up the postcards that fell as Dash rose.

As they walked to the house, Beau added, "Oh, Cav called and wants to get together Friday night. He's bringing his wife so Landon has decided to fix you up with a date; if I recall his exact words what you need is a 'buxom broad who's good in bed'. You okay with that plan? He thinks you need a bit of love to spice up your life."

Dash stopped and turned to Beau. "Okay, but don't count on me being more than polite. Landon might think I need a bit of loving, but I don't. Had too much of that in Clover Pointe and you saw where that got me.

But it'll be nice to see Cav and Cora again. Good food, smooth jazz and great conversation."

The following Friday evening Dash, Beau, Cav and his wife, Cora, sat waiting for Landon. He was bringing Dash's date. Jazz played in the background as the quartet reviewed the menu.

Smiling, Dash realized he felt better than he had in days. He and Cav discussed the merits of one dish over the other when he heard a very throaty laugh.

Looking at Beau, he dropped his shoulders and then the menu saying, "I *know* that laugh."

Dash stood and turned to watch the very beautiful curly-haired woman sashay toward him.

Shaking his head, he said to Beau, "I *paid* for that green dress. Landon nailed it alright: Buxom broad who's good in bed."

Thanks to

My readers' circle: Theresa Berry, Debi Huff, Patience Martin, Kristin Munsch, Laura Barda Thomas and Patricia West for spotting the good, the bad and the inconceivable.

The Derby Rotten Scoundrel Chapter of Sisters in Crime for their words of encouragement.

The booksellers at Barnes & Noble #2705 in Louisville who go the extra mile to support all the fledging writers on staff.

Dr. F. Richard Schmitt, D.D.S., for his wonderful insights on dental identification.

Rick McMahon, a 'Peach' of a guy who tirelessly answers all my weapon-related questions.

Pamela Cooley, R.N., for your advice on medical issues.

Michael Guzy, my old classmate, for your very positive accolades.

Finally,

Murphy Jane Munsch, (1990-2007),

best feline ever!

With apologies to Millie Jane

and Daisy Rose.

E. M. Munsch grew up on the shores of Lake Erie. An avid reader, bookselling seemed to be the ideal profession which she has practiced for over forty years. She now resides in Louisville, Kentucky.